WITCH'S DOZEN

by

STEWART FARRAR

This book is a work of fiction. The characters, incidents, and dialogue are drawn from the author's imagination and are not to be construed as real. Any resemblance to actual events or persons, living or dead, is entirely coincidental.

WITCH'S DOZEN

WITCH'S DOZEN

by

STEWART FARRAR

OTHER BOOKS BY STEWART FARRAR

<u>Fiction</u>

The Snake on 99
Zero in the Gate
Death in the Wrong Bed
Delphine, Be A Darling
The Twelve Maidens
The Serpent of Lilith
The Dance of Blood
The Sword of Orley
Omega
Forcible Entry
Backlash
Witch's Dozen

<u>Non-Fiction</u>

What Witches Do

with Janet Farrar:

Eight Sabbats for Witches
The Witches' Way
The Witches' Goddess
The Witches' God
The Life and Times of a Modern Witch
Spells and How They Work
A Witches' Bible: The Complete Witches' Handbook

with Janet Farrar and Gavin Bone:

Pagan Path: The Wiccan Way of Life
The Healing Craft: Healing Practices for Witches and Pagans
The Complete Dictionary of European Gods and Goddesses
Progressive Witchcraft

Contents

ABOUT
STEWART FARRAR

Stewart Farrar was born 28 June 1916, in London, England, son of bank official Frank Farrar and schoolteacher Agnes Farrar, nee Picken (a Scottish family). Stewart went to the City of London School and to University College, London, where he obtained a Diploma for Journalism, coming second in his year for the whole University.

He has worked as an author, journalist, and scriptwriter for drama and documentary, for film, radio and television. Ever since, with thirteen books to his name, he also co-authored seven books with his wife, Janet Farrar, and then co-authored four books with Janet Farrar and Gavin Bone. His first three books were detective novels, and his fourth a romance. Since 1971 all of his books have been occult, whether fiction or non-fiction.

On 19 July 1975 he married Janet Ewer, nee Owen. He and Janet moved to Ireland that year.

Their books became increasingly well-known internationally within the occult movement, with the result that they have visited the United States of America by invitation every year since 1991. By 1995, the Farrars had been to twenty-eight of the fifty states, plus Washington D.C., and three Canadian provinces. They have been interviewed by press, radio and television in Ireland, England, Scotland, the USA, the Netherlands, and Germany.

Stewart Farrar

Stewart passed away 7 February 2000 after a brief illness.

For a full biography of Stewart Farrar please read *Stewart Farrar: Writer on a Brookstick* by Janet Farrar and Elizabeth Guerra.

INTRODUCTION

Two years ago, I embarked on a journey that would take me onto a path I did not expect. It started with the inspiration to republish *High Magic's Aid* by Gerald Gardner I wanted to do this because I did not want to see this extremely important novel be relegated to the abyss of out-of-print books. Once it was published, after a lot of hard work, incredible help from Philip Heselton in tracking down the copyright holder and providing a wonderful introduction to that edition, I was asked if I would be republishing Gerald's other fictional novel, his first, *A Goddess Arrives*. Again, the quest for the copyright holder, gaining the rights and republishing it occurred. It was during my work on *A Goddess Arrives* that I realised that there were many works of fiction, geared towards Pagans and Wiccans that were becoming lost to the annals of time.

During my restructuring of my home library, I saw that I had a copy of Stewart Farrar's *Witch's Dozen*, a cute take on the 'baker's dozen' in which Stewart had written thirteen wonderful fictional stories. *Witch's Dozen* had been originally published by the small, independent publisher, Godolphin House, in November 1995. In a time when print on demand technology was nonexistent and offset print runs were expensive, the small publishing house's publication of *Witch's Dozen* was clearly unprofessional. Even still, I had purchased it way back when it was a new publication. How did I find it when it clearly was not available in book stores as Godolphin House did not have a distributor? I had found it at *The Occult Shop* in Toronto,

Canada. Richard James, the owner, who also was the High Priest of the Wiccan Church of Canada at that time, had ordered it directly from the Frosts' publishing house. Lucky me!

Upon republishing *A Goddess Arrives*, I was on a mission. I wanted to republish this almost unknown anthology from well known and highly influential Witch, High Priest and author Stewart Farrar. This meant I needed to see if Godolphin House was still in existence. A short internet search proved it was not. In fact, Gavin Frost had passed away in 2016 and Yvonne, as of this writing, is 94 years old. My next step was to try and contact Janet Farrar, Stewart's widow, High Priestess and co-author of many incredible books on Wicca. Thanks to social media, I contacted her current partner in life, Wicca and book titles, Gavin Bone. As Stewart's widow, the copyright was held by Janet and the publishing rights reverted to her as well. With Gavin's assistance, my proposal to republish *Witch's Dozen* was approved by Janet and a publishing contract was signed, sealed and delivered, so the saying goes.

The next step was transcription of the book, an arduous task to say the least. I spent numerous hours typing. Why did I not just scan it into the computer? I chose not to for several reasons: 1) *Witch's Dozen* clearly had not been professionally edited and required some clean-up. Excessive and inaccurate uses of m-dashes and ellipses were evident, as well as other issues, though I tried my best to not fiddle too much with how it was originally published so as to keep to the 'spirit' of the original, right (or is that write) or wrong. 2) When the Frosts published, they did so in American English. I wanted to return it to British English. After all, Stewart was British. I tried my best to catch as much as possible and return it to British English, but if I missed some, please forgive me. 3) Had I scanned the book, I still would have to go through the manuscript with a fine toothed comb, taking probably as much time or more than transcription would have. It also gave me the opportunity to re-read the anthology as it had been thirty years since I had read it.

WITCH'S DOZEN

Transcribing *Witch's Dozen* proved fun. I had forgotten the stories, so I was thrilled to re-discover them. What struck me about Stewart's short fiction proved that he could write in multiple genres. From Romance to Horror, from Paranormal to Fantasy, and from Science Fiction to Literary, the stories in *Witch's Dozen* do not disappoint. In fact, the mixing of these genres in one anthology is unlike a baker's dozen where thirteen loaves are baked in the expectation one loaf does not come out perfectly. *Witch's Dozen,* to extend the metaphor, is a bakery shop that provides thirteen exquisite stories to consume, each different from the other yet as delicious to the eyes and imagination.

I hope you enjoy *Witch's Dozen* by Stewart Farrar.

Karen Dales
Toronto, Canada
July 2025

I

APRHODITE'S
DAUGHTER

think,' Jeremy Stock told his wife, 'that I must be the luckiest man alive... Hell, no, I *am* the luckiest man alive.'

Dora turned at the gas-cooker and smiled at him. 'Why, darling?'

'Do that again.'

'Do what?'

'Face the cooker—that's right. Now turn towards me again.'

Dora obliged, not looking puzzled at his request because she was used to him. Jeremy shook his head.

'How any woman, cooking on a second-hand gas-stove in a wretched, cramped, shabby two-room London attic, can still move as beautifully as you, defeats me. *And* smile like an angel, after a nine-hour day at a dress shop... You can cook, too,' he added.

Dora laughed, a silvery sound, and answered him obliquely, woman-like. 'If you really were the luckiest man alive, you wouldn't me stuck in a wretched, cramped, shabby...'

'Don't interrupt. I stick to my point. I'm twenty-two, demobbed a year after somehow surviving three years in the trenches. I come home to the prospect of a lifetime in my uncle's shipping office, and dam' lucky to have a job at all in the year of doubtful grace 1919. I haven't been there a week till out of the blue I meet this angel. Within another week we're both in love, and she knows everything about me—including the fact that my impossible dream is to be a writer. Impossible my foot, she says. But I've got to eat, say I. Right, says she. And before I know where I am she's married me, ordered me out of the shipping office and to hell with my uncle cutting me off with a shilling, found me a typewriter from God knows where, and insisted on working six days a week to keep us both, so that I can be a writer. And what have I sold in six months of it? One story to *The Strand*...'

'You see what I mean? Loyal and unquenchable—and on top of everything, the loveliest human being I have ever set my eyes on.'

'You're biased.'

'Biased, but accurate.'

She kissed the top of his head as she crossed the room to fetch two dinner-plates.

'You know what, Dora?' he continued. 'I have a theory. You are not really human at all. I think you are Aphrodite's daughter...'

'I am the daughter of Albert and Georgina Whitehead, of Croydon, and if you tell them any different they'll cut *me* off with a shilling, or would if they had one.'

'So you pretend, but I know better. Listen to my theory.'

'Yes, sir.'

'I've come to the conclusion—on the evidence of *you*—that once in every human lifetime, Aphrodite, Goddess of love, beauty, and all things erotic and delectable (such as you), has a daughter. And that daughter is bestowed upon some incredulous, undeserving male, for reasons known only to inscrutable Olympus. This time round, I am he. And that *makes* me the luckiest man alive.'

Dora sighed contentedly. 'I don't know about the luckiest,' she told him, 'but you're certainly the most adorable.'

*   *   *

Jeremy's flight of fancy, which had come to him on the spur of the moment, wouldn't leave him alone. Next day, after Dora had left for work, he found himself unable to concentrate on the novel he was supposed to be writing; his imagination kept being drawn back to the idea of Dora as Aphrodite's daughter, and to the daydreams arising there from. They were delightful but all too distracting.

In the end he decided that the only way to get back to work on his novel was to exorcise the intrusive fancy by putting it down on paper in some form. He pushed the typewriter away, took out a pad, and started scribbling. An hour later, satisfied, he returned to his novel.

When Dora got home from work, he presented her with the single sheet of paper before she had even taken off her hat and coat. She stood by the gas-fire, reading it.

The Gift

When Cyprian Aphrodite first arose
In naked splendour from the foaming sea,
Dazzled Olympus rubbed its eyes, and chose
The most unlikely God her mate to be:

Lame-foot Hephaestus, black with furnace smoke,
Mocked for his countenance, though not his craft,
For that alone was God-like; metal spoke
Beneath his fingers, and the jewels laughed.

Since then, through all the ages, one by one
The Queen of Heaven's daughters come to earth
To bless some mortal underneath the sun;
Each lifetime once, the Cyprian gives birth.

I know it to be true; yet cannot see
Why, of all man, the gift should come to me?

Dora just stood there, moist-eyed in her loveliness, unable

to speak, until Jeremy removed the poem gently from her fingers and put his arm round her.

It was siesta time on the slopes of Mount Olympus, for mortals at any rate—such as the shepherd girl drowsing i the shade of an outcrop of rock well above the tree line, or the young hunter who had taken too long in bagging his hare and now, sweating, approached the outcrop a little diffidently, wondering if it would be an impertinence to share that shade; the girl was, after all, a married woman, and her middle-aged husband was strong as an ox and notoriously jealous.

The two immortals who watched them, amused, were indifferent to siesta time, though by their natures never indifferent to potential drama. Although they stood in full sunlight a few paces from the hesitant hunter, there were of course invisible and inaudible to them.

'Eros...'

'Yes, mother. I think so too.'

Eros flipped the bow from his shoulder and an arrow from his quiver, aimed, and loosed the shaft in what seemed to be one continuous movement of his graceful muscles. The shepherdess' half-closed eyes opened in a moment of puzzled surprise, which changed immediately into a smile of shy welcome as she caught sight of the hunter. Eros turned slightly and loosed another arrow.

'The second was quite unnecessary,' Aphrodite pointed out. 'That smile of hers would have been enough.'

'I know, mother. But it would have taken them a little longer. Why waste their time, in this heat?'

For about ten minutes, motionless, they watched the sequel to its climax, when the Goddess let out a sympathetic contralto grunt of delight and then set off again up the mountain with Eros following. In a cave-mouth high above them a dark, gnarled figure in a leather apron, leaning on a hammer, watched them approach.

'That was unscrupulous, my dear,' he said mildly when they

reached him. 'The girl is married to somebody else.'

Aphrodite laughed, giving him a quick affectionate hug. The soot on his shoulders left no mark on her creamy skin. 'You *know* that's no concern of mine, darling.'

'I should, by now.'

'Dear Hephaestus—the millennia have mellowed you a little, but you're still incurably stuffy.'

'And you are still incurably amoral. The millennia have had no effect on you whatever.'

'You know you love me exactly as I am. Which is just as well, because future millennia won't change me, either... And take that grin off your face, Eros. I may mock your father—you may not.'

Eros winked at Hephaestus, who winked back, both of them forbearing to point out that there was some doubt as to whether Eros was the son of Ares, Hermes, or of Great Zeus himself, but that he had almost certainly not been fathered by Hephaestus. Aphrodite was incurably forgetful, when it suited her.'

One of Eros' putative fathers chose that moment to materialise, wing-heeled and wing-helmeted, in a shimmer of light.

'Greetings, Hermes,' Hephaestus said politely. 'Though I'll have to leave you to these two, if you don't mind. The afternoon shift is due on, below.'

Hermes gave them an unusually (for him) hasty salute with his caduceus. 'Stay a moment, though, Hephaestus, if you don't mind. This is rather important.'

Aphrodite looked bored. 'If you're going to talk business, I'm leaving.'

'*Your* business, I'm afraid, Aphrodite. And something will have to be done about it, or you'll be in trouble with *him*.' He pointed his caduceus at a thunderhead which crowned the summit above them, temporarily quiescent.

'Great Zeus!' Aphrodite swore, the boredom vanished.

'Don't invoke him, for all our sakes,' Hermes said quickly. 'The fact is, one of your human beneficiaries has realised the truth.'

'One of...?'

'The husband of your current daughter. He has just written her a sonnet—rather a second-rate one, for my taste, but alarmingly specific. He knows, Aphrodite. Even down to the one-a-lifetime clause.'

'A *sonnet?*' Aphrodite paled, and then suddenly turned on Eros in magnificent fury. 'It's all your fault—you choose the husbands. And ever since that Dante and Beatrice thing, I've told you—no poets, not artists! They're *always* the ones who find out an give trouble.'

'But he wasn't *meant* to be a poet!' Eros protested. 'What's his name? Jeremy Stock, that's right. Demobbed soldier, shipping clerk. He seemed ideal. I steered Dora his way...'

'Without *her* realising, I hope?'

'Mother, really! I'm not *that* incompetent. She hadn't an inkling.'

'She still hasn't,' Hermes intervened. 'Got the poem tucked in her under-bodice, but believes it's just a charming fantasy.'

'A daughter of mine wearing an *under-bodice?*' Aphrodite shuddered.

'Don't change the subject, mother,' Eros said. 'Anyway—one arrow and the job was done. I never dreamed a shipping clerk could...'

'Well, he has,' Hermes said glumly. 'Dora is too much her mother's daughter, that's the trouble. She found out he really wanted to be a writer, and out of sheer love she's working to keep them both while he scribbles hopefully.'

'If Zeus finds out—you remember how angry he was about that Pre-Raphaelite creature.' Aphrodite shuddered again.

'Only one thing for it,' Hephaestus said practically. 'Bring 'em here and talk to them. Explain the risk.' He hefted the hammer on to his shoulder and stumped off into the cave, the matter settled as far as he was concerned.

'Dear Hephaestus,' Aphrodite sighed when he had gone. 'Always so sensible.' She turned on Hermes. 'Well, don't just stand there. You heard my husband. Fetch them.'

Hermes vanished.

'Mother,' Eros suggested, 'I think you'd better put some clothes on. It'll be enough of a shock to them, being brought here, and post-war London is still remarkably prudish.'

Aphrodite shrugged. 'This do?' Hellenistic drapery suddenly arranged itself on her splendid body, from the hips down, the style of her Venus de Milo representation.

'Better than nothing,' her son conceded. 'After all, they may have been to the Louvre.'

'Under-bodices!' the Goddess muttered under her breath. 'Disgusting.'

The man at the door was so charming, so good-looking, and so impeccably dressed that Jeremy was immediately distrustful; he could only be a salesman. But when he presented his card, which was engraved '*H. Psychopompus, Literary Agent*', Jeremy's wariness changed to excitement. Literary agents were salesmen, all right, but on *your* side. And no agent had so far thought it worth his while to call on Jeremy Stock.

'Come in,' he said. 'I'm afraid we're a bit cramped here, but...'

'What a delightful flat,' the man said. 'So compact. And this is Mrs. Stock?' he bowed over Dora's hand. 'You'll forgive me for calling unannounced, but one is so *busy*... My card, Mrs. Stock.'

Dora read it and she, too, melted at once; her faith in Jeremy's genius was absolute, and anyone who might conceivably help it to find recognition was a potential ally. In no time at all the visitor was seated by the gas-fire with a cup of tea in his hand, and Dora was slicing a cake she had meant to keep for the weekend.

'It as your exquisite little masterpiece in *The Strand* magazine that aroused my interest, Mr. Stock,' he explained. 'Tell me—and I shall be terribly disappointed if you say "yes"— have you an agent already?'

'Actually, no—I...'

'Good, good. And what are you working on at the moment, may I ask?'

And so Jeremy found himself summarizing the theme of his half-finished novel, while the man with the odd Greek name nodded and smiled and interrupted occasionally with shrewd and encouraging questions, in between mouthfuls of Dora's cake. When Jeremy had finished, the man nodded several times, and then said: 'You know, Mr. Stock, i have some people who would very much like to meet you.'

'Publishers?' Jeremy croaked.

'Shall we say, patrons. But very powerful ones. Would you like me to introduce you to them? And you too, Mrs. Stock?'

'Of course,' they both said at once.

The man smiled. 'No sooner said than done.'

'I'm sorry about that,' the man said. 'But you both had to agree, you see—if you want to get back, that is. One way journeys are usually involuntary.'

Jeremy and Dora started up at him, open-mouthed, from the sun-hot mountain grass on to which they had collapsed from the shock of the instantaneous transit. H. Psychopompos no longer wore his Savile Row suit. A skimpy, one-shouldered tunic barely concealed his athletic frame, and little golden wings sprouted from his sandals and his close-fitting helmet.

'I remember what Psychopompos means, now,' Jeremy said in wonder, when he could find his voice.

'The advantage of a classical education. Call me Hermes— it's simpler.'

'Are we dead, then?'

'Anything but. This is Mount Olympus, by the way. And for your further reassurance, this is still 1919.'

'I don't understand,' Dora whispered 'And I'm frightened.'

Hermes sat gracefully on the ground in front of them. 'Dora, my dear—if I may call you that—there is nothing whatever to be afraid of. In a sense, this is your home from home.'

'Mine? What do you mean?'

'You'll understand later. Just get your breath back, and in a moment we'll climb a little further, to meet the others.'

'Others?'

Hermes smiled. 'The patrons I promised you. I just thought it'd be easier if you took it all a step at a time.'

Jeremy would never have believed he could be so resilient. His courage and self-possession were returning fast—partly under the stimulus of having Dora to look after, and partly because of the fact that writers are notoriously impertinent towards the Gods or they wouldn't dare to be writers.

'Since you are Hermes,' he ventured, 'you must also be Thoth.'

Hermes looked pleased. 'I'm glad that you at least recognise it. In the Greek environment, Apollo's lot have done their best to take it from me...' He chuckled. 'But you're right. My claim to be a literary agent was not entirely fraudulent. And our interdepartmental jealousies need not trouble you, because I'm here and Apollo's Nine aren't, at the moment. Besides— wouldn't you agree, Dora?—it isn't *inspiration* that Jeremy needs. It's encouragement and recognition.'

With that, of course, he had her as well; so when he rose and led the way upwards, she followed him unafraid, her hand in Jeremy's.

After about ten minutes of climbing, they rounded a spur of the mountain and found themselves face to face with the Three.

They halted and gasped.

The glorious creature in the centre of the group moved a pace or two towards them, a small cloud of butterflies follow- ing her, and little flowers springing up instantaneously in her footprints. There could be no question who she was. She gave Dora a slow up-and-down appraising examination, appeared satisfied, and then looked Jeremy straight in the eyes. His head swam, but he managed somehow to stand his ground. 'I am Aphrodite,' she announced.

'I know, madam' Jeremy said.

'Yes, you would... Well, mortal, you have heard all about

me. What do you think of the reality?'

As though to enable his complete judgement of that reality, her lower-half drapery disappeared, revealing her splendidly naked. Her divine arrogance was complete, relaxed, and—Jeremy could hardly deny—utterly justified. He was about to reply, but then he became aware of the trembling of Dora's hand in his own. He never knew quite what impelled him, but he gently disengaged his fingers, but his arm round his wife's shoulders, and committed himself to the ultimate impertinence.

'I think, madam, that you are the second most beautify lady that I have ever seen.'

For a moment, he thought the Goddess' eyes were going to shrivel him where he stood, and he was conscious of a distinct earth tremor beneath his feet. Then suddenly Aphrodite laughed, and the tremor was stilled.

'You chose well, Eros,' she said over her shoulder. 'At least no one can say he doesn't *appreciate* my gift. But you should have realised. Anyone who takes that kind of risk could only be a poet.' She turned her attention back to Dora. 'Oh, dear—the crimes that fashion commits against my offspring! Do something about it, Hermes, will you?'

Hermes nodded and waved his caduceus. Jeremy always remained proud of the way Dora retained her composure; it must have been traumatic for any girl to find herself suddenly clad in about a yard and a half of what looked like chiffon, with her lipstick and powder gone, and her hair not merely down but also decorated with flowers. But after no more than a quick squeal of surprise, she drew herself up proudly and smoothed the chiffon to her satisfaction.

'That's better,' Aphrodite said. 'I must say, you almost do his audacity justice... Now, my dears, sit down and make yourselves comfortable. Oh, by the way, this is Hephaestus and this is Eros, as you probably guessed... I expect you wonder why you're here?'

'Well,' Jeremy said, 'we're honoured and delighted, of course, but...'

'Quite, quite. The fat is, you've presented us with a problem.'

'How, madam?'

'The other day, you wrote Dora a poem.'

'A sonnet,' Hermes amplified, 'beginning *"When Cyprian Aphrodite first arose..."*'

'It's a *lovely* poem,' Dora said defensively, and then caught her breath. 'Oh dear. You mean it's—well, sort of blasphemous?'

Aphrodite laughed. 'Child, child—if poets were called up here for blasphemy, there wouldn't even be standing room on Olympus. No, just the opposite. Jeremy's poem is the literal truth.'

After a moment of astonished silence, Jeremy whispered: 'I knew it. I knew it. She *is* your daughter.'

'But I can't be!' Dora protested. 'I *know* who my mother is. She's Georgina Whitehead, and she lives in Croydon, and...'

Hermes coughed discreetly. 'I know it's a shock to you, Dora, but you are a changeling. I can confirm that, because I made the exchange myself. Part of my job, you know. And you must admit I chose you two very kind foster-parents.'

A tear started in Dora's eye. 'Oh, poor Mummy!'

'But my dear—she never knew.'

'*Must* never know,' Aphrodite emphasized.

'And don't worry about her real daughter,' Hermes went on. 'She had an idyllic childhood and adolescence in Arkadia, and is now happily mated to one of the more eligible satyrs.'

Dora, too, had had a classical education, so she blushed slightly and changed the subject. 'Then you are my real father?' she asked Hephaestus.

The sooty face smiled at her in a mixture of kindliness and resignation. 'I'd be delighted to think so, Dora, but to be honest I can't say for certain... Aphrodite?'

The Goddess looked immortally vague. 'Oh, for goodness' sake, it's twenty years ago... What matters is that she is *my* daughter. And you were quite right, poet. For the past—I *think* it's about two thousand years—Great Zeus has permitted me to send one daughter at a time to live among humans and marry one of them. It all came out of one of those silly wagers that tend to arise up here after too much ambrosia. I can't remember all the details, but anyhow I won. Zeus had a terrible hangover next morning, but of course he can't go back on his word. Nor could I, even if I'd wanted to—the bargain was made, and it's eternal. But he *could* lay down conditions. And the one that matters is nobody must know. My daughters must remain unrecognised for what they are. After all, they are goddesses, even if only with a small *gamma*. Don't look so worried, Dora, it's something you learn to live with.'

('A *theta*, to be accurate, Hermes muttered.)

'And flesh-and-blood, acknowledged goddesses wandering about loose would be too much for humanity to swallow.'

('Especially the Vatican,' Hermes muttered again.)

'Stop interrupting in parentheses, Hermes. Exposing my daughters could cause riots and schisms and letters to *The Times* and heaven knows what—metaphorically speaking, because heaven includes me, and I daren't event think of it. Anyway, that is the Divine rule. And that is why you are here, my dears. If this gets out, I, and Eros who selected Jeremy for the honour of being my son-in-law, and Hermes who ought to have kept a better eye on you, will be in very, very serious trouble with Great Zeus. So it's quite simple, isn't it? All you have to do is to promise to burn that sonnet when you get home, and never, never let anybody suspect Dora's true nature. Agreed?'

The silence drew out for so long that Aphrodite began to frown. Then Jeremy said, clearly but firmly, 'No. I am sorry, madam, but it is not agreed.'

'I do not understand,' the Goddess said. Ice was creeping into her voice, and one or two of her attendant butterflies sheered off, nervously.

'With all respect to you, my divine mother-in-law—you gave me Dora, for which I am eternally (or perhaps I should say, mortally) grateful. I did not know until this moment that she was a goddess, even with a small *gamma* or *theta* or whatever, but it doesn't surprise me. In fact, I must have known it intuitively, which is why I wrote that sonnet. I love her very much indeed, whether she's human or divine; and she is my wife, entitled to whatever I can give her. But you are asking me to underrate her. I can't do it, madam. As a writer and as a man, I have to… to celebrate her. Do you really ask me to do less—for your own daughter? For one who carries about with her something of the splendour of *yourself?*'

The butterflies were creeping back, and the ice in Aphrodite's voice had melted perceptibly. 'We-ell…'

'Mother!' Eros cried, sharply. He added something obviously pointed in Ancient Greek, which Jeremy's classical education wasn't quite up to.

Aphrodite squared her shoulders, insofar as their graceful curves lent themselves to squaring. 'You're right, Eros, of course. I'm sorry, Jeremy—you put your point very charmingly, but I must insist.'

Jeremy hesitated, and was about to speak when he glimpsed the adoring pride in Dora's eyes, which were fixed on him all too humanly. They hardened his resolve. 'And if I still don't agree—can you compel me?'

'You dare to ask Olympus *that?*'

The divine bluff might have succeeded, had it not been for Hephaestus' sense of justice. 'Be fair, my dear. The lad's been honest with you, and stuck up for himself, Olympus or no Olympus.' He turned to Jeremy. 'Got to tell you the truth. That's one of the rules, too, about her daughters—once they're given, the gift can't be revoked. She's yours for life, and that's that. We can't put the screws on you. All we can do is appeal to your good sense. How about it?'

Aphrodite looked daggers at her husband, but said nothing.

Jeremy shook his head. 'I'm sorry, sir. I appreciate your frankness, I do really. But it's not a matter of good sense. It's a matter of treating my wife as I feel she deserves to be treated. So I'm afraid it's still "No".'

Aphrodite sighed. 'You know, I like this man. I like his

outrageous impertinence, defying Olympus itself in honour of his wife's beauty. He *deserves* a daughter of mine. Oh well, I suppose I'll have to face Great Zeus after all. It will not be pleasant. He's been in a bad temper ever since Versailles.'

'Would it help if *I* faced him, too?' Dora asked, determined not to fall behind Jeremy in courage. 'After all, it's my fault, in a way.'

'I wouldn't dream of letting you, child. You're too lovely to bring to his notice. I don't want to be in trouble with Hera as well.'

'Again,' Hermes amended.

'I share your admiration for Jeremy's audacity, mother,' Eros said. 'After all, it's a tribute to my marksmanship, too. But the implications are still alarming.'

Aphrodite shrugged. 'I've been in trouble before and I shall be again. And if you can't suggest anything helpful…'

'But I can.' They all looked at Eros–Jeremy suspiciously. 'A compromise. I hesitate to call it a bribe, even though it's one I think Jeremy and Dora would appreciate.'

'I have made it quite clear…' Jeremy began stiffly.

'Bear with me, Jeremy. I would just like to remind you of one of my divine mother's many titles. Among other things, she is known as Aphrodite Amologera.'

Jeremy and Dora looked at each other hopefully, and then helplessly. 'I'm afraid,' Jeremy admitted, 'that without a lexi-con…'

'It means,' Eros told them, 'Aphrodite the Postponer of Old Age.'

This time the silence was longer, while Aphrodite began to smile mischievously, Hephaestus to chuckle in his deep chest, and Eros merely to wait while his meaning sank in.

Stephen Patterson, of the third generation of literary agents of that name, was nervous and conscious of still being wet behind the ears. After all, Jeremy Stock was pretty well their most distinguished (and profitable) client, full of renown and royalties. This was 1979, and Stephen's grandfather had handled Stock's first novel in 1921; fifty-eight years of steady output, a book every eighteen months without fail, including five best sellers and seven made into films.

Clients at that level were for Stephen's father to handle. But his father was in America, and Stock and his wife had turned up on one of their rare London visits from their home in Cyprus with only forty-eight hours' warning. So here was Stephen left with no choice but to take them out to dinner and to do his best.

But his nervousness vanished over the hors d'oeuvres. Somehow it was easy to relax with this friendly and incredibly handsome couple. Stephen had done his homework. He knew that Jeremy Stock was 82 and Dora Stock was 79, but he found it hard to believe. The man's hair was gray, but his voice was crisp and he carried himself like a tennis star. The woman's hair was pure white, but her eyes sparkled and most women of forty would be delighted to have her figure. If it hadn't been patently absurd to Stephen's 25-year-old imagination, he would have described her as sexy.

By the time they were halfway through the steak, he was trying to think of some enterprise he could pull off independently of his father. He even asked if Mr. Stock had ever thought of a book of poems. After all, critics had often praised the lyricism of his prose.

Jeremy smiled. 'I haven't written a poem since I was your age.'

'But couldn't you...'

'No. This Nuits St. Georges is excellent, don't you think?'

Stephen was not so inexperienced that he failed to recognise a head-off. So he changed the subject with good grace and called for another bottle.

He had never enjoyed a business dinner so much in his short professional career, and his guests seemed as vivacious over the brandy as they had been over the sherry. What an amazing couple!

He felt suddenly reluctant to have the evening end. 'Would

you like to go on to a night club?'

Jeremy Stock laid a hand on his wife's and looked at her, seeming amused about something. The glance she gave him back made Stephen's heart jump—and she was three times his age, for God's sake.

'It's very good of you, Stephen, but thank you, no,' Jeremy Stock said. 'My wife and I rather enjoy going to bed early.'

II

ACTION REPLAY

he morning sun through the floor-to ceiling net curtains bathed Connie in light, brilliant but soft. From four stories below us, the early clamour of Athens rose out of Omonia Square.

'Come back to bed,' I said.

She smiled at me. When Connie, naked, smiles, she seems to smile all over; in that incredible light. Well. 'Don't tempt me, insatiable. There isn't time. The tour bus leaves at nine, and I want a bath and breakfast.'

I looked at my digital watch. It said 7:56, June 10.

'You underrate me, but I'll let you off this once, or you might get indigestion.' I got out of bed and reached for the Pentax while her back was turned. She heard the shutter click and glanced over her shoulder, and I caught her again. She sighed, not really meaning it. We'd only been married three months, but she was used to me by now—and anyway, with a fortnight of Greek sunshine and bikinis and things ahead, she know she was in for a lot of it. Besides, I'm not bad, and some of the results I'd got already would have done any girl's ego good.

'Put that thing away and get shaved, darling,' she said, and added not very relevantly, 'Beside's, today's the day for Grandpa's letter.'

'Not before noon on the tenth of June, 1980, the

instructions are.'

'You lawyers! You've got it right there in your case. What do four hours matter?'

'Oh, I don't know. Call it professional ethics or superstition or something. Anyhow, it's been waiting half a century, so it can wait another four hours.'

'Are we taking it with us to Cape Sunion?'

'Why not? From what I hear, it'll be a nice dramatic setting for reading it.'

'I wonder what it says,' she murmured, not for the first time. Come to that, the family had been wondering for years. My father had lived till 1972, but he'd never know now. Apart from me, all that was left of the direct family was my sister, her husband and the twins, and me—and now Connie, of course.

There it had lain, for half a century, in the old boy's dead box in our office, clearly addressed in his own hand. 'To be hoped not earlier than noon on the tenth day of June nineteen hundred and eighty by my eldest surviving heir and successor.' In other words, no, by myself, Marcus Braithwaite Duffy.

It had always been the object not merely of natural family curiosity, but of a degree of puzzlement. The will of my grandfather, Norman Paul Duffy, had been straightforward and well drawn up, but the firm of which I, at thirty-four, am now the middle of three partners. There were no mysteries or complications about his estate, and so far as anyone knew, no skeletons in his cupboard. He had been an author, and his agent was his literary executor. He had *his* successor had handled that side of things perfectly competently.

So what could Grandpa possibly want to tell us, half a century later?

I'd always swished I had know him. He seemed to have been a character. His forte had been the supernatural, and I think in that field he was ahead of his time. As a writer, much better informed on it than most of his contemporaries, who seem to me to have relied more on atmosphere-building than authenticity. He had been a council member of the Society for Psychical research, and a personal friend of a remarkable number of relevant people, from Yeats to Margaret Murray. He had been a less gloomy writer than Lovecraft, and an infinitely better one than Wheatley, though he equalled Wheatley's gift for telling a compelling yarn. He had been an inveterate traveller. Incidentally, he had known Gerald Gardner in Malaya years before anyone else had heard of him. He had (so he used to boast to my father) clashed with Crowley and won, though the details of the encounter remained vague.

His books had gone on selling quite well for a few years after his death, and had then tapered off. But with the occult book of the 70's, he had been rediscovered, reprinted, anthologised, and generally re-established in a hagiography of the Genre. More than our family pride was gratified. Over the past few year, my sister and I had done very nicely out of royalties, and we'd been viewing the impending lapse of copyright with considerable regret, especially as Universal had been talking about another film and obviously postponing it with the same thought in mind.

But back to Grandpa's letter. It seemed highly unlikely that it could have anything to do with his estate, so my own theory had always been that it must concern his supernatural and psychic interests. I'd suggested to my sister that maybe it would ask us to contact a medium to try to contact *him* at a particular time, perhaps to tie in with other arrangements he's made, on the lines of the famous Cross Correspondence. But Sheila had pointed out that this wouldn't have tallied with Grandpa's views, because he had been a firm believer in reincarnation, so he wouldn't have expected to be contactable on the astral plane half a century later. He'd expect to have been reincarnated already. ('Perhaps *you're* Grandpa,' she'd suggested, and the thought made me feel queasy for days.) I'd had to concede her point, but I still felt the letter must have something to do with his special subject.

Anyway, in four hours we'd know. I put the letter in my camera case, we had breakfast, and at nine o'clock we climbed into the bus along with the rest of the package tour.

*   *   *

'You were right about the setting,' Connie admitted.

Neither of us had been there before, and it gook our breath away.

Way back when Greece was young, the prudent Athenians had built a temple to Poseidon on Cape Sunion as a consolation prize, after having rejected him as their city patron in favour of the rival candidate Pallas Athene. It must have done a lot to soothe the sea-god's ruffled pride. They couldn't have chose a better place for him; surrounded on three sides by the jewelled sea, far below, it is still magnificent even though the temple itself is now no more than a stone floor and a double row of roofless pillars, more skeletal even than the Parthenon.

At noon, when everyone had 'done' the temple and had gone down to the beach for a swim or to a cafe for an ouzo, Connie and I sat in the shade of one of Poseidon's pillars and opened the envelope.

It contained a two-page letter in Grandpa's small precise script, and a disc of parchment about three inches across carefully protected in a fold of tissue paper. The parchment was mass of symbols and of Hebrew lettering, but the central figure around which they were all grouped was the sign of infinity, ∞, coloured violet. All the rest of the characters were in black, with the exception of a scarlet Eye of Horus facing right at the top, and a blue one, facing left, at the bottom. As we don't read Hebrew, the infinity sign and the two Eyes of Horus were about the only things we could recognise, though some of the other symbols looked like the name-sigils that ritual magicians plot on planetary magic squares. We'd have needed the traditional squares as templates even to attempt to unravel them and I don't carry such things in my camera case.

We put the parchment disk back in the envelope for safety and turned our attention to the letter, which I read out loud to Connie.

'Dear Descendant,' it began. 'I am afraid I do

not know how else to address you. You may be my son, Joseph, or one of his children if (as I fondly hope) he has any, or a nephew or niece. Our family is at least large and fruitful enough for me to be reasonably certain that you are a blood relative.

'I am about to die. I would know that even if my doctor, who is a capable if unimaginative fellow, had not told me so. I am not alarmed at the prospect, and if (as I am conceited enough to assume) you have read some of my works, I do not need to tell you why, because I have made my beliefs perfectly clear. I am convinced of the truth of reincarnation, both from what I regard as valid personal awareness, and from a formidable mass of other evidence. However, it is not the purpose of this letter to convince you that my belief is right—merely to explain to you why I am un-afraid. My beloved wife preceded me four years ago. Joseph is well launched on his own life. So I have no reason for regret, either

'One thing, however, does annoy me—a personal and perhaps foolish thing. Allow me to explain. It may be that, by the time you read this, my published works will have gone the way of all literary flesh, and—to put it in practical terms—are no longer paying royalties to my heirs. That would be true of the great majority of authors, so why should I be one of the favoured few? I take pride in my craft, but I am no Shakespeare or even Dickens.

'However, it is possible that some chance of public taste will have persevered or revived a demand for my writings, and that you who read this letter will still be benefiting from their sale. If so, I am glad. Blood ties mean a great deal to me, and even if you have never met me, you are the fruit of one of my incarnations. But if you are still benefiting, by the law of the land (unless it has changed meanwhile) you will cease to do so very soon after you read this letter, because my works will be out of copyright. And that galls me. Call it undue family bride (and if it is, the fault is part of my karma, not yours) but if there are still rewards to be harvested from my efforts, I do not see why publishers should enjoy them unshared. I would like you, too, to go on sharing them.

'And by a strange coincidence, my researches into what is loosely called magic have offered me a solution. I have come across a formula which, I have every reason to believe, can evade the seemingly inevitable. It is contained in the enclosed talisman. Though I should warn you, not in what is written thereon alone; the talisman has undergone other processes without which it would remain ineffective.

'To reveal how I obtained the formula would, even in 1980, betray both a confidence and an oath. For the same reason, I may not explain to you why the particular date and time I shall give to you is important. All I can ask you to do is to follow my instructions exactly. I can at least promise that you will not be either physically or psychically harmed. It is of the nature of the process involved that it will either work, or fail completely, in which case nothing whatever will happen. But in my judgement—and I'm not altogether ignorant in the field—failure is an extremely remote possibility.

'The only other thing I should say is to admit that I do not know how it will work. I do not know the precise sequence of events, or development of circumstances, by which the formula will achieve its objective. But if it does work at all, the objective will be achieved. The copyright will never lapse.

'Here, then, are the instructions. The time of the operation will be 12:32p.m., Greenwich Mean Time, on June the twentieth, 1980, which is the moment of the first quarter of the moon. (To avoid any misunderstanding, I do mean 32 minutes past noon, G.M.T.)

You will perform the operation alone if you are unmarried, or with your wife or husband if you are married. You will prepare yourself, or yourselves, beforehand by complete immersion in a bath of water to which a handful of salt has been added. After drying, you will anoint every inch o your skin with pure olive oil. You will then sit cross-legged, on the floor or a bed or whatever is comfortable. One minute before 12:32, holding the talisman with the thumb and forefinger of both hands, you will start repeating your own name—the full Christian names and surname— out loud slowly but clearly, over and over again. If there are two of you, you will sit opposite each other, hold the talisman with all four of your hands, and repeat your own names alternately. You will continue to do so until you are certain that 12:32 is well past.

'You will perform this operation without clothes, jewellery, wrist-watches, make-up (in the case of a woman), spectacles, hair-clips, or anything else on your bodies, which must have nothing attached to them except the olive-oil anointing.

'That is all I have to say, except that my love and good wishes go with you.

'Norman Paul Duffy.'

When I had finished reading, Connie and I just stared at each other without speaking. If I had opened my mouth, I don't know what I might have said; that Grandpa was as mad as a hatter. That I couldn't wait to try his formula. That I wouldn't dream of trying it. That I was excited, embarrassed, impressed, frightened... I just didn't know. Nor, I could tell, did Connie.

After a while I re-folded the letter, put it back in the envelope with the talisman, and hut it away in my camera case. We stood up, still without speaking, and started down the hill towards the beach.

Halfway down, Connie said in a small voice, 'At least the

olive oil will be no problem.'

'No'

'Where will we be on the twentieth?'

'At Amnissos, in Crete. Last day but two of the holiday.'

'Oh,' she said.

That night I rang my sister from the hotel, as of course I'd promised, since she was as curious as I'd been. 'I was right, Sheila. It was magical stuff. He wants me to try out a formula. A sort of spell.'

'*What* sort of spell? What for?'

'You won't believe this, but to stop his copyrights from lapsing.'

'Good God! Well, that I *am* for. There's only a couple of months to go. You'd better get weaving right away.'

I never have been able to tell when Sheila's joking, half-joking, or serious, so I kept it light. 'Can't, I'm afraid. It's got to be done at the time of the first quarter of the moon on the twentieth. Ten days' time. We'll still be in Crete.'

'Too bad. I'd have liked to join in.'

'The letter says me only, plus wife or husband, if any.'

'Oh, well, it's up to you two, then. How is "if any", by the way?'

'Fine. Right here beside me.'

'Lovely. Put her on.'

I handed over to Connie, who chattered with her in that semi-telepathic language of half-finished phrases women communicate by. It's hard enough to follow if you can hear both ends, and practically incomprehensible if you can only hear one end.

Afterwards, I asked her, 'Well?'

Connie lit a cigarette. 'Whether we think it's nonsense or not, Mark, we're going to have to do it. Sheila will be so disappointed if we don't at least try.'

And so it was decided. Cowardly, really, as we admitted to each other later. We were both dying to try out Grampa's spell, but we'd have felt foolish admitting it. Sheila's (doubtless exaggerated) eagerness gave us the perfect excuse to go ahead, while pretending to ourselves that it was against our better judgement.

The decision made, we proceeded to enjoy our holiday. And a wonderful holiday it was. Six days on the mainland, starting with two in Athens and then visiting Delphi, Mycenae and Corinth. Then a night sea-journey to Crete, for a week there, which was to be followed by a final day and night in Athens and the flight home, but we resolutely closed our minds to the end of it.

We fell in love with Crete, with the tremendous impact of Knossos and its more enigmatic twin Phaestos; with the Shangri-La remoteness of the Plain of Lassithi and the candle-lit descent into the cave where Zeus was born; with the sun and the sea and the mountains; and above all with the people, who are at the same time the most dignified and the friendliest in the world.

For Connie and me, as comparative newlyweds, it was a time of personal alchemy. Three months ago, for various reasons, we hadn't been able to take a proper honeymoon. Now we did. I'd always believed Connie and I were made for each other, and the days on Crete proved it. The last barriers faded and the last incomprehensions were made clear. We had reached that precious state, known only to lovers, when it seems at the same time as though everything is known and yet there is infinity awaiting discovery.

Without that closeness, I don't think we could have survived what has followed. By now (whatever 'now' means) we might well have escaped into madness or suicide.

But for those days, life was cloudless. We visited all the wonderful places, and in between we lazed at our idyllic hotel, a cluster of pleasant little chalets around a blue swimming pool by the beach at Amnissos where Odysseus once landed. We grew brown and we drank ouzo and retsina and we made friends and we learned Greek dances and I photographed everything in sight but mostly Connie. We made love in the warm silence of the night, and sometimes on impulse with our bodies still salty from the water of the pool.

We rarely mentioned the parchment talisman or our appointment with the first quarter of the moon, and yet the knowledge of it somehow added a little tang of excitement to our euphoria, like the slice of lemon in a bland cocktail.

When June the twentieth finally came, we prepared for Grandpa's 'operation' as though it were the most natural thing in the world. The time difference with G.M.T. made it early afternoon, so we skipped lunch. We filled the bath and put in the handful of salt, and immersed and dried each other, hair and all—Connie's is long, so we allowed an extra ten minutes to use the hair-drier. Then we opened the can of olive oil I had bought in Heraklion market, and carefully and rather enjoyably anointed each other all over. Out of consideration for the hotel, we had decided not to sit oily on the bed, so we spread towels on the floor, and sat cross-legged opposite each other with the talisman between us. We had obeyed instructions meticulously. I'd laid my watch where I could see it, and Connie had even removed her nail-varnish.

'Which name should I say?' Connie wondered suddenly. 'My married one, or my maiden one?'

'Oh... that's a point.'

'How about both? Constance Mary Duffy nee Chalmers?'

'Covers all contingencies. You'd make a good lawyer yourself.' I glanced at the watch. 'Three minutes to go.'

We picked up the talisman and held it between us, with our thumbs and forefingers.

'Good luck, darling.'

'Good luck, my love.'

When the minutes on my digital watched flicked to 31, we began.

'Marcus Braithwaite Duffy.'

'Constance Mary Duffy nee Chalmers.'

'Marcus Braithwaite Duffy.'

'Constance Mary Duffy nee Chalmers.'

The two names, male and female in counterpoint, became

hypnotic and then uplifting. Just our two names, in our two voices, rhythmically repeated, seemed a twofold mantra of declared love, sealing us off from the outside world.

We lost all sense of time. Then, without warning, we seemed to be sitting inside a living rainbow, which held for a moment, swirled vertiginously, and plunged us into oblivion.

The morning sun though the floor-to-ceiling net curtains bathed Connie in light, brilliant but soft. From four stories below us, the early clamour of Athens rose out of Omonia Square.

'Come back to bed,' I said.

She smiled at me. When Connie, naked, smiles, she seems to smile all over, and in that incredible light...

You know how the feeling of *déjà vu* creeps up on you like a quiet tingling in your nerves. Well, what do you do if instead it hits you like a steam-hammer?

I will tell you what you do. You stare at each other stupidly, with your mouths open.

It was Connie who moved first. She came and sat on the edge of the bed, trembling a little. 'Amnesia?' she suggested throatily. 'This must be our last morning in Athens. We've forgotten a day and a half.'

'So you're lost, too. How did you know *I* was?'

She shrugged. 'Your face... Darling, how did it *happen*?'

I think I knew the truth even then. Without thinking, I said, 'Con, we aren't tanned. You've no bikini marks.'

She looked at me, wide-eyed, and then at herself.

'Dare I look at my watch?' I said, foolishly.

Connie nodded. I looked. It said 7:56, June 10.

'My God.' I whispered.

Then, somehow, we pulled ourselves together and started checking properly. None of the things we had brought were among our luggage. The brooch which Connie had lost in the sea at Amnissos lay on the dressing table. The 35mm colour films I'd expended so lavishly were still in their cellophane-wrapped packs of six cassettes each. Connie's tube and bottles of make-up which she'd stocked up for the holiday were still practically full. And so on. There was no doubt about it at all. Somehow, we had jumped back in time, by ten and a quarter days.

Still unable to take it all in, we nevertheless found that we were ravenously hungry. We dressed and went down to breakfast.

'Now that I've got used to the idea,' Connie declared, 'I'm really quite excited about it.' She grinned at me in that quirky way of hers. 'Whatever else, we're getting two holidays for the price of one.'

We were leaning in the same shade against the same pillar of Poseidon's temple on Cape Sunion. In our suddenly elated mood, we had decided it was well worth a second visit.

'One thing seems clear,' I said. 'We're the only ones who are affected. Everyone else is behaving quite normally. People we've known for twelve days are treating us as though they've only known us for two, and they obviously believe they have. After all, we were prepared for *something* to happen. It's pretty staggering, but at least we've got a cause for it—Grandpa's spell. You can't tell me that if all those other people had suddenly found themselves jumping back in time, without *any* warning or explanation, they wouldn't all be screaming their heads off. No, this really *is* June the tenth. As it was. And we really have come back to it—all by ourselves, in some way, though God knows how.'

'Partial success for Grandpa, at least,' Connie pointed out. 'For us, the lapse of copyright has been *postponed* for ten days, if nothing else.'

'That's what puzzles me, Con. Grandpa's letter was positive that it would work either completely or not at all. And somehow I'm inclined to believe him. So why this bit of back-tracking? Where does it fit in, and what happens next?'

'We shan't know that till after the twentieth, shall we? Oh, talking of Grandpa's letter—where is it?' Still unopened in your suitcase?'

'Oh, Christ, I forgot to look. We'll see when we get back.'

But it wasn't in my suitcase, or anywhere else. The letter had simply vanished.

Oh a sudden thought, I rang my sister. She sounded pleased and surprised to hear from us so early in the holiday, and we exchanged family pleasantries. Then I said casually, 'Today's the tenth. Aren't you curious about Grandpa's letter?'

A moment's silence from Sheila's end, and then, sounding genuinely puzzled. 'What letter, Mark?'

I got out of it somehow, pretending that it was a laboured joke which ha misfired, and changing the subject.

Afterwards, Connie said, 'Well, that's it. Grandpa's letter has been cut out of history, except in your memory and mine. All part of the spell, I suppose, however it's working. Let's forget it, darling, and enjoy our bonus ten days.'

We did. We had an even better time, because we knew which places we wanted to spend more time on, and which less. We knew the little cafes, from the start, which we hadn't discovered till near the end first time round. We knew which members of our tour were worth making friends with quickly, and which were better kept at a polite distance. We swam and we got brown and we made love.

We coasted happily along till midday on the twentieth. Then suddenly Connie looked at e and said, 'Darling, I'm scared. I don't know why. I just want this afternoon to be *over*.'

'I'm a bit on edge myself, love,' I admitted. 'Silly, isn't it? Let's have a swim and take our minds off it.'

So we skipped lunch again and played around like dolphins in the warm sea-water of the swimming pool. We forgot our apprehension, and we forgot time, too.

Until, without warning, the water round us was a liquid rainbow, which steadied, swirled, and flung us into darkness.

The last thing I remembered was our two hands, reaching out and clutching for each other.

*   *   *

The morning sun through the floor-to-ceiling net curtains bathed Connie in light, brilliant but soft. From four stories below us, the early clamour of Athens rose out of Omonia Square.

Connie screamed. I think I did, too.

So far, we have lived through those ten and a quarter days eighty-seven times. That is nearly two and a half years of our own private calendar.

Our Greek is now fluent and idiomatic. We know the life histories of our fellow holiday-makers in wearisome detail, and we have had to be very careful to hide the fact with each fresh start. We know Knossos, Phaestos, Delphi, Mycenae, Corinth, and the Athens and Heraklion Museums rather better than our guides. We know every street of Heraklion and Hagios Nikolaus, and we have quite an extensive familiarity with Athens and the Piraeus. I have taken upwards of fifty thousand photographs, none of which have ever been processed, because to stop taking them, or to mime with an empty camera to satisfy the fellow-travelers who already knew, before June the tenth, that I was an enthusiast, would be finally to admit defeat. We have got brown eighty-seven times over. How many times we have made love we would neither count nor guess, because that would somehow be to violate the one continuity which keeps us sane.

Connie has spent two and a half years practically certain that she is seven weeks pregnant, and her ability to live with that endlessly postponed hope is quite enough by itself to define her as a very remarkable woman.

We have wondered sometimes whether to try a dash home for a few days in London. But we had let our house to someone else for the fortnight—and to face our much-loved families, and our old friends , across an iron curtain of incommunicable knowledge would be more than we could bear. While this limbo lasts, Athens and Amnissos must be our home, and a handful of tourists, waiters, guides and couriers, whom we have known for two and a half years but who have never known us for more than twelve days, must be our friends.

We have learned some techniques to make repetition less repetitious. We tend to alternate between being the life and soul of one tour, and being virtual hermits on the next, or between being dedicated amateur archaeologists and being philistine hedonists. We have even been able to do a little good, perhaps. We were able to save the marriage of one sad couple, after watching it reach breaking-point for maybe the fiftieth time, because by then we knew so much about them that we knew the precise catalyst needed to heal their wounds, and applied it. The only trouble, is of course, and that we've had to apply it anew each time since; it has become a duty we haven't the heart to neglect.

But if we are not careful, we may come to hate even these evanescent friends we have. Hate them through sheer envy of the fact that *they* are going home, while we seem doomed to reawaken again and again in that sunlit hotel room four stories up from Omonia Square. For ever and ever amen.

We are tired. *We* want our child to be born, not to remain for always a bundle of cells in Connie's grieving womb. We want to live our lives. We want to die of old age.

Damn you, Grandpa, what went wrong? Get us out of here!

III

THE SALZBURG PROJECT

ou're joking,' Markov said.

'Have you ever known me to joke about work, Yosif Mikhailovitch?'

Markov sighed and shook his head, resisting the temptation to answer that he had never known Rodzianko to joke about anything. Whatever it was that had brought Rodzianko up to the rank of colonel in the KGB, it had not been a sense of humour. Nor, Markov thought drily, had it been field experience. The man was an apparatchik through and through. While he, Markov, had spent most of his career abroad, doing the dirty work, and dodging the dirty work of his Western opposite numbers, Rodzianko had been at home saying the right things to the right people and learning to live with computers. That was why Markov, at fifty-two this year, 1963, was sitting on the wrong side of a desk in Moscow and taking orders from thirty-eight-year-old Rodzianko, who sat on the safe side of it. The patronizing show of respect with which Rodzianko treated him, as 'one of our most experienced field operatives', only made it more tedious. My God, you needed a sense of humour in this business, or you might forget your manners.

'Who is this woman, comrade Colonel?'

'Anna Khrushcheva. She is a—'

'Any relation to—?'

'No. She is a photographic darkroom assistant on *Komsomolskaya Pravada*, age thirty-one, unmarried, no close family.' Rodzianko paused slightly, then shrugged. Markov understood the shrug. No close family meant an advantage in that fewer questions would be asked if she went on a 'holiday', but a disadvantage in that there were no hostages for her good behaviour. Clean but undistinguished Party record,' Rodzianko went on. 'Hobbies: piano and swimming. Good reliable worker but unambitious. Extcetera etcetera. Here.' He passed the biog over to Markov, who memorized everything he needed to know in little more than a glance (a trick you learned, out there where the real work was done) and then spent rather longer studying the girl's photograph, which he found more informative.

It reminded him somewhat of a bush-baby he had watched a length in an Amsterdam pet shop while he was waiting for a contact who was unforgivably late. The astonished vulnerable eyes, the warily cuddly appearance, the little hands that might, in panic, prove deceptively strong. As a man with unfulfilled paternal instincts, the picture appealed to him. As a professional agent, it alarmed him.

'And she's a telepath,' he said unhappily.

'She is a telepath. A remarkably gifted one.'

'It isn't something I have any experience with.'

'You mean you think it's a lot of mumbo-jumbo.'

'I didn't say that, comrade Colonel.'

'But I'm sure you think it. You are, after all, a severely practical man, which is why you are so valuable to the organization.'

Unctuous little bastard, Markov thought. 'I know there were experiments in the sixties—the Popov people with Nikolaiev and Kamensky, and so on, but I presumed they'd faded out.'

'that is what the public—here and abroad—were meant to think. We couldn't fool the Pentagon, of course, because they're working on it as hard as we are. But research into telepathy and associated matters had become a top security project—or rather, a cluster of projects. The KGB has its own laboratory.'

'Which means the Army has too, and keeps our noses out of it.'

Rodzianko smiled thinly. 'Doubtless. As we keep theirs out of ours. But you and I are not concerned with that at the moment. What we are concerned with is that our own researches, under the leadership of Academician Runitch, have discovered and trained several telepaths at least as gifted Karl Nikolaiev, two or three of them being considerably more so. Their outstanding product is Anna Khrushcheva.'

'If I know anything about scientists, she can't have spent much time in her darkroom, playing the piano, or swimming.'

'She has had a lot of "sick leave" in the past couple of years. The point is, Yosif Mikhailovitch, they are ready to try her out on a field operation. And since she is not a trained agent, she must work under the guidance of a real professional, such as yourself.'

'You say she's not a trained agent. Presumably she's had some sort of...'

'I mean she's a completely untrained in weaponry, un-armed combat, code procedures, or any of the hard realities of an agent's life.'

'But for God's sake! Why not? The poor bitch could have had the basics, couldn't she? She'll be a babe in arms!'

'In your very capable arms, comrade. That is why you have been chosen. Let me explain. During the research program, one unexpected and unfortunate fact has come to light. The research team's first two star pupils—a man and a woman—were very promising indeed. Their telepathic ability was of the same order as Khrushcheva's. So when they were ready for work, from that point of view, they were given the very training which you naturally assumed would be necessary. They went to the School and learned everything. They were very good. In particular, the man became a first-class shot, and the woman was brilliant at unarmed combat. There was only one snag. The training destroyed their telepathic faculty. It would seem that there is something inherent in the training of an effective KGB agent which is incompatible with psychic sensitivity.'

'You surprise me.'

Rodzianko seemed impervious to irony. 'Anyway, that's how it is. But the telepathic weapon is too valuable to waste. So...'

'So, I'm to be nursemaid and bodyguard to a defenceless spook... Oh well. Something to tell my grandchildren if I had any. Right, then, comrade Colonel. What's the job?'

Rodzianko took a file out of his drawer and laid it in front of Markov. Markov read the title on the cover and gasped. 'The Salzburg Project! In the name of all that's holy, couldn't they try her out on something simpler? You know how delicate that one is. You know how touchy the Austrians are at the moment, after that Klagenfurt business. One mistake, and there'd be red faces from Leningrad to Ulan Bator. Which is where you and I would probably end up.'

'easy, now, Yosif Mikhailovitch. That is precisely why we are sending you and Khrushcheva. We have to know what the Americans are up to, up there in the forest. The Austrians don't know they're up to anything, and we don't want them to know, for various good political reasons. We have to find out what it is, without drawing either the Americans' or the Austrians' attention to ourselves, or even the Austrians' attention to the Americans. Never mind the background—that's at Politburo level—but that is the situation we have to deal with.'

'Infiltration?'

'Impossible. The unit is too small. Two men and a woman, without servants. One of them at a time comes down into town for shopping, once a week. Their cover is accepted—American novelist and wife, and wife's brother. In fact they are three thoroughly professional CIA operatives. We could only find out what they're up to by a direct attack on the house—which is ruled out. Do you get the picture?'

Markov sighed. 'I get it. Psychic spying, if it works, would be undetected. Find out, get out, and no one any the wiser except us.'

'Precisely. Now, the cover. Khrushcheva has a Moscow University degree in English.'

'So I noticed.'

'And your English is excellent, if slightly accented. .So you will be Joseph and Ann Levy, father and daughter. London Jewish, on holiday in Salzburg. Any English ear will accept your trace of accent as Jewish rather than Slavonic.'

'I do know that, comrade Colonel. I've done it before.'

'Of course, of course. And her musical interests will make a Salzburg holiday seem natural. With an inexperienced agent like Khrushcheva, it helps if she can believe easily in her own cover.'

Teach your grandmother to suck eggs, Markov thought sourly, and slipped into another professional trick of listening with half an ear why still looking interested and missing nothing.

The bush-baby eyes gave a misleading impression, Markov soon realised. Anna was certainly sensitive (in the everyday sense, never mind the 'mumbo-jumbo') but neither so helpless nor so vulnerable as her appearance suggested. During their familiarisation week at one of the department's dachas fifty kilometres from the capital, he found her to be relaxed, self-possessed, and spontaneous. Thank God, she also had a sense of humour. She referred to the week as 'the parental honeymoon', and to Rodzianko as 'Colonel Rubberstamp.' (From the start they had spoken in English, and in character. She had seen the sense of that at once.)

'You should watch your tongue while we're indoors,' he warned her when they were strolling in the woods on the second day. 'I take it for granted and dacha is bugged.'

'Haven't you searched it to find out? I thought that was the first thing James Bonds always did.'

'Modern equipment is micro-miniaturized. You might have a chance in a hotel room. But in the department's own dacha, you'd have to take the building apart.'

'Maybe they've sewn something into my clothes,' she

laughed.

'No.'

'You've looked?'

'Every stitch of it, I'm afraid. Including that lot, while you were swimming in the lake. Are you offended?'

'Reassured. It means you're looking after me, Dad.'

'It's my job. My safety as well as yours depends on such little details.'

'And you don't like it?'

He smiled. 'I thought you were a telepath?'

'Oh, but that wouldn't be fair,' she said quickly, and apparently genuinely. 'We've got a week to learn to be an English father and daughter. How could we do it naturally, if I tried that on you?'

'Now *I'm* reassured,' he told her.

'You still haven't answered my question, though. You don't like this job, do you?'

'Let's put it this way, Ann. If we were ordinary citizens, I should be very happy with you as my daughter but as a pair of agents, going on a delicate assignment in a neutral country, I am scared stiff.'

'I suppose I am a bit of a handicap.'

He didn't want her disheartened, so he said, 'Only in one sense. With your gift, you should be a considerable asset.' She did not answer, so he went on, 'Could you read my mind, if you wanted to?'

'The odd thought, maybe. If I tried. But it doesn't work quite like that.'

'You'd better tell me how it does work.'

'Yes, I had, hadn't I? What I do isn't really telepathy at all, in the Nikolaiev sense. It's astral projection. I make my physical body comfortable and safe—it'll be part of your job to watch over me—and then I project my consciousness outside it. My astral body and my consciousness. In that condition I can leave my physical body behind and wander about, looking at things and people. And I can hear what they're thinking. It's very hard to describe.'

'And for someone like me to accept,' he said ruefully. 'Academician Runitch or no Academician Runitch.'

'Oh, he's a pet. A bit fussy, but very clever.' She halted, glancing around. 'Look, Dad, let me try to show you. It's a lovely warm day, but you'd better put your jacket over me, because my body temperature drops. Here.'

She chose a soft patch of grass and lay down on her back, wriggling till she was comfortable. Obediently, and very curious, Markov laid his jacket over her and sat down beside her.

'I'll look pretty well dead,' she warned him. 'You may even think I've stopped breathing, but I won't have done. Just don't disturb me, or let anything else disturb me, till I come round of my own accord. Right?'

'Right. How long will you be like that?'

'It depends. Anything from five minutes to an hour or more. It's hard to judge time when I'm out. But I can come back when I want to, so I'll try not to make it too long this time.'

She was 'out' almost at once, and the first thing that struck Markov was that all her appearance of vulnerability had come back. He found himself trying to remember, absurdly, if he had ever seen a bush-baby with its eyes shut. Automatically, he had triggered the stop-watch function of his digital watch, and he smiled at himself for such a habitual observer's reflex.

My God, she does look dead, he thought. But she must know what she's about. He sat very still, watching her and waiting.

It was shorter than he expected. When she stirred, muttered to herself, and sat up with a little shiver, he stopped the watch. 'Four minutes forty-seven seconds,' he told her. 'Are you all right?'

'Fine. Give me a minute to rest, and then we'd better start back. Colonel Rubberstamp's on his way to visit us.'

'You know that? I didn't.'

'Yes, he's got a warning of some kind. He'll tell you, but not me. He's not happy about it. A tip-off from London about a man called Stanek, Stanitch, something like that.'

'Oh, Christ.'

'Important?'

'Could be. We'll see. Forget it for now.'

She got up and gave him back his jacket, and they started walking back towards the dacha. He was silent, trying to sort out his thoughts. He realized that he had still been sceptical, unready for the possibility that she might be all Rodzianko had said she was. But how could she possibly have known of Stanek's existence—let alone that he was under suspicion? And was Rodzianko on his way?

'Poor Yosif,' she said unexpectedly, in Russian.

'Dad,' he corrected her, in English. 'And why "poor"?'

'Sorry. I must remember. I tried not to peek, honestly, I did. But that thought about the bush-baby was so funny you caught my attention. And then it came in such a wave, how if things had been different I could really have been your daughter—that girl in Odessa.' She broke off, looking almost tearfully apologetic.

'That was a long time ago,' he said without expression.

'I know. I broke away then. You'd just caught me out, that's all. I'll be more careful another time. I've upset you, haven't I?'

He thought for a moment, determined to be honest with her. 'As a person, not too much. That was a memory I might well have put into words some time. And I've already told you I'd be happy if you were my daughter.' He smiled deliberately, to ease it. 'But professionally, being so transparent goes against all my conditioning.'

She took his arm, and they walked without speaking for a while. 'I'll try not to be too much of a pain in the arse,' she said at last.

'We'll manage,' he told her. 'At least your English is idiomatic.'

'I must emphasize that it's unconfirmed,' Rodzianko said. They were sitting in front of the dacha, out of the girl's hearing.

'Spider only had a hint to go on, but he thought we should be warned.'

'Could it affect the Salzburg Project?'

'If Stanek is a double agent, there is a remote possibility.'

'And so?'

'The decision is that you go ahead, but with the possibility in mind.'

Markov knew that when Rodzianko said 'the decision is', that meant higher authority and no argument. Markov's limited right to express doubts about an assignment stopped at Rodzianko's desk. So he shrugged and said nothing.

'How are you getting on with Khrushcheva?' Rodzianko asked.

'From yesterday until the assignment is over, she is Ann Levy,' Markov relieved his feelings by saying.

'Very sound procedure. How are you getting on with Ann Levy?'

'I think a week will be enough for her to behave convincingly as my daughter and an English tourist, provided that we do not run into trouble in Salzburg. And by 'trouble', I mean any situation which requires quick professional thinking, which cannot be expected of her. She is quick-witted, but that cannot entirely replace experience and training.'

'Obviously. That is why you are going with her.'

'Obviously.' No point in raking over that again. 'And incidentally, you were right about her abilities. My compliments to Academician Runitch.'

'You've had a demonstration?'

'An hour ago we were sitting in the woods. She told me that we must come back here, because you were on your way with a warning which you were unhappy about, and which you would give to me but not to her. About a tip-off from London concerning a man called Stanek or Stanitch.'

'Rodzianko pursed his lips. 'Well. *Well!* The tip-off only came in this morning. I decoded it myself, and the only other person I have told is the Chief.'

'Impressive, isn't it?'

'Almost too impressive. I knew she was good, but...' He shook his head. 'One wonders if our organization can really contain such people, valuable as they appear to be. Security could become meaningless.'

Markov felt all-too-familiar icy sensation in his plexus. 'She has had maximum clearance,' he said defensively.

'To know what she needs to know, yes. Not to know anything she may care to pry into, without us being aware of it.'

'The decision is to use these people. The risks must have been fully taken into account. And after all, comrade Colonel— the fact that firearms are occasionally known to backfire doesn't mean we go back to bows and arrows.'

'You are right, of course,' Rodzianko said. But his eyes were still thoughtful, and Markov's solar plexus felt no warmer.

'They're flying out one of the weirdoes right away,' Donelli explained. 'Pan-Am Flight 137, due Vienna oh-nine-fifty. His name's Jacob Trench, schoolteacher from Colorado Springs, age thirty-four, Caucaian, single. One day's briefing here, then you and he will high-tail it up to Salzburg on Thursday. I've booked you both in the Liliengarten, under your own names. The Commie pair are booked from Saturday at Zum Roten Hirsch, as Joseph and Ann Levy, father and daughter, British. The girl is the telepath, said to be good. Hope our man Trench is better. Your hotel faces theirs across the street, and I've got you front rooms, second floor. So quite apart from the spook bit, you'll be able to keep an eye on their comings and goings.'

'Is the tip-off reliable?' Potter asked.

'We checked the booking, and it tallies. That's all we know. Frankfurt says the source has proved good before. We'll just have to take it from here, Walt, and see how the cards fall.'

'What are they after?'

'Our man couldn't say, or didn't. But Salzburg's too damn near to Operation Pumpernickel for my taste. Only fifteen kilometres up towards the Altersee. That must be what they're sniffing at.'

'So if I confirm that that's their caper, why not just eliminate 'em?'

'Negative, repeat negative. The word is no dust-up, Walt. Not without further orders. The Austrian situation's too hair-triggered as of now. They know too many of us, and we could all be persona non grata tomorrow if we put a foot wrong. What the Austrians *don't* know is about Operation Pumpernickel, and they mustn't. We didn't think the Commies knew either, but it seems we were wrong. This is a private war, Walt. We can't afford to expose them, and visa versa. So it's *molto pianissimo.*'

'But we've got to keep their snowy boots out of Pumpernickel.'

'Precisely. In the ordinary run of things, it wouldn't be too difficult. After all, you could hide the Pumpernickel hardware in three separate components each no bigger than a deck of cards. So what could they find out, without actually going in and grabbing the stuff? But they're as hog-tied as we are, in today's Austria. They've been told nothing conspicuous too, that's clear. Otherwise they wouldn't be sending in just a man and a girl, would they? Especially since she's a spook.'

'She may not be just a spook. I knew a girl once who I thought only read tarot cards, and I got a sprained shoulder to prove how wrong I was.'

'I've got news for you, sonny. You may not be fully briefed on the spook racket.'

'"Not fully" is understating it.'

'I got a quick run-down on it, last time I was back home, in case we had to use one suddenly, like now. It seems you can't teach 'em the delicacies of professional mayhem, or they stop spooking. The two don't mix. If we've found that out, so has Moscow. So young Ann will sprain no elbows.'

'It was a shoulder.'

'Don't quibble.'

Potter lit a cigarette. 'Oh, well, it figures. They can't get at Pumpernickel without starting a brawl, and right now a brawl is out, for KGB and for CIA. (Why can't politicians mind their own business and let us brawl in peace? Don't answer that.) So they bring in a spook, a non-brawling voyeur...'

'Voyeurs, in this case.'

'Don't *you* quibble. A psychic keyhole-peeper. It's the obvious answer, *if* spooking works. Does it?'

'Yes, they say it does. Our own handful are trained and the boys are eager to try them out. And on the principle of technological parallelism, Moscow...'

'Should be ready and eager too. Yes, it does figure. So what do you want me to do?'

'They promise me this Jake Trench is their best. But he'll be—remember what somebody said about Wilson at Versailles? —"Like a virgin in a bawdy-house, calling piteously for a glass of lemonade." He may be a grade one spook, but when it comes to James Bondery he'll be way out of his league.'

'So I'm the baby-sitter.'

'Affirmative. Look after him, change his diapers, give him whatever conditions he needs, and get him spooking on the spook.'

'I hope he plays chess. It sounds like one hell of an assignment.'

'A lousy one, I agree. But you have consolation. There's someone else in exactly the same predicament.'

'Oh? Who?'

'He has all my sympathy,' Potter say, with feeling.

For Anna at least, the first three days in Salzburg were a real holiday. Markov was too old a hand to be in a hurry unless he must, and he decreed an acclimatization period. 'Learning to be an English tourist in the Moscow woods is one thing. Being one in Salzburg is quite another,' he told her. 'Besides, you've only been abroad once before, for that London trip the university fixed up. And I've no illusions about what *that* must have been like.'

'Actually, it wasn't too stuffy at all,' she said. 'I didn't learn *all* my colloquialisms from films and books. The professor in charge of our party got a reprimand afterwards, I believe.'

'Which means he'd been doing the job properly, poor devil. By the way, remember it was eleven years ago. Some of those colloquialisms may be dated.'

'Don't worry too much, Dad. Thirty-one-year-old spinsters *do* use dated colloquialisms, thus betraying their retarded emotional development and general insecurity.'

Markov laughed. He was—almost—enjoying the holiday himself.

Zum Roten Hirsch was a delightful hotel, with a garden that gave a view of the Salzach River, and their interconnecting rooms overlooked both. Markov entertained her by doing his 'James bond bit' in search of electronic bugs. He found none, but was still not satisfied on principle, and ordered that all significant conversations must be out of doors. Anna's astral projection sessions required no speech, only a code of signals they quickly devised. She could make notes afterwards if necessary, and report the results to him later in the garden— burning notes, of course. Barring unforeseen developments, the assignment might prove more straightforward than Markov had feared.

Meanwhile, they were Joseph and Ann Levy, on holiday from London.

They 'did' the Mozart house and museum, from which Anna could hardly be torn away. She got into animated conversation with a couple from Birmingham who were fellow enthusiasts. This put Markov's nerves on edge, especially when it was extended to a drink together afterwards. But Anna conducted herself admirably, steering away from tricky subjects with a natural skill which greatly reassured him.

They admired the archbishop's old and new residences and the town hall, and the seventeenth-century cathedral modelled on St. Peter's in Rome. They wandered along the Salzach banks. When they explored the big and little shops, Anna was naturally fascinated by the musical ones. When her 'father' confessed that his own musical abilities were limited to the harmonica, she bought him a Hohner and presented it to him in the shop with a kiss on the cheek and a '*Neets gezunt!*' He smiled, played a few bars of *Eine Kleine Fruehlingsweise* for the benefit of the sales clerk, and asked her when they got outside, 'What was that bad German you tried?'

She shook her head reprovingly. 'And you're supposed to be Jewish! It was Yiddish, and it meant "Use it in good health". Really, you armatures!'

'One to you,' he admitted, unsure whether to laugh or worry.

They took a trip up to the Altersee, and on the way he was able to point out to her, from a kilometre away, the isolated Alpine chalet which was the target of their assignment. He was very relieved that she did not want a closer reconnaissance. She assured him that a mental picture of the house and its environment would be all the help she needed in getting an astral fix on her objective. He hoped she was right.

On the third day his mood of qualified optimism received a jolt.

They were in the hotel garden, Markov sipping a tall glass of lager and enjoying the sun while Anna held a laughing conversation with a young Austrian woman, matching her schoolgirl English with less-than-schoolgirl German (in what Markov had to admire as a very plausible London accent). They drifted casually close to him, and the woman, without changing her expression, switched to quiet, precise, obviously college Russian.

'There is a CIA man staying in the Liliengarten Hotel opposite, in Room 8. His name is Walter Potter. He has a younger man with him, Jacob Trench, in Room 9, whom we have not seen before. We do not know why they are here, or whether they are aware of you.' Then she moved away with Anna, still laughing, and a few minutes later gave her a friendly wave and left.

'Keep looking cheerful and relaxed,' he warned Anna when she rejoined him. 'That girl was an Embassy courier.'

'I know. I do pick up some things without astrally projecting, and she stuck out.'

'Not to anyone else, I hope. Did you hear what she said to me?'

'I heard.' She repeated the message to him in English by way of confirmation. 'What do we do now?'

'First of all I identify them by sight. Leave that to me—it's routine stuff, but I won't be caught doing it and you might. When I know, I'll point them out to you. Steer clear of them. You're very good with your casual tourist chat, but these are pros.'

'Right. And then?'

'I'll find out if it's us they're watching.'

'How?'

'I'm a pro, too. Have a lager.'

It was as Markov had said, routine stuff, made almost too easy by the circumstance that the Liliengarten had a newsstand in its lobby and Zum Roten Hirsch did not, so everybody crossed the road to buy a paper. Markov had been doing so himself ever since they arrived. He did so again now, as soon as he had finished his lager.

As he came away from the stand with the *Daily Express* (today's already—capitalism had some advantages, if only competitive speed) he glanced at the key board behind the desk. Keys 8 and 9 were in place. Good, his men were out. Less waiting, with any luck. He noted carefully their position on the board.

Back in Zum Roten Hirsch, he looked back across the street through the window of the cocktail bar. The Liliengarten had a modern plate-glass entrance, revealing most of the lobby, but from here the key board was out of sight. The coffee lounge, perhaps?

He tried it, and found that from a table behind the net curtains of the window he could just make out the Liliengarten key board. Not too clearly, but enough to see that keys 8 and 9 were still there. He rang Anna's room on the house phone and she came down.

She needed little explanation, and her eyes were better than his. Markov ordered coffee and cognac, and they settled down to wait. 'Which is nine-tenths of an agent's job,' he told her, 'and not always so comfortably.'

In fact, they were rewarded in less than an hour, and it was Anna who said, 'This might be them,' as the pair came up the street. Markov looked and agreed. A man about his own age with another in his middle thirties, the older probably American, the younger unmistakably. If they are, Markov thought, the older's the pro—too consciously unremarkable—and the other's the new boy. His suspicion was strengthened when the young man glanced almost surreptitiously across at Zum Roten Hirsch and the older one did not. If that's our pair, he thought glumly, it's our hotel they're interested in. He heard Anna suck her breath in sharply, and wondered if she'd drawn the same conclusion.

The two men turned into the Liliengarten and were given keys 8 and 9.

'So there we are,' Markov said. 'Have you got their faces fixed in your mind?'

'More than their faces,' she said, and for the first time since he had known her he could see that she was shaken. 'The younger one's a telepath. I pulled away just in time. He felt something, but I don't think he was quick enough to know what it was.'

'Oh, *Jesus!*' He put down his cup, carefully, feeling his hand shake. He must be getting too old. 'Now we have trouble.'

They were silent for a moment, then Anna asked, 'It means they're really on to us, doesn't it? That Stanek man *has* tipped them off.'

'I'm afraid so. And they're on to us in the worst possible way—with our own weapons. Ordinary surveillance we could have ridden out, because we're doing nothing it could detect. But *this...*'

'Don't panic, Dad. It may not be as bad as all that. At least I *know*, and there may be ways round it. After all, a situation like this was bound to arise sooner or later. Academician Runitch did warn us, and we've got at least a provisional plan for it. So take it easy while we think. Go on, drink your cognac. Do we warn Moscow?'

Markov sipped pensively. 'No, we don't. Stanek's being watched already, if he's not under lock and key by now. And there are too many unknowns. What we don't tell, can't leak. As long as the CIA don't know if *we* know they've a telepath on the job, we have a slight advantage. In our business, Ann, you don't trust even your own people father than you have to.'

'So I gather.'

'Then we get on with our job as best we can, and keep our own counsel till it's over. Right?'

She nodded. 'There's one thing I should warn you of, though. Telepaths differ a lot—in their strengths and weaknesses, in their methods, in what you might call the *shape* of their talents. This man Trench and I will be scouting around each other, very cautiously, both trying not to be noticed, try-ing to get the measure of each other. But *because* we don't know each other's "shape", there's always the chance we may make contact suddenly and accidentally. If that does happen, we'll *both* know. The cards will be on the table, and the rules of the game will change. And what the rules are will depend on our two "shapes". Do you understand me?'

'Yes, I think so. It happens in *our* world, too. Like Potter knowing me and me knowing Potter, and both knowing what the score is, while we play it cool on the surface and circle round each other with one eye on the Austrians. It could come to that with him and me, just as well.' He paused, and then said very seriously. 'But in our world, the rules of the game may mean that one of us has to... dispose of the other, if he can get away with it.'

'You mean kill him.'

'I mean kill him. I've done it myself, and more than once I've narrowly escaped having it done to me. We all know it, and you could almost say there's no hard feelings. I have to ask you, Ann. How about *your* world?'

She did not move or speak for quite a time. 'I thought we were told, no rough stuff,' she said at last.

'In your world, wouldn't the thing be undetectable? Long-distance?'

Again she was slow to answer. 'It isn't impossible—psychic killing. It has been done, far more often than people realise. But let me tell you the rules of *our* game, Dad. In a... a murderous confrontation between two trained psychics, the advantage isn't necessarily with the attacker. It's more like what the English call Russian Roulette. If the defender is psychically stronger—which neither of you may know for sure till you try it—the attack will bounce back. In other words, if two presumed psychic equals commit themselves to a fight-to-kill, they might almost as well toss a coin to see who wins. So even if I could bring myself to try to kill Trench by psychic attack— and I do know how, in theory—you could very easily find yourself with *my* corpse on your hands. You just wouldn't know till afterwards.'

Markov sighed. 'Thank God for that, anyway.'

'Eh?' She sounded surprised.

'Don't you see? It means Trench won't try it, either. *He's* got to assume you're equals, too. You must be, approximately, or you wouldn't have been sent on this job, either of you. You said, "If I could bring myself". *Could* you kill, in the line of duty?'

'Only in extreme self-defence, I'm afraid, Dad. I'm not a natural soldier.'

'You know what?' he said, smiling at her. 'Maybe I shouldn't be, in these circumstances, but I'm glad. One professional bastard in the family's enough.'

The fragile holiday mood had been shattered. There could be no doubt about that. Anna was under constant strain. She tried to explain to Markov just what mental, or psychic, disciplines she was having to impose on herself, but they were as difficult to communicate to a non-sensitive a colour to a man blind from birth. They seemed to amount to a constant watch for any mental probing from the American telepath, and a quick mental switch to 'innocent' thinking the moment she felt it'; 'but more complicated than that, actually,' she had to say with every attempted explanation.

The danger was, of course, that Markov's mind would be under surveillance too, and he was utterly dependent on her for warning, which meant he could never leave her side for more than a few minutes at a time, and while he had to be away from her—even to go to the toilet. He had to fill his mind with 'innocent' thoughts. At night, they left the door between their rooms open. Fortunately, his training enabled him to be instantly awake if she called his name.

They invented a defence. If she started talking about Mozart (sometimes in the middle of a sentence about something quite different) it meant 'Trench is probing'. Then Markov would do his best to think of Mozart and nothing but Mozart. Anna, of course, knew a great deal more about Wolfgang Amadeus than he did, so these incidents were more teacher-and-pupil sessions than discussions. In the first twenty-four hours, it happened six times. The shortest was two minutes ('he was only trying casually, I think') to nearly half an hour ('that one must have worn him out'). *Much more of this,* Markov told himself, *and I'll be an expert on Mozart and all his works.*

'So they know,' Potter said.

'They have to know, Walt,' Jake nodded. 'Her mental defences are up every time I try, and so are his, and he's no telepath. And I can't believe they think and talk of nothing but Mozart, round the clock. They start it every time she hears me coming.'

'She's good, you say.'

'Damned good. I just can't catch her unawares. But it means she has to reveal herself. If she didn't have Markov with her, she might be able to fool me—but obviously they have to have a procedure to protect his mind from me, too. And that means a simple cue, like Mozart. *And Markov's mental discipline is pretty solid. He* can't sense me, but the moment she warns him, his mind is nothing *but* Mozart.'

'What kind is she? An astral projector with occasional normal-consciousness pickup, like you—or a direct-liner?'

'I just don't know yet, Walt. She can certainly pick me up when *I'm* astrally projecting, but then any of us could do that. It's like a... Well, you can't mistake it, anyway. And this morning I'm pretty sure she picked me up when I tried direct-lining her for a few seconds. We won't know what kind she is till he starts trying to do her job. About Pumpernickel, I mean.'

'And you'll know when she does.'

Jake hesitated. 'I can't guarantee that, if she tries it when I'm asleep. It depends how good she is. She just might be able to pussyfoot around me. But I'll do my best. Unfortunately I need my six hours, or the old psyche gets bleary-eyed. But I can give myself orders as I go to sleep. I don't *think* she'll slip by me.'

There wasn't much Potter could say to that, so he just grinned reassuringly at him and set up the board again. Jake was a good man, and a mean chess-player. Shrewd and unexpected, but honest. He'd given his word he wouldn't telepath, and Potter believed him. It was a pleasant change, in Potter's world, to be involved with someone you *could* believe.

'Our best chance is to try it while he's asleep,' Anna said. 'And that means when he's most deeply asleep—about an hour after *going* to sleep.'

'No way for you to spy on him and know when he does?'

'It wouldn't be wise, Dad. He might pick me up and that'd warn him.'

'Right, then. It's up to me.'

That night Markov made repeated trips to the front window of their landing, and at ten past midnight he was able to report that the lights in rooms 8 and 9 of the Liliengarten had gone out. An hour later, Anna lay warmly wrapped up in her bed with Markov sitting watchfully beside her.

Within minutes, he saw that she was hardly breathing.

She had warned him to keep his thoughts away from their objective, as an extra precaution. He obeyed her meticulously, but he had had enough of Mozart, and observing Anna—or rather his 'daughter' Ann—offered a pleasant if self-indulgent alternative. He did not lust after her. He was more than content with the relationship their cover provided. She was indeed the daughter he would have liked to have, and as such he had grown increasingly fond of her. No emotional involvement, the rule book said, and he knew the rule was wise. But surely a parental emotion was less dangerous than a sexual one? He was honest enough to admit to himself that the argument was weak. Love for a surrogate daughter could prompt wrong decisions in a crisis almost as surely as that most notorious of trouble-makers, sex. But he knew he could not help himself. Casual bed mates were two a rouble, and could be kept within bounds. A daughter (no, Yosif Mikhailovitch, be really honest—*this* daughter) was a rare being, not casual at all, not so easily dismissed afterwards.

'It must have been hell, being Mozart's librettist,' Ann said suddenly. 'He had too many ideas of his own.'

'If he hadn't been a musician, I wonder if he'd have been a poet?' So Trench had reacted. Markov had no sooner registered the thought than he steered away from it firmly, and joined Anna in a lively discussion of Mozart's relations with his librettist, scraping the barrel of their knowledge and even making facts up—it didn't matter. The thing was to keep going. They carried on for a good ten minutes, then Anna held up her hand, her head on one side as though listening.

'Tell you in the morning when Jake's busy shopping or something,' she told him. 'But it's cards on the table now.'

'It must be, if you know he thinks of himself as Jake.'

'You're on the ball, Dad. But cheer up. I think I've got most of what you want. So go to bed now and sleep easy.'

'Good girl.' He bent down and kissed her on the forehead.

'Sleep easy yourself.'

She called, 'Good night, Daddy,' softly as he went through the door. It was the first time she had used the diminutive.

They had their opportunity soon after breakfast, when Jake and Potter did in fact go shopping, and were plunged into noise and movement. Anna needed to be less wary now, so she was able to keep a mental watch on Jake and assure Markov that, for a while at least, he was effectively screened. So they went into the garden and she started talking, in quick burst with regular pauses to check on Jake.

'The three at the chalet; one man's an electronics expert, the other's an air force colonel in civvies, and the woman's the CIA liaison. The operation is called Pumpernickel. Its purpose is to pinpoint TN41. What's that, do you know?'

'Oh, Christ! That's about the most top secret equipment we have. All I know about it is that it's as far ahead of radar as radar is of binoculars. I only know even that much because I had to for my last assignment, and I was told to forget it afterwards.'

'Well, the equipment in that chalet can get a bearing on it. The reason it's here, on neutral territory, is it takes a minimum of four observation posts like that to get a fix accurately enough to be operationally useful. And the geographical layout is critical. They *have* to have a post somewhere around here.'

'How bulky is the equipment?'

'It's tiny. That's the real breakthrough. They were able to discover the principle by which they could locate TN41, and then micro-miniaturize it to a fantastic degree. They had the stuff on the table, and I saw it. Three grey boxes, two of them about as bit as a packet of twenty cigarettes, and the other a bit larger. Two of them have no controls but on-off switches and small tell-tale lights which show red when they're switched on, and green when they're on target. The other box has two rows of six digits—you know, LEDs—with buttons so that you can set them on the grid reference on your position, one for eastings and one for northings. Then there's a third display, of the date and Greenwich Mean Time. Those three are needed because they apply certain corrections according to the Earth's magnetic field and the position of the sun as a source of radiation. What a moment...'

She cocked her head in silence, then nodded. 'The fourth display gives you the answer, in the form of a true compass bearing accurate within plus or minus ten minutes of arc,' she went on. 'That's why they need at least four Pumpernickels, suitably spaced. Then they can pinpoint TN41 By triangulation to within a half a kilometre, at the range of the area in which the TN41's are currently deployed. The only other equipment, if you can call it that, is three outlines marked on the floor where you place the three boxes, because the placing is critical. That patch of floor is covered by a rug when it's not in use.'

'How the hell did you get all this?' he asked. 'I know you're good, but that's all technical...'

'Because two of then—the electronics chap and the woman—were up and about and very pleased with themselves. The Pumpernickel set-up had just tracked a TN41 on the move from Lvov to Mukachevo. "Our" Pumpernickel had contributed its readings, and got confirmation yesterday afternoon that the network as a whole had successfully tracked the move, even down to the halts for meal-breaks. Their minds were wide open, Dad. I'm just dishing it out to you as it came to me, and I don't understand half of it myself. But it was as clear as newsprint.'

Markov was thinking rapidly, knowing they might have little time to talk. 'Right. You've done wonderfully, Ann. Now there are two things we need to know. First: where are the other Pumpernickels?'

'These two didn't know. Perhaps the Air Force colonel does, but was fast asleep and I couldn't get anything clearly from him because he was busy with a randy dream. But my guess is, none of them will know. They'd be safer that way, wouldn't they? They didn't *need* to know the other locations, just to send their own readings to headquarters.'

'Right. Then where is Pumpernickel headquarters?'

'My two don't know that either. I'll have to try the colonel, when I have a chance.'

'Point two, then—and it's rather more subtle. Has Pumpernickel a weakness? Something they hope we won't find out about, even if we know about Pumpernickel itself? Some way we could jam it, for instance?'

Anna hesitated. 'No one was thinking about it, if so. Maybe they were too cheerful to bring out their worries. Perhaps, if I can catch the electronics man in a worrying mood.'

'Okay, then. What are your chances? You say it's cards on the table.'

'Yes. Jake knows about me and I know about him. How can I explain it? Dreaming is half astral projection anyway, and Jake caught up with me as he came out of a dream. For a moment we were—well, sort of face to face. A very intense mutual recognition, and then I switched off, but fast. I'm sorry, Dad. I did warn you. It had to come sooner or later.'

'I know. I'm not criticising. I said, you'd done marvellously.'

'But how am I going to get these other things? He'll be watching me like a hawk now. And we won't catch him again by waiting till he's asleep. He'll be on to my wavelength, so to speak. I'm pretty sure any concentrated effort on my part would wake him up, even from a deep sleep.'

Markov considered. 'Maybe we could...'

'Hold on,' she said. 'They're coming back to the hotel. No, they're not. Well, the cheeky buggers! They've decided on a drink in *our* garden.'

'Right.' Markov snapped his fingers. 'Can you lock yourself in your room, take the phone off, and project without me to watch over you?'

'Yes, but.'

'Synchronise watches. It is ten thirty-two... now.'

'Got it.'

'You be projecting in—well, let's say at eleven o'clock exactly. Try not to make it longer than about a quarter of an hour. I'll be doing my best to keep him off your back. Do what you can with the colonel, but if you feel Jake really getting at you, pull out.'

'How will you do it?'

Markov smiled. 'Believe it or not, Ann, there are times when it is even an advantage for the cards to be on the table.

The morning sun was pleasant in Zum Roten Hirsch's garden. Potter leaned back in his chair, sipping his Campari. 'Don't wear yourself out, Jake,' he told the younger man. 'Now that we know her form, just keep an eye on her for when she projects. She won't get any real information otherwise, you say?'

'Well, *I* couldn't, and her pattern's very like mine.'

'You learned a lot in what you described as a fraction of a second, didn't you?'

'If *you* saw a girl, head on, six feet away, by camera flash and then darkness, wouldn't *you* be able to say how tall she was, whether she was blond, brunette, or read head, how she was dressed, what sort of figure she had, and so on, and *know* her face if you saw it again? If you memorised all that the minute the light went off, I mean, because you knew it was important?'

'I guess so, yes.'

'Well, it was rather like that. I studied the after-image, as well as hanging on to the initial impact.' He grinned. 'You can safely bet she'll have done the same. We may be amateurs, but we're not stupid.'

'This ain't a game, Jake,' Potter's voice was menacing.

'I know, Walt. I was just being realistic.'

'Okay, okay. And you can't say what she'd been doing, before you—er—met?'

'No. She was too quick. Gone before I could get more than her mental pattern. When I tried to chase her thoughts, she was already yakking Mozart with her Dad. Sorry, Walk. She could have been just about to start on Pumpernickel, or she may already have taken 'em to the cleaners. There was no way of knowing, and believe you mean, *I* was pretty quick myself. And since then, she's shielded herself like armour-plating.'

'Well, all we can do is... Hold your horses and look straight ahead. Markov's going to walk by. Don't react.'

Potter sipped his Campari again, ignoring the Russian and hoping Jake would be able to do the same.

'Good morning, Mr. Potter, Mr. Trench.'

Jake gasped as Markov, smiling amiable, sat down at their table and put down his glass of lager.

'Good morning, Mr. Markov,' Potter said, inwardly praying Jake would gather his wits. 'Enjoying your vacation?'

'Very much. Though escorting a telepath takes a bit of getting used to, don't you find?'

'Mine plays a good game of chess, Markov. It helps to pass the time.'

'Does he, though? I used to be pretty good myself.' He turned his smile on the younger man, who was still open-mouthed. 'Perhaps you'd give me a game some time, Jake, while we're all stuck here? I hope you don't mind me calling you Jake. After all, I feel I know you rather well by now.'

'Er—no, not at all.'

'Good, good. And how do you like Salzburg? Have you been here before?'

'Well, no, I...That is, it's great.'

Potter laughed. 'Give 'im a break, Markov. Like your so-called daughter, he's in our racket but not of it. He doesn't know we sometimes suck lemons together at half-time.'

Markov beamed at Jake. "He's right, you know, Jake. Take our selves, now. Our more extreme forms of mutual annoyance are ruled out by the fact that neither of us can afford to draw attention to ourselves in this delightful but determinedly neutral country. Each of us knows what the other is up to, so in a sense, we have nothing to hide.'

'Only how much, if anything, we've achieved,' Potter pointed out.

'Of course, of course. And nobody expects us to tell each other. But in between rounds, Jake, why shouldn't we enjoy a drink together? If only for the pleasure of teasing each other?'

'I suppose now,' Jake conceded. 'Seems a bit cynical, is all.'

'On the contrary. You and Mr. Potter are loyal American citizens, and I am a loyal Soviet citizen. A pleasant exchange like this does not harm the interests of either country. And if anything, it is a brief respite from cynicism. Admittedly, ours is a cynical profession. But one cannot be cynical round the clock.'

Jake seemed to relax a little. 'It's a point, I guess.'

'I'm glad you see it.' Markov sighed. 'And anyway—and I'm sure it's as novel an experience for Mr. Potter as it is for me—with a telepath on each team. In the long run there isn't much we *will* be able to hide from each other. Each of us can only hope for a temporary advantage.

Jake tensed, and Markov realised his mistake. He had reminded the psychic of Anna.

'You bastard!' Jake hissed. 'Shut up now.' He lay back in his chair and closed his eyes. In a moment he appeared not to be breathing. The other two men watched him unsurprised.

'Forgive my young friend for his bad manners,' Potter said. 'He's not used to taking a sneaky punch gracefully. Smart, Markov. I should have seen what you were up to.'

'I muffled it, though,' Markov sighed. 'If I hadn't reminded him of her, she might have had a few more uninterrupted minutes. I had his attention nicely.'

'Win one, lose one. You've had your chance now. Once they're both projecting, those two can't dodge each other. As I'm sure Anna's told you.'

They looked at Jake in silence for a while, and then Potter said, 'He's taking a long time, isn't he? He'll have headed her off already. We both know that. So don't get me wrong, I'm not worried. Just that this spook business is weird.'

'I believe the American phrase is, "You can say that again."'

'Right. I'm only curious. What's keeping him?'

'Perhaps,' Markov suggested, 'they are sucking a lemon at half-time.'

When Markov an Anna were alone together, and she had assured him that Jake was not listening in to her, he asked, 'Did you have time to get anything?'

'Only a mental picture of the Pumpernickel headquarters. It's in Dortmund, above an antique shop called Wolfgang Jucho.'

'An *undercover* HQ, on their own ground?'

'Yes. I gather the US Air Force still has it under wraps. They haven't told their NATO allies yet. Sorry again, Dad. That's all I'd got when Jake turned up.'

'Not to worry, it's very useful.' He went on, curiously, 'What happened when he did "turn up"? We noticed he didn't exactly hurry back.'

'It was strange. We sort of looked at each other, and then he made a joke about sucking lemons at half-time.'

'Do you actually talk on this astral plane of yours?'

'Oh, yes. Like you do in a dream, only real—you know? He was very polite. Said he wouldn't ask what I'd found out, because if he did he knew I'd go. So we just, well, chatted, like you would over a drink. About Salzburg and that.'

Markov shook his head. 'Weird is right. Is he listening now?'

She paused, and said, 'No.'

'Right, then. *I* need him off *my* back for an hour, while I get a report off on what you've discovered already, and ask for instructions. Don't ask what channels I use, and don't look into my mind to find out, there's a good girl. You're better not knowing. I'm right in saying we're stalemated, aren't I? That we've used up all our chances to find out about Pumpernickel?'

'I'm afraid so, Dad. Jake has...'

'I know. I know. Where's he now?'

A pause again. 'Still in the garden. Potter's gone back but Jake's sitting there brooding.'

'Ideal. Go and have a drink with him. Keep him occupied while I get my report off.'

She looked startled. 'But I...'

'You've been introduced, haven't you?' he smiled. 'You even like him, I think. I certainly do, though he's kind of angry at me. So go out and enjoy yourself. And let CIA pay for the drinks.'

Her bush-baby eyes seemed anxious. (Strange, he'd forgotten that simile until this moment.) Then she smiled, and said 'all right', and refreshed her lipstick before she went.

He watched through the window till he saw Jake jump up at her approach, hesitate, and then signal to a waitress. As soon as they were sitting down together, he turned briskly to his report.

It was three days before the answer came from Moscow. There was nothing to do meanwhile, except to keep Potter guessing, so they saw more of Salzburg, went to a concert, did a little more shopping (nothing too bulky, Markov warned Anna, not knowing what their orders might be), took photographs, and ate well, they even had a couple of drinks with Potter and Jake, being guardedly light-hearted, but though Markov and Potter could have relaxed together with professional ease. It was clear that both of them were slightly nervous about their charges, so the occasion was not repeated. Anna showed no desire to see Jake alone again. She said their hour in the garden had been 'quite fun' but made no further comment.

Anna and Markov had kept up the habit of leaving their inter-connecting door open, and during the small hours of the second night he woke suddenly, thinking he had heard her cry out. He was halfway to the door before he realised that the cry—if it had been a cry—had been very soft, probably only a dream. Still, he'd better look.

Her face was quite clearly visible in the reflected glow from the street lamps. She lay on her back, and seemed not to be breathing.

Markov frowned, puzzled, then reminded himself that dreaming was often a form of astral projection. All the same, she looked so like she did when she was doing it deliberately. He tiptoed back to his own room and put a dressing gown over his pyjamas, then sat by her, watching, mysteriously concerned for her, for nearly two hours. Then he heard her breathing become normal, and her face was almost smiling. It was hard to tell, because she immediately turned on to her side and snuggled into the bedclothes.

Markov went back to bed.

The third night he woke again, at about the same time. This time he was certain he had heard no cry, but nevertheless he felt impelled to go and look. She lay on her back and seemed not to be breathing. Markov shook his head. Maybe this was ho she kept in training.

Back in his own bed, he took a long time to go to sleep, and realised he was waiting for the sound of her turning on to her side. It was dawn before the sound came.

Breakfast next morning was a strange meal. Anna seemed quiet and withdrawn, yet treated him, in some way he could not define, with a thoughtful tenderness which disturbed him. She agreed readily to his suggestions for the day's plans, offering none of her own. When the meal was over, she said she'd see him in the garden, and crossed the street to by a newspaper.

An hour later, she had still not returned.

At first he thought she must have run into Jake and Potter, and was being as guardedly sociable with them as she had been two days earlier. But when Potter walked into the garden, looked round without acknowledging him, and walked out again, he began to worry. Perhaps she'd gone out with Jake, but she'd arranged to come straight back here, so surely she'd have come and told him.

After two hours, he knew he would have to start looking for her. But where? She could be anywhere by now.

He stood up, uncertainly, but just as he was deciding to start with her favourite shops, Potter came into the garden again and strode across to him, his face deliberately expressionless.

'All right, Markov. What have you done with him?' The quiet voice was far from expressionless.

'Done with him? Nothing, man! What have *you* done with *her?*'

They glared at each other, then Potter said more calmly, 'Maybe we'd better sit down. Now. Are you really saying...'

'Of course I am. I haven't seen Jake since yesterday. And Ann was to have met me here, in the garden, two hours ago.'

Somehow the genuineness of their anxiety became apparent to both of them. Potter said, 'You don't suppose those stupid spooks have done a Romeo and Juliet, do you?'

'For God's sake, I hope not. If they have, you and I are in trouble.'

'But they've only met twice! And the second time you and I were there.'

'That's what I thought, too. But now I believe we may have been wrong.'

'Eh?'

'Have you looked in on Jake while he was asleep, the last night or two?'

'No. Why should I?'

'The night before last, I thought I heard Anna cry out. I went to her room to look. I am certain she was astrally projecting. I know the signs by now, as I'm sure you do. She was like that for about two hours before she changed to normal sleep. Last night I looked in again, and she was the same. This time it lasted for at least three hours. At breakfast she was very quiet, but very nice to me.'

'Jake was the same, come to think of it.'

'My friend, I think our two spooks, as you call them, have spent the last two nights in consultation. And I would be the pension which I shall doubtless not live to enjoy that they met this morning, by appointment. And where they are now, God alone knows. What did Jake say to you?'

'The same. That he'd meet me here in the garden. Look, Markov, we'll have to work together on this. For the sake of our skins and those pensions you spoke of. Agreed?'

'Agreed. And as a sigh of good faith, I may tell you that the young Austrian woman in the blue sweater who has just arrived will have a message for me. I had better find out what it is. She may not deliver it while you are looking her way, so don't. I will go and find a waitress to bring us drinks. Campari?'

'Right.' Potter looked studiously down the river.

Markov made his way slowly towards a waitress beyond the embassy courier. As he passed her he paused to light a cigarette. Without looking at him, she said in her quiet Russian, 'You will both go to Dortmund. Catch the BEA plane to Frankfurt from Vienna at ten thirty hours tomorrow. Tickets at the desk. You will be met at Frankfurt.'

Markov found his waitress, ordered his drinks, and went back to Potter. 'Worse trouble now,' he said. 'Marching orders. We must be in Vienna by early morning. Which means, if I do not find her in the next couple of hours, I shall have to report her missing. And, of course, that your boy's missing too.'

'So I'll have to do the same. Oh, Christ. What can we do in two hours? It really *has* hit the fan.'

They were still discussing, with little hope, where they might possibly look, when the waitress brought the drinks.

Markov was paying her as Jake and Anna walked into the garden together. 'I think,' he said to the waitress, 'that our friend might like one too.' He pointed, so that Potter would see them as well.

'*Bitte scheon,*' the waitress said obligingly, and waited.

Jake and Anna came and sat down with them, and drinks were ordered, very calmly. When the waitress had gone, Potter asked, 'Where the hell have you two been? We should send 'em back to school, eh, Markov?' His relief was plain. Markov nodded, sharing Potter's relief but something in Anna's eyes made him delay sharing his rather forced jocularity.

'We've come to report,' Jake said seriously.

'That's rather a strange way of putting it.' Markov's voice was cautious.

'It's a strange situation, Mr. Markov. But we want to make

one thing quite clear from the start. You won't like what we're going to do, and we're sorry. But neither of us is a traitor, and neither of us is defecting to the other side.'

Potter drew in his breath sharply, and said, 'Come on! Come on!'

'One moment,' Markov said. 'Ann, does Jake speak for both of you?'

'He does, Dad. Absolutely.'

It hurt him to ask. 'Are you sure it is appropriate to call me Dad?'

'It is how I think of you.'

Markov was silent. Potter said, 'Drop the other shoe, Jake.'

'The second thing is that when we go, you two will take no action. The man sitting over there by the rockery is an Austrian plain-clothes policeman. He knows nothing except that we want to be taken to Major Friedrich in Vienna, and that some-one—we haven't specified who—might try to stop us. When we've finished talking, we'll join him, and he'll take us to Vienna in his car.'

'How did you know Friedrich's name?' Potter asked, and the same question was in Markov's eyes. 'Don't tell me. You picked our brains. You wanted to know the one man who could really help you, and you picked our brains! Shit.'

'I'm afraid we had to, Walt. We really are sorry.'

'Don't keep saying that.'

'But we are,' Anna said. 'We like you both, and I think you know that. But we just had no choice.'

'And what will you tell Friedrich,' Markov asked, 'in ex-change for the freedom he can arrange for you?'

'As little as possible, and no one will be hurt. In forty-eight hours' time—at noon the day after tomorrow—we'll tell him about Pumpernickel and about the Feldkirch *apparat*,' Jake said. 'That will give you time to get Pumpernickel out of the country, and you, Mr. Markov, time to get the Feldkirch people out of the country. Call it our gift to Austrian neutrality, which is ours too from now on. And since both America and Russia will be paying for it equally, we're not favouring anyone. We'll persuade him that that's all we know, and we won't tell him we're telepaths. But *you'll* remember that we are, and that if anyone tries to come after us, we'll know. And if there's one attempt—even one, from either side—we'll let Friedrich know we're telepaths, and put ourselves at his disposal. Otherwise, you have our word we'll keep quiet. So you see, we'll be safer left alone.'

The waitress chose this moment to reappear with Jake and Anna's drinks. When she had gone again, Markov asked, 'But why? *Why?*'

'Because the idiots think they're in love, of course,' Potter said sourly.

'*I* think they are, too,' Markov said. 'But there's more to it than that, isn't it Ann?'

Anna gave him a half-sad smile which he carried with him for the rest of his life. 'Yes, Dad, we are, and there is. I think it's my turn to explain. Jake's right, all along the line. We're not traitors, we love our countries, and we don't want to hurt either of you. But we *have* to opt out. We *have* no choice. Do you know why?'

Markov sighed. 'Because it won't work.'

'What won't work?' Potter demanded.

'Yes, Dad, you're right. That's just it. Once they come up against each other, like we did, telepaths can't do this job unless they're psychotics. They can't practically, because it blows all security wide open. Look at the four of us. We know all about each other and *we can't help it*, after the first encounter. So how can we play at being spies? How can spies even exist, once we're involved? And it can't be done emotionally, because it's like asking someone to lie to himself, in full consciousness. In the very act of trying to fight each other, Jake and I became one. Ad you just ask if we're in love!'

'So why don't you just come home, explain yourselves, and resign?' Potter asked.

'Two reasons,' Jake told him. 'One, Anna's just given you; it's too late. We are *one*. And the other reason...'

'That you'd never be allowed to live,' Markov said. 'By

either side. Don't tell us. You can only survive by the way you're taking.'

Potter opened his mouth to protest, and then slumped. 'Screw it, that's the truth. I wish I could say it wasn't.'

Jake stood up. 'I think it'll be less painful for everyone if we leave right now. Good luck to you both.'

Anna kissed Markov on the forehead, and the two of them walked away together.

Markov and Potter sat in silence for a long time after they had gone, staring at the two untouched lagers on the table. 'You and I've got a hell of a lot of explaining to do,' Potter said at last.

'Yes.' Markov shook his head slowly. 'Do you know what? I would like to send them a wedding present. Care of Major Friedrich.'

Potter said, 'Count me in on it,' and they walked out of the garden their separate ways.

IV

FAIRY GODMOTHER

There can't be many people who've got a fairy god-mother these days. I mean, a real one. I have.

I've never been quite sure how I got her. If I'd been born in Llangollen or Lisdoonvarna or somewhere like that, she might have been an understandable part of the local scene. But I was born in Thornton Heath, a respectable suburb of London where they don't go in for such things.

My parents didn't warn me. In fact, I think they tried to keep it from me. Perhaps when they asked Aunt Julie (courtesy title, of course) to be my godmother, they didn't even realise it themselves. After all, my godfather Uncle Robert has been thoroughly conventional, from the cuddly-tow stage to the bottle-of-scotch stage. But Aunt Julie's quite a different cup of tea, and you can't fool kids about fairy godmothers, not for long.

I remember when my parents found out that I knew. I was about four, and Mother was reading me a story, with me interrupting a usual. She had come to the bit about the Princess' fairy godmother, and I said, 'Like Aunt Julie?'

Mother went pale, and Dad popped up from behind his newspaper. 'How do you know?' they both asked at once.

' 'Cos she made the poker and tongs do a dance for me,' I explained. 'She just said something magic, and they did a dance, all by themselves. It was fun.'

Mother looked at Dad, and sort of moaned, 'Bill, she *promised!*'

Dad said, 'Oh well, it can't be helped.' He told me that it was a family secret (which was true), and that if I breathed a word about it anyone else, the magic wouldn't work any more (which wasn't, but I don't blame him). Anyhow, it certainly kept me quiet. A fairy godmother is too good to waste.

She looks the part, I must say. Not the nutcracker-jaw type, but the firefly-wings type, though without the wings of course. A knowing little wedge of a face, huge eyes, and pale hair, long and straight. She might be anything between twenty and forty, and she hasn't changed a fraction since I was a baby.

'You'll be just the same till the day you die,' I told her.

Aunt Julie smiled and said, 'Don't be silly, darling. I shan't die. I shall *withdraw.*'

'Whatever that means, don't do it for a long time yet,' I begged her. 'You're too useful. And besides, I'd miss you.'

She promised.

I meant what I said about her being useful. Not only about practical things like school exams (for one of them, my form master almost demanded a recount), but with little surprises that sneaked up on you, like the gaps in a stamp album filling themselves up overnight, or a Paul Jones coming right six times out of six. (You probably won't have heard of that, but we still had it at dances in Thornton Heath in those days; boys and girls circled, and you danced with the one opposite you when the music stopped.)

Actually, dances could be a bit dodgy. I don't mean she couldn't fix things. She could and did, often. Sometimes she went over the top a little, like when George Paterson was making out too well with my current heart-throb. Aunt Julie was samba-ing past, and caught my eye. Thirty seconds later George got hiccups, which wouldn't stop. It sort of took the edge off his particular brand of charisma, so he packed it in and went home.

But in the matter of girls, she had to approve before she would help, and if she didn't approve, then *I* was the one liable to end up with hiccups. Even while I was still at school, I knew in the back of my mind that the day (and the girl) would come when I'd have to be very, very careful about Aunt Julie. That's the snag about fairy godmothers being women. They tend to behave like them. To be fair, she was very understanding on the whole. But I always had the sneaky feeling that the crunch would come.

It came all right, and her name was Anne.

I'd been in my first job for two years, and I wasn't doing badly. It was with an estate agent. I'd managed to get it (I think) without Aunt Julie's help, and to hold it (no, I really *do* think) the same way, because I have *some* principles, and I felt that fairy godmothers and hustling houses to unsuspecting customers shouldn't mix.

Though there was that time, of course, when I weakened to cover up a blunder. I'd written up the particulars of a house in Boundary Avenue, and for some draft reason I'd described it as having fruit trees in the garden. It wasn't till I'd given a prospective buyer on Order to View and the key, that I suddenly realised I'd been thinking of another garden, and that the Boundary Avenue place hadn't a tree to its name, fruit or otherwise. I was up the creek all right, so I broke my rule and got Aunt Julie on the blower.

But the time the buyer got there, the garden had two Cox's Pippins, three Beauty of Bath, and a Worcester Permain, all bearing like mad (and a gooseberry bush thrown in). Fortunately the house was already vacant, so there was no resident to end up in a mental hospital. I still the trees when I pass the place.

But to get back to Anne.

She came as a temporary when Maggie Bennett was in hospital with appendicitis, and she was a doll. Bubbly black hair and a dimple. I was hooked at first sight, and I got nowhere fast. She was polite, she was efficient, but as a man I might just as well not have existed.

It wasn't till I was really desperate that I went to Aunt Julie. I wouldn't have, even then, if I'd seen a glimmer in any other direction—but what could I do? Anne was only booked with us for two weeks, and if I couldn't rouse her interest when I saw her all day, what chance could I have after she'd left?

So at the beginning of the second week, I admitted to myself it was Aunt Julie or nothing. Even though I knew she hated dimples, whether for some technical reason concerned with her private magical system, or because of union rules or something. I'd never got it quite clear, and until now it had not mattered enough to try. This time, I just hoped I could talk her round.

If Aunt Julie doesn't know her 'patient' personally, she works better if she has something tangible to latch on to, a lock of hair is ideal, or nail clippings (yuk!), but in this case I had to make do with a photograph. Anne had scattered a few of her things around Maggie's desk, and among them was a wallet of holiday snaps. While she was at lunch I borrowed one of Anne playing tug-of-war on some beach with a large Dalmatian dog. (The fact that the dog's name was Hoppy was the most intimate conversational exchange Id had with Anne in six whole days, and that was wrong out of her because a client had been in with a Dalmatian who looked like him. Which shows you the completeness of my failure.)

That evening I showed the photograph to Aunt Julie, and pleaded.

'She's got a dimple,' Aunt Julie said.

'So what? I'm the one who's in love with her, and I like her dimple.'

'And I'm the one who's supposed to be bewitching her,' Aunt Julie pointed out, 'and I don't. I'm sorry, darling—but no.'

And from that she wouldn't budge.

But as I told you, I was desperate. And suddenly I had an idea.

'All right,' I said, pretending to give up. 'You're the fairy godmother around here. And to show there's no ill feeling. I'll take you out to dinner.'

'Lovely.' She was all smiles again.

Normally, I like taking Aunt Julie out to dinner. For one thing, she's a looker, and undeniably sexy—not that I'd do anything about that, even though by then you could have taken us for the same age; one just *doesn't*, with fairy godmothers, but it does my ego good to be seen with her. And anyway, hell, I *like* her.

For another thing—you can order, say chicken, and chicken is served, and chicken is charged for on the bill, but when you get your fork into it, it's pheasant. And what she can do to a bottle of the cheapest rotgut is nobody's business. If the French knew, they'd demand her extradition.

We went to Soho, to a dim exotic place we both like, and Aunt Julie was in splendid form, starting with a caviar-spell on the pate. This suited my plan excellently, and I goaded her on.

Especially with the drinks.

I flatter myself I know a thing or two about alcoholic content, and I kept betting her she couldn't do various things which would step it up considerably. Of course, she kept winning.

Within a couple of hours my fairy godmother was a good deal higher than any kite. She was brimming over with wit and good humour, though having a certain amount of difficulty with her muscular coordination. When she reached the stage of having to use magic on her cigarette-lighter because her fingers wouldn't work it, I judged my moment had come.

I laid the photograph of Anne and the Dalmatian on the tablecloth, and looked at her beseechingly.

Aunt Julie gave me a benevolent if unfocused smile, and said, 'Oh, all *right*, darling.'

She poised an unsteady finger over the picture. 'Look me in the eyes!' she ordered. I did. They grew bigger than ever. Then she lurched slightly, and I heard her finger plonk down on the photograph.

'*Blexum, hexum, smile and sigh—*
You shall love him till you die!'

I felt an electric tingle in the back of my neck, and then her eyes smiled. 'An' that's that, darling. You're a cunning old fox, but I forgive you. Let's have another.'

And that *was* that. It was a very powerful spell, and quite irreversible. But I took a solemn vow never to get Aunt Julie tight again. At least, not so tight that she doesn't know whereabouts on a photograph she's putting her finger.

I got over Anne after a while. Of course, I had to. But what can you do about a ruddy great Dalmatian who sits outside your window and whimpers—all night and every night?

V

WATER, WATER

Some people (like Dubliners who've been there) describe Moinvara as the most desolate spot in the West, and make jokes about 'next parish Boston' and so on. Miles of peat bog dotted with white cottages, ringed by mountains which reach out like a crab's claws to embrace the bay. Mulkerrin's Bar which is also shop and post office, and itself a dozen miles from the next pint of Guinness north or south. A church which is always open because a cow ate the key back in old Father Quinnelly's time. Two of the parish's three Protestants go there too, *and* take Communion, reservations notwithstanding, because the nearest Protestant church is twice as far away as the next Guinness, and who wants to be lonely on Sunday morning? Garda Pat O'Grennan, whose unofficial headquarters is also Mukerrin's Bar, maintains law and order according to his own civilized interpretation. There is one bus a month to the county town, but everybody knows whose car is going in and when, so that's no limitation. Half of the population have lived in Moinvara for ever, and the other half live in Cleveland, Ohio, where their cousins call them collect, from the phone box with the winding handle outside Mulkerrin's. That sounds like one hundred per cent, but of course there's the unusual handful of foreigners, like the New York couple who inherited Rosfada house from a grandfather, or the German who imagines he can farm sheep on Inishdearg (his father's a Ruhr industrialist, so the consensus is that it's really a bolt-hole), or the Canadian divorcee with an obsession to get people organised (it works, too, or Moinvara wouldn't have its little Health Centre), or Clarice the English witch, who writes books on folklore and speaks passable Irish with a Northhamptonshire accent.

Let the Dubs call it desolate. When their central-heating oil costs a bucket of gold a gallon, the people of Moinvara will still be sitting on a million tons of their own good peat, there for the effort of a few days' annual cutting and stacking. While the price of whiskey soars, Moinvara proteen remains unparalleled, unreported, and unprosecuted. Moinvara is surrounded by the kind of scenery the Bank of Ireland make their prestige calendars of. Television tells Moinvara all it needs to know of the ways of the world. And anyone who things the locals are ignorant or stupid should try talking with them.

And now Moinvara has water.

It's always had water, of course, by the skyload, but collected off the roof into big storage tanks, from which it was pumped by hand (or more recently by electricity) into little tanks in the loft. Dr. Shevlin always maintained that it was the cause of half Moinvara's ailments (the other half being bad feet) because no one took a blind bit of notice of his pleas that they should never drink it unboiled.

By the time that Marje Graham, the Canadian divorcee, had got the Heath Centre going in what used to be the curate's house when Moinvara still had a curate, he and Tom Shevlin were naturally firm allies. That done, Marje had felt at loose end, with nothing really substantial left to organise. So she'd got together with the doctor again, and hit upon a project which won his even more enthusiastic support: the Moinvara Group Water Scheme.

Marje wasted no time. She formed a committee of herself, Dr. Shevlin, and a sighing but resigned Father Horgan, who was not allowed to wriggle out of calling a parish meeting. There Marje, who had done her homework, told the people of Moinvara what they wanted and what their spontaneous civic initiative was about to demand. It would cost an estimated £150 per household, but she softened that blow by talking largely and convincingly about Government and EEC grants, and dragooned the reluctant by announcing the households which did not join the scheme, and pay £50 deposit, by a deadline of October 1ˢᵗ would have to pay a lot more if they wanted to join it later.

The scheme was to bring down nice clean water from a lake in the mountains, six miles away, but a plastic pipe tap to every house in the straggling village. It could be done, and Marje waved documents to prove it. Fascinated by her oratory, which was well up to national standards and herself with not a drop of Irish blood in her, and remembering to her credit that her Health Centre at least meant they could queue for treatment in sociable comfort, the parishioners approved her scheme, confirmed her committee, and added Sean MacMenamin to it, because he'd made the longest and most colourful speech in support. One or two of the better-off farmers (or those who wanted to be thought better off) actually paid their £50 deposits on the spot, which meant the Moinvara Group Water Scheme could have letterhead printed right away, much more impressive for claiming grants on.

Having secured her brief, Marje did her own survey, which was not a matter of geology, mathematics, and cartography so much as of muscle and diplomacy. The muscle came into it because the route involved mountain slopes of an eerie loneliness up which tractors and trench-diggers would be able to go, but Marje's six-year-old Toyota certainly couldn't. They had to be covered on foot and in rubber boots. The diplomacy concerned many things. First, the many family holdings the pipes would have to cross, which in turn involved lengthy correspondence with cousins in Cleveland, Ohio, who had a finger in every pie. Next, the strange Irish laws of commonage, comprehensible only to those capable of lateral thinking, and again always involving cousins in Cleveland. Next, local politicians with one eye on the coming election. And finally, Marje's fellow North American the owner of Rosfada House, who held the fishing rights not only of the proposed source, but of a network of bogland rivers and streams which interwove the whole Group Water Scheme layout. She showered him with statistics and expert opinion till he was almost persuaded that the Moinvara Group Water Scheme was the one thing his trout and salmon had been waiting for all their lives.

Over the long months, the paperwork and footwork plodded ahead. Marje completed her survey, compared bids, chose the contractor, and got the grants authorised subject to the village's own contribution being paid in full. (This last called for a certain amount of nagging from Father Horgan's pulpit.)

The Group water Scheme had been talking point for so long that nobody in Moinvara (not even Marje, sometimes) could bring himself to believe that it might one day actually happen, that water from Lough Gorm might actually run out of the taps. But on a chilly day in March, a year and a half after that first parish meeting, a contractor's trailer started unloading black pipes on to the bare batch beside Mulkerrin's; impressive straight lengths for the main pipeline, and great coils of smaller calibre for the branches. The very next morning, a praying mantis of a trenching machine started work, and the black pipes were disappearing into the ground.

It was all happening at last.

It might have gone on happening, smoothly and uneventfully, if Sean MacMenamin's wife hadn't been seized by a fit of spring-cleaning, just at the beginning of the school vacation when the house was bedlam anyway, and Sean had wisely concluded that he was better off out of it for the day. At Mulkerrin's he ran into Terry Boyle the contractor, who was on his way up to Lough Gorm to prepare some blasting. Sean remembered his duties as a committee member, noticed that the sun was shining, told himself that blasting would at last be a different kind of noise, put a six-pack of Guinness under his arm, and climbed into Terry's Land Rover beside him.

An hour later the phone rang in Father Horgan's house.

'Father, it's Sean MacMenamin here,' a breathless and

agitated voice told him. 'I'm up at Mulchrone's Can' you come quick, and bring the doctor and Marje?'

There were five Mulchrone families in Moinvara, but Father Horgan was unconfused. Only one of them had a telephone—a lonely sheep farm about a mile from the downstream end of Lough Gorm. An urgent call from there for priest and doctor might have meant that someone was dangerously ill. But that would not have required Marje Graham's presence, especially with the extra delay of a three-mile detour to pick her up, she still having no phone in spite of two years' pestering of P & T. And since Sean was making the call, that meant Group Water Scheme committee business. One of the advantages of village life is that intricate shared knowledge saves a lot of unnecessary explanation.

'Is Terry with you?' the priest asked, showing similar economy of words, for they both knew four adult Terrys and two boys.

'He's over at the Lough. Can you be meeting us there, father?'

'What's the trouble, Sean?'

'He's after wanting to blast the Rock of the Mass.'

'Holy Mother! I'll be up as fast as I can.'

While Father Horgan is rounding up the doctor and Marje, let me explain. During the penal centuries, which did not entirely end until O'Connell the Liberator won Catholic Emancipation a hundred and fifty years ago, the Mass beloved of the people could only be celebrated in hidden corners and in wild and secret places. Lonely rocks became unofficial altars, charged with generations of a devotions proscribed by faraway Parliament. All over Ireland, from Vinegar Hill to windy Donegal, you will find these Rocks of the Mass, still venerated as holy and magical places, even though they are usually unmarked except by local memory.

One such Rock of the Mass, a flat-topped slab of creamy-grey quartzite, stands at the mouth of Lough Gorm in the secretive mountains above Moinvara.

To be fair to Terry Boyle, it too is unmarked, and not being a local man he didn't know that it was anything more than an obstacle to his black plastic water-pipes, easily penetrated by a few pounds of well-placed gelignite. Moreover, he had agreed the route with Marje Graham, who although a Catholic was also a newcomer and didn't know either. And when Sean had realised and explained the sacrilege which Terry had been on the point of committing, Terry had paled, and had needed one of Sean's Guinnesses to steady his nerves.

Father Horgan luckily found Dr. Shevlin at home, and Tom understood the seriousness of the situation at once. They hurried off to pick up Marje. They found Clarice the English witch with her. Clarice, though an unconcealed pagan, was friend with everybody, including Tom and the priest, so they took her along as well, since she'd never seen the Rock of the Mass and wanted to.

The Rock was ideally situated for its ancient purpose. Here the valley narrowed to a tumbling steam at the mouth of the Lough, with about half an acre of flat ground beside it, hidden under the mountainside. The Rock stood near the lake shore, at the edge of this half-acre. Immediately behind the Rock, on the very edge of the water, stood another rock, known as *an Snathaid*, the Needle, a fifteen-foot upright, freakishly isolated by some primeval erosion, looking remarkably and appropriately like a church spire. The half-acre could (and in the old days did) easily hold the entire population of Moinvara, and the Rock and the Needle even faced east.

'I'd no idea at all, father,' Terry apologized a little plaintively. 'Do you think I'd be wanting to put a curse on my own work, at the very source of it?'

'Oh, well, Terry, now you know and there's no harm done. Can you get round it, do you think?'

'I'll be having to, won't I? You see my problem, though. I can't put my inlet in the stream, it's too shallow up here, and if we go farther down for it, we're into the turf, and then where's the nice pure water you're after? Not to mention the cow shit, begging your pardon, father. So I'd had in mind, and Mrs. Graham agreed, that the inlet must be in the Lough itself. But the Rock stands in the way, unless I'm to blast a tunnel in the mountain, and that'd send your costs soaring, never mind the danger of starting a rockfall, which I wouldn't know without a survey.'

'Let's have a closer look,' Father Horgan said.

He led the way round the Rock, the others trooping behind him, and stood for a moment looking thoughtfully at the Needle. 'I'm no civil engineer, Terry, but there's a good four yards between the Rock and the Needle. Couldn't you dig a fair-sized sump there, without disturbing either of them? Line it with concrete, and let it fill from the Lough, and place your inlet there. There you could take your pipe round the edge of the Rock and across the flat ground. Or am I talking non-sense?'

Terry tilted his head, frowning. 'Wait a minute, now. Father, you just might be on to something. How low does the water fall, in a dry summer?'

'Not more than three feet below what it is now,' Sean said, 'and I know this place like the palm of my hand.'

'That's right,' Marje said. 'I checked.'

'Then I reckon it *could* be done. Father, you're a genius, and if you're not an engineer you ought to be.'

They plunged into technicalities, and the doctor wandered off to join Clarice, who was sitting on a little outcrop at the foot of the cliff enjoying the sun and the view. 'They've lost me,' he told her, 'Outside my own job, I'm a technological infant. Well, how do you like it?'

'Marvellous,' Clarice said.

'Magical vibes?' he teased her.

'Can't *you* feel them?'

'To be honest, yes. All the generations who worshipped here, their emotion sharpened by illegality—they can't help leav-ing their mark on the place. And it might have been designed for it, don't you think?' He waved a hand towards the Needle. 'I'll bet not many Rocks of the Mass have their own steeple, as well.'

'And *I'll* bet it's a lot older than that, Tom. As a holy place,

I mean.'

'You think the Needle's an artefact? Put there by the megalithic people?'

'Oh, no, it's natural enough, I'd say. And the site's too closed-in for a megalithic one. If it'd been on a skyline, I might have thought twice, but that's my point. Like you said, it's *made* for it. For worship, including pre-Christian. Take another look at it, my Freudian friend.'

Tom did. 'Well, yes, I see what you mean. Female lake in a womb-like valley. Phallic stone at the entrance. Ready-made altar, and assembly place for worshippers. And at a rough guess, the dawn sun shines down the length of the Lough from the vee in the hills at the other end. Fertility temple, made to measure.'

'No wonder the people gravitated here naturally, in the penal days.'

'Conceded,' he smiled. 'We are, after all, *Celtic* Catholics. Our sense of magical continuity is unique.'

'Why do you think *I* live here and am put up with?' she smiled back.

'Seriously, though,' he wondered, 'which of our predecessors *would* have used it that way? Like you said, it doesn't seem quite to fit into the megalithic pattern. Their layouts were precise and interrelated, like a ruddy National Grid.'

'We don't understand it fully yet, remember,' Clarice pointed out. 'And we don't know what else they did on the side. We know little about them, apart from their stone jobs which happen to be indestructible. They doubtless had their own fertility rite, and if so, they'd be very likely to take advantage of a natural set-up like this. Tell you what you would find here though, if you excavated—bet you anything.'

'What?'

'Viking remains.'

'Well, there *was* a little Viking settlement at the river mouth, that's true. They seem to have used it as a raiding base and repair shipyard, for a generation or so. There are quite a few finds from there in the museum in town.'

'I know, I've seen them, and another thing, Tom, this is Lough Gorm, the Blue Lake. Did you know it had an older name? I discovered that in the museum, too.'

'Oh? What?'

'Lough Fraigh.' She spelled it for him. *Fraigh* or *frigh*, which means all—sometimes rafters or a roof. I don't get it. "The walled-in lake", I suppose it could be. But it doesn't sound right.'

'Suppose the root isn't Irish at all? Suppose it was the Lake of Freya, the Norse Earth Mother?'

Terry found that Father Horgan's solution worked perfectly. He didn't even have to use much cement. When his men dug out the hollow between the Rock and the Needle, they found that these two surface features were the continuation of buried vertical rock strata, providing natural walls for a rock tank which, when its bottom and ends had been concreted, held a good ten thousand gallons. The tank filled from the Lough, the inlet was available for inspection and cleaning when necessary, and almost the only visible difference was that Rock and Needle were now separated by a not unattractive pool instead of by a patch of gravel.

Father Horgan joked to Terry that if ever he got tired of being a priest, he'd come to him for a job. Terry swore he'd give him one.

The Group Water Scheme sailed ahead from that day on. Within months, the houses nearest to the main pipe were being connected up, and more houses every week. The public analyst tested the water yet again and pronounced it excellent. The day the first four homes (which included Marje's, not by privilege but by geographical chance) had their main valves opened, the beneficiaries, men and women, celebrated their new water by gathering in a body in Mulkerrin's and drinking anything but, all evening. Even Marge, a teetotaller, was too elated to keep an eye on what went into her orange squash, and had to be driven home at closing time as defined by Garda Pat's extremely tolerant watch.

Terry Boyle, who of course was there too, rashly foretold, after his fifth Jameson's, that he'd have every bloody house in Moinvara connected by Samhain even, the last day of October. He was alarmed when he remembered his boast in the light of his morning hangover, but he was a proud man, and he made it good, even if he did have to pay some overtime out of his own pocket outside the budget in the last week or two. (He got that back anyway, by offering a flat price for redundant electric pumps, which he disposed of profitably elsewhere.) At 4p.m. on October the twenty-ninth, old Bridie Lardner, at the northernmost end of the Group Water Scheme's area, proudly turned on her tap and made Terry and his weary men a pot of tea. Terry was not a teetotaller, but for once a cup of ordinary tea tasted to him like the nectar of victory.

Winter in Moinvara is a time of virtual hibernation. Its simple economy of cattle, sheep, and peat, and the Atlantic weather, gear its people to a busy summer and a restful winter. So from Samhain on they settled down as usual, with the additional luxury of piped water. Even Marje allowed herself a few months' sabbatical before looking for the next thing to organise.

Tom Shevlin and Clarice (whose surname she used as rarely as possible, since it was Sidebotham) were among the exceptions. Her typewriter did not hibernate, and she went on doing whatever a witch does, which cannot have been very sinister because Tom often teased her that she had more satisfied customers than he had. ('Of course,' she would reply. 'Most of yours ignore your advice, but mine are scared to ignore mine.') And in Tom's surgery, winter meant more work, as it does for all doctors. Having made such an issue of unboiled roof-water, he felt-bound to insist that he now had fewer intestinal upsets to treat, and he even began to believe it himself.

Tom and Clarice were seeing more and more of each other. He was still a bachelor at thirty-five, not through choice, but because in this, his first and rather isolated practice, he had not yet met anyone he could fall in love with, and he stubbornly believed that to be essential. He had often been drawn to Clarice, not only for her looks but for her warmth and her dry humour, and had known that she liked him. But he had kept his distance, afraid that for a Catholic doctor (even if his Catholicism was privately unorthodox) to marry a pagan witch might produce difficulties, both internal and external to marriage.

This winter, however, he found himself worrying less and less. As they got to know each other better, their personal contrast seemed to lose importance, to offer a stimulation to harmony rather than a threat. And as for external problems, he was surprised to realise that nobody seemed upset by their friendship. People were beginning to invite them out together, to have that 'Well, when are you going to...' look in their eyes. Could it be that, since their clientele overlapped, people might actually feel reassured by seeing that the doctor and the witch were in partnership?

He stopped worrying altogether, and as soon as he did that he knew he was in love with her.

'About time too,' she said when he told her. 'I was begin-ning to think I'd have to ask you myself.'

They fixed their wedding day for the following May, so that they could get some Mediterranean sunshine on their honey-moon. But they soon found that they were even more in love than they had realised, and had more passionate natures than they had allowed for, and one evening in January she told him, a little pinkly apologetic, that if they were going to on living in this village, perhaps they had better get married right away. An eight-month gap between marriage and childbed might be glossed over, and was indeed not all that uncommon in Moinvara, but four months would be pushing it.

So they did and were very happy. They had to cross the Border for a civil wedding, but nobody minded. Even father

Horgan just shrugged and smiled.

It seemed to Tom at first to be no more than coincidence that he had rather more than the usual number of pregnant patients to give advice to. But by April he was beginning to be puzzled.

'It's ridiculous,' he told Clarice. 'Half the married women in Moinvara seem to be expecting, including at least three in their forties.'

'Only the married ones?'

'Confidential information,' he said, mock-sternly. 'I wouldn't dream of telling you the names of the four unmarried ones.'

She made four guesses without drawing breath, and three of them were right. At next morning's surgery, he discovered that all four had been right.

'It must be the water,' Clarice laughed.

'You know what, darling? I'm beginning to wonder.'

'That's what they're saying in the village, though, seriously. After all, every pint of our water flows against the Rock of the Mass on its way here. As they see it, it's practically holy water. Certainly magical.'

'How did I ever manage without you? I didn't know half of what goes on around here.'

'They could be right, too. After all, I was pretty immediately fertile myself, wasn't I, and I'm thirty-two.'

'Thanks to the holy water?' he mocked.

She smiled. 'I wasn't thinking only of the Rock of the Mass. The water flows against the Needle, too. And remember what primordial power *that's* charged with.'

They enjoyed provoking each other, so he just smiled back. 'My line of investigation would be the chemical constitution of the water. Maybe there are trace elements conducive to increased fertility. I think I'll get it more carefully analyzed.'

'You do that, darling,' she said.

In the first three years of the lake water, Moinvara's population doubled, give or take or few.

Clarice's daughter was safely born and thriving, and Clarice was pregnant again. Tom, who loved children from one minute old upwards, was delighted with little Finola and with the promise of the next, and although he complained about how hard he was working. ('I'm just a dam' male midwife') he was really pleased with the village too, and enjoying himself.

The phenomenon of Moinvara's fruitfulness had by now, of course, become national news, and with increasingly familiarity, a source of affectionate national amusement. Moinvara jokes ranked second only to Kerryman jokes in turnover. The scientifically-minded had naturally cottoned on to the possibility that the water of Lough Gorm had something to do with it (an enterprising heath food story in Dublin's Gaiety Green did a roaring trade in bottles of the stuff) and Tom, a little sadly, had found his private research outstripped by interested experts with well-equipped laboratories, and before long had confined himself to obligingly supplying them with on-the-spot statistics.

The research got nowhere. Lough Gorm water was admirably pure mountain water, the experts all agreed. That, and nothing more.

But the babies kept on coming. Some couples who had had enough moved away. Some childless couples hopefully (and almost always successfully) moved in. Property values in Moinvara rocketed. The Department of Education subsidised an enlargement of the village school.

Tom had given up wondering why. Sometimes Clarice would say yet again, 'Well, darling, what do you expect, when our water comes straight from a very ancient and powerful temple of fertility?' And he would laugh it off, too proud to admit that by now he half-believed her.

But one day, relaxing after his third delivery in two weeks, he laughed it off once too often, and perhaps with too little conviction. She came and sat beside him.

'Tom, love, I hate undermining your convictions, but don't you think it's time you faced facts?'

'What facts?'

'The one thing nobody seems to have noticed. Ninety per cent of the people of this village—the adults, I mean—have black or brown hair. Right?'

'About that, I'd say. Yes.'

'Then why are all these kids—*all* of them—perfect little blonde Vikings?'

Tom thought, for a fraction of a second, and then stared at his wife, dumbfounded.

'Except Finola, of course,' she went on comfortably. 'Her hair's as black as night, like yours and mine. I saw to that. And so will this one's be.' She patted her pear-shaped belly and blew Tom a kiss.

Tom Shevlin took a very long, very deep breath. 'Thank God you're a witch,' he said.

'And if she doesn't?'

'Well, what does it matter? As long as we are happy—you'll be as faithful as she, and won't give me away either.'

VI

NIGHT SHIFT

Philip Andrews found it extremely difficult to concentrate on the last patient on his list, and this annoyed him, because he was a conscientious professional. A straightforward molar filling, too—though perhaps its straightforwardness made it worse. An intricate problem would have left his mind less free to wander. As it was, his movements could he virtually automatic, leaving an attention-vacuum to be filled, and Nurse Codd to fill it, as thoroughly as he himself was filling his patient's molar cavity. And Philip had a tidy mind which he liked to be occupied by one thing at a time. The agenda was supposed to be patients first, Nurse Codd afterwards.

But 'afterwards' was drawing so tantalisingly close, and Nurse Codd herself was so tantalisingly close already, that the agenda was becoming blurred at the edge. He wondered if she, too, was finding it hard to concentrate on her pestle and mortar as she ground away in the background. It would be personally flattering, but professionally disturbing, to think that she was.

Codd was really an absurd name for her, he thought. If she had to be called after a fish, why not Eel, smoothly sinuous, or Trout, shapely and delicately freckled, or Salmon, leaping nobly in concupiscence.

He jerked his thoughts hurriedly back to his work.

89

Very few words had been exchanged in private between Philip and Nurse Codd in the weeks they had known each other. The busy dental clinic had offered them little opportunity, usually at least two of Philip's three partners, and the other nurse, were around, not to mention the steady stream of patients. They lived six miles apart, Philip with his sister and Nurse Codd with her mother, so neither had suggested the all-too-definitive step of meeting at one of their houses. And his senior partner's positively Victorian attitude to professional relationships made any restaurant or bar meeting, in this observant community, inadvisable.

Fortunately, at least once every eight working days, they had an evening free of their colleagues. The clinic remained open every evening, Monday to Friday, from 6:00 to 10:30p.m., with one dental surgeon and one nurse, and Philip lived for the evening, like this one, when his and Nurse Codd's night shifts coincided.

And tonight, in plain terms, was the night.

So little had been said, but neither had been able—or, after the first few shared shifts, had even tried—to conceal the charge of mutual desire that was building up between them. The verbal sparring, such as it was, had been long finished with. All that remained, tonight, was the knowledge that for one reason or another none of the other partners could possibly drop in, and that after the last patient had gone, the couch in the little Recovery Room at the back awaited them.

Philip's hand slipped, and he had to re-shape the filling.

At last, it was done. Trying to smother their eagerness to get rid of him, they both escorted the patient to the door and saw him out.

Impatience was their downfall. They shut the door and were kissing each other greedily before either of them though to lock it. Halfway through the kiss, the door reopened, and if Nurse Codd's bottom had not been six inches from it to check its swing, the man would have burst straight in on this unprofessional spectacle. As it was, they managed to jump apart just in time.

'Could you handle an emergency?' the stranger asked. 'I realise it's rather late, but I would be most grateful.'

He was a striking figure. Tall and thin, with rather long but well-groomed black hair, he had deep-set eyes which it was difficult to look away from, and a forehead too wide for his concave cheeks. Philip tore his gaze from the eyes to take in the clothes—full evening dress and a crimson-lined black opera cloak.

The man smiled, embarrassing Philip with, 'Ah, yes, the clothes. A little ostentatious, these days, but they're expected of us, you know.' He walked in, closing the door behind him, apparently taking it for granted that his request for treatment would be met. Philip and Nurse Codd exchanged agonised looks behind his back, but there was nothing they could do. The clinic was still technically open, and if it was an emergency...

'What exactly is the trouble?' Philip found himself asking.

The stranger took off his cloak and dropped it casually on the reception desk. 'I think perhaps I had better show you. Which surgery is it?'

'Er, the second one on the left.'

The stranger led the way, with Philip and Nurse Codd hurrying to catch up with him. He sat himself gracefully in the operating chair (a thing which Philip had always thought impossible) and said, 'The problem is a loose right upper canine.'

Philip pulled himself together enough to express annoyance. 'A loose canine is hardly an emergency!'

The man smiled, 'In my occupation, my friend, it is.'

Philip and Nurse Codd had moved, from habit, to the right and left of the chair. 'What occupation?' Philip asked.

Still smiling up at them, the man drew back his lips.

Nurse Codd gave a stifled scream, and Philip gasped. The strangers' two upper canines gleamed white and sharp, each a good half an inch longer than the rest of his teeth.

'Well, Mr. Andrews?' the man asked. 'That is your name, I believe?'

Philip stammered, 'Yes,' grasping the chair arm because he felt faint.

Nurse Codd said incredulously, 'You're a vampire.'

The man returned his lips to normal, the tips of his canines none the less still showing. 'Certainly I am, my dear. And that explains my problem, which I am sure both of you will appreciate. I can only come here, or indeed anywhere except my...er...*pied-a-terre*, during the hours of darkness, which at this time of year do not begin until nearly ten o'clock. And secondly, a loose canine tooth, which for you would be a mere inconvenience, is for me a very serious handicap.'

'Yes,' said Nurse Codd thoughtfully, 'it would be.'

'But the way, I would rather not give you my name, because it is a little too well known among those who take an interest in such matters. I am not an insured patient—a serious omission in the system, I may say—so I shall naturally pay for the treatment upon leaving. And since I have no opportunity to obtain banknotes except by theft, which is distasteful to me, I shall pay you in gold. I trust that will be acceptable?'

Philip realised that Nurse Codd had been doing what talking there was on their side, and felt shamed into trying to seize the initiative. 'Why should I treat a vampire? I'd be an accessory to a crime!'

'My dear fellow, do not prisons have dentists? And are they accessories to whatever crimes their patients may have committed?'

'No, of course not, but...'

'I don't know,' the man went on, ignoring the interruption, 'whether dental surgeons take, or acknowledge, the Hippocratic Oath. But I imagine your code of professional ethics, like that of doctors, requires you to treat those in need of your services regardless of their moral worth.'

'Well, I...'

'Human beings, yes,' Nurse Codd came to his rescue. 'But vampires aren't human, are they?'

'An interesting question, my dear, which I would enjoy discussing with you if we had more time. In the broader sense, there are cogent arguments both for and against. But dentally speaking, I should have thought there was no doubt at all. Even if two of them are unusually well developed, these are unquestionably human teeth.'

He drew his lips back to display them, and Philip had to admit he was right. But he suddenly remembered something else, and stepped back a pace, involuntarily.

'All right, I'll accept that, ad teeth, they come within my sphere and not a veterinarian's.'

'Thank you for that.'

'But I don't see why I'm called upon to put myself in personal danger, especially when, dentally speaking, a loose tooth is not an emergency.'

'Danger? I'm afraid I don't follow you.'

'Oh, come now. I don't know much about vampires, but I do know that anyone who's bitten by one, and has his blood sucked, becomes a vampire himself. Am I right?'

'Perfectly. Otherwise we could not maintain our numbers. Unfortunately,' he said with a gallant little smile to Nurse Codd which infuriated Philip, 'while we are sexually neither unappreciative nor incapable, we are infertile.'

Philip snorted. 'Well, I have no desire to become a vampire. So do you really expect me to spend the next half hour with my jugular vein a few inches from your teeth?'

The man looked instantly and genuinely remorseful. 'Oh, my dear chap, I *am* sorry. I should have explained. We, too, have our Code. Dental surgeons are sacrosanct—but absolutely. It's understandable, really, we are so dependent on you. The day you qualified as a dental surgeon, you became taboo to any self-respecting vampire. Your throat, Mr. Andrews, is perfectly safe with me. You have my word as a gentleman.'

Philip looked into the deep-set eyes, and in spite of himself, believed him. 'Very well,' he said.

It was a long and difficult operation, and Philip carried it out skilfully. He had the man's assurance that the inconvenience of a brace behind the offending tooth was acceptable in view of the vital importance to his way of life of having it fully functional. So Philip fitted one, admirably unobtrusive, in the circumstances. He became fascinated by the unique problem, for the leverage exerted on the root by a canine which extended almost an inch beyond the jawbone was quite outside his experience. But by the time he had finished, he was professionally satisfied that he had met the challenge.

He had become so absorbed that he had even forgotten all about Nurse Codd, except as a skilful and reliable assistant.

He realised the fact when he finally straightened his back and faced her across the chair, and her temporarily forgotten seductiveness hit him with full force. Her eyes shone and she glowed with excitement—doubtless in admiration of his own brilliance—and the glow made her doubly, trebly luscious.

Philip felt faint again, and after such a professional triumph, that would never do. On no account must he appear flustered.

'Excuse me a moment,' he said as briskly as he could. 'Some routine to attend to.'

He managed to leave the surgery without running. Somehow he found himself in the Recovery Room, leaning over the handbasin and splashing his face with cold water. He felt better, but still strangely weak, so he went and sat on the couch. That, in turn, brought Nurse Codd and the delights to come vividly back into his mind, and he remained there in a dreamy erotic euphoria. He had no idea for how long.

He was vaguely aware of sounds from the surgery. Even of a low laugh from Nurse Codd. Good, she's being polite to him and seeing him out. Yes, that's the front door shutting and the key turning.

Deliberately tantalising himself, he did not even look round when she came in and turned off the light.

'At last,' he whispered.

'Yes, darling. At last.' Her husky voice was the final trigger to his desire.

He could hear her garments falling one by one on the floor, and he jumped up and started feverishly tearing off his own. Then, out of the impenetrable darkness, she was suddenly in his arms, soft and silky and infinitely desirable. They fell together on the couch, their limbs entangled.

'It's been so long, this waiting,' Philip gasped.

Nurse Codd gave a deep, enchanting laugh. 'Only a few minutes for me, darling. Not even long enough to learn the Cod, I'm afraid.'

And with that she sank her canines firmly and voluptuously into his jugular vein.

VII

THE
YELLOW BOX

My Name is Dugald Mackenzie, and I am (still) the Middle East Correspondent of the London *Announcer*. That's not a very arresting opening to a story, as the rawest sub-editor could tell you, but I start by introducing myself because some of you may remember the series of features I'm talking about, from the heady days when Fleet Street was bursting out in a rash of colour supplements. The *Announcer* had been left in the dust by the *Sunday Times* and the *Observer*, though at least we beat the *Telegraph*. And I would like to think that our six-partner on the Fertile Crescent, by myself and photographer Elizabeth Derry, helped us to make up in impact what we'd lost in precedence.

It started with Issue No. 1, and it was a bloody good series, though I say it myself on Bess' behalf. And if you did read it I hope you enjoyed it, which you must have done because our Circulation Department were more than happy. What you don't know, and after all these years I think I can honourably tell you, is the tale of one of our adventures that never got written up, and of one 120-size roll of Bess' Ektachrome that never even got processed, let alone published.

It all came about through Bess' lust for black tents.

I'd found her enough for a Scout jamboree, you'd have

thought. We'd been on the move for a fortnight, working our way south from Damascus, over the frontier at Ramtha, taking in the ruins at Herash, the honey-and-green quilt of the Jordan valley, Jerusalem, Bethlehem, Hebron, the lot. (You could still do it like that in those days, before war altered the map.) Bess had hot, to my knowledge, forty-two cassettes of black-and-white and fifty-seven rolls of colour. Colour was her real love, and nothing less than 2 ¼ square would do her for that. So in those days, before newspapers had Hasselblads, for an assignment like ours she needed three wide-angle, standard, and her pride and joy a Rollei specially fitted with what she called a 'Long Tom' lens. Plus of course a 35mm. Pentax and *its* lenses, for black-and-white. Sorry to blind you with science, but being a gentleman I had to lug most of it for her, and in that heat, by God, I remember it.

She was half drunk with delight at the harvest she'd gathered, and convinced that our Editor would be the same. Except that she still wanted 'proper' black tents in a 'proper' desert.

'I found you two lots in the Wilderness of Judea,' I reminded her. 'What was wrong with them?'

'Call that a desert?' she asked, with as much scorn as her rather cuddly good nature would allow. 'From smack in the middle of it, you can still get home to your hotel in time for tea.'

'It still *looks* like a desert.'

'Dugald, darling, for my sort of pictures I want real Bedouin who wouldn't recognise a Coca-Cola sign if they fell over it.'

I tried to explain to her that they were all the same Bedouin. The ones she'd despised at the Herodium well, because their kids wore plastic hair curlers, or the ones she'd ignored near Jericho, because they were surrounded by vegetation, or the ones in the Judean Wilderness who'd failed to qualify because of the accessibility of hotel teas. Any of these might well be the same individuals who'd turn up a week or two later in the empty lands to the east, plastic hair curlers and all.

Bess wouldn't believe me. She'd been reading up her Gerald Sparrow, and threw me quotations about tribal territories. I agreed in principle but argued on detail, as well as insisting that greatly as I admired Mr. Sparrow, I'd been Middle East Correspondent since before 'O' levels were even a glint in Bess' eye, etc., etc. We were still arguing as the Land Rover pushed south from Amman through the Devon-red Land of the Moabites on the way to Petra, our next major chore.

Don't get me wrong. Arguments or not, I was thoroughly enjoying our joint assignment. Bess Derry was good company. A whizz-kid who'd used the Regent Street Poly like a launching pad to get her where she now stood at twenty-nine. She was apparently stuck for life with her springtime enthusiasm and her springtime puppy-fat, both of which she carried charmingly under the tumble of short yellow hair. She was also, thank God, as professional as I.

But obsessed with black tents.

She started building up the pressure again as we crossed the Mujib gorge. 'There's a desert off to our left soon, isn't there?'

'Only about a million square miles of it,' I admitted.

'We could take in some of it on the way.'

'No.'

'Why not?'

'We're going to Petra.'

'I said, "on the way."'

'You're a defenceless female under my care. I'm not going to risk—'

She interrupted that with the indifference it deserved. 'We've got enough petrol and food and water to add a day or two to the journey. And a tent.'

'No.'

'Why not?'

'I daren't trust myself. I'm a sex maniac, with seventeen convictions.'

'I can hardly wait. So am I, and I've only got sixteen.'

I tried another tack. 'Too many days of this heat, and your

colour stock will deteriorate.'

'Buster,' she asked, 'are you looking for a demarcation dispute?'

'Neither for that, nor for black tents in the desert,' I said firmly. 'Once and for all.'

Our first night off the road (and I still don't know how she wheedled me into admitting I knew a tract) I enjoyed more than I was prepared to admit. It had been a year or two since I'd really been in the middle of nowhere among the silence and the stars, and perhaps every journalist should do it more often. Preferably in the company of someone who can whip up a meal that transcends the tins it comes from. Bess had it cooked by the time I'd pitched the tent. We climbed into our sleeping bags in a state of well fed mutual benevolence and with enough jokes about their regrettable narrowness to add spice to our goodnight dialogue and flatter both our self-esteems. I don't remember falling asleep, but her head was on my shoulder when we awoke in the abrupt dawn, and that and her coffee started me off in a good temper.

I don't think Bess had ever known such heat. She kept smiling through the sweat and dust, but she was too limp to make more than a token fuss about the complete absence of black tents.

'We may still see some,' I consoled her. 'This is a busy route, by desert standards.'

'I'll take your word for it. When do we stop?'

'Another couple of hours.'

I was wrong. We stopped three minutes later, with the nasty jarring of a wheel rim on small rock.

'Oh, charming!' I said, and climbed out. The near front was as flat as a Glagow Sunday. Five seconds' inspection showed that a pump wouldn't help, so I unclamped a spare, propped it against the side, found a wheel brace...

And failed to find a jack.

Bess came to help me. We searched the Land Rover from

end to end. No jack.

I looked at her. 'Yusif swore he'd checked the kit.' I pleaded. 'I'll wring the bastard's neck when we get back. It's my own fault. I should have double checked myself.'

'Skip the breast-beating,' Bess suggested, 'and let's think of something we can do.'

'Oh, it's easy. We find a rock to put under the front axle, then we dig a hole under the wheel till the rock takes the weight, then we change the wheel and fill the hole up again.'

'Nice weather for digging.'

It was. By the time we'd found a rock the right size and succeeded in manoeuvring it into place (Bess working as hard as I did) we were both dizzy with heat and weariness. I practically forced her to sit in what shade the vehicle offered, and after five minutes' rest myself, gathered up enough strength to lift the shovel.

I'd managed to hack away an inch or two, and was wondering whether to wait till sunset anyway, when Bess called to me in sudden excitement.

'Dugald—look!'

There were twelve—no, fourteen of them—tall undulating camels, making their way up the track from the south, with half a dozen horse-men flanking them as outriders.

'Now I know why they call them ships of the desert,' Bess said wonderingly. She was already getting out the Rollei with the Long Tom.

I had to smile at her. They all say that, first time they see a caravan on the move. Even I could remember the awestruck moment when I realised that the cliché was true, and today I saw them again through her eyes—the tawny schooners nose to tail, rising and falling with the swell.

I let her click and wind on twice, then said, 'Now stop pointing that thing at them. They've got eyes like sparrowhawks.'

She obeyed me at once, putting away the Rollei, but slinging a Pentax with a wide-angle lens round her neck and folding her arms casually. Bess had learned, in the past fortnight photographing Moslems, a few things which they hadn't taught at the Poly.

We stood by the Land Rover watching them approach. When they were half a mile from us, one of the horsemen drew ahead.

'*Salaamu aleikum*,' I greeted him when he reined in beside us.

'*We-aleikum as-salaam*. You have trouble?'

He was about sixty, as nearly as I could judge. By his bearing, and by the fact that he had investigated us personally, I guessed him to be the paterfamilias.

'Your servant has had a small misfortune, *ya sheikh*,' I said, pointing to the wheel. 'By my own foolishness, we lack the tool to lift the car, and I must therefore dig a hole that I may be able to change the wheel.'

He nodded slowly, and then turned to speak to a young man who had followed him. 'We stop here for the night.' He waved to the side of the track. 'Let the women dismount and the men gather to help this man.'

'Blessings descended at your approach,' I told him, with feeling. And to Bess, in English, 'He's getting his lads to help us.'

I hadn't looked her way, but could guess the trick she'd been using, shooting from the waist by guesswork, without looking in the viewfinder or even at the camera. That way, she could usually get what she wanted within the lens' field, and enlarge that section of the negative in due course. As long as you don't raise the camera to your eye, few of your camera shy Arab victims will realise that they are being photographed.

'Good for him' she said. 'He's splendid, isn't he?'

'Yes, but be careful, even with the wide-angle. He's not so dumb. Oh, and you'll get your black tents. They're pitching right here.'

Bess' eyes lit up.

The wheel changing was child's play. Half a dozen of Yub al -Ali's sons, nephews and grandsons braced themselves to lift the corner of the Land Rover long enough for me to whip the wheel off, the spare on, and have the nuts finger tight. I grinned at them gratefully as I braced the nuts home.

'*Inshallah,* may I never be far from men as strong as you,' I told them. They smiled deprecatingly.

'For tonight, at least, it will be so,' the eldest said. 'You travel no father, surely?'

I looked at my watch, and at the sun. 'If i may pitch my tent by yours, I shall consider myself honoured.'

They assured me that the honour would be entirely theirs, and half an hour later our tent was up and our kit unpacked. Bess was beside herself with joy. 'Dugald, *darling*, I asked for a Bedouin camp, but I didn't expect to be part of one!'

'Perhaps I won't break Yusif's neck after all.'

'I should think not! You ready for something to eat?'

I hesitated. 'We'd better wait till we discover what the form is. Don't look now, but I've a feeling we won't be seeing each other for a few hours.'

'You mean I'll be with the girls?'

'Here comes your invite.'

Bess glanced at the shapeless bundle of black which was sidling up to us, and purred. 'I'd have given my right arm for this. You know what? Yusif deserves a bonus.'

I said hastily, 'Talking of right arms, eat everything with your *right* hand, never touch food with your left, and don't turn the soles of your feet towards your hostess.' Black Bundle was on us. I politely ignored my host's woman, but listened as she spoke shyly in Arabic to Bess.

Bess smiled at her. 'Sorry, sweetie, but I don't understand a word,'

'She's asking you to be their guest.' I stared at the horizon and told it in Arabic, 'May Allah grant that this woman learn quickly the language of the Prophet, on whom be the blessing of Allah, and peace. Then she will be able to express, to those who are kind to her, the gratitude with which her heart is filled.'

Black Bundle giggled and took Bess' hand. Soon after they had gone, Yub al-Ali's eldest arrived and led me to his father's tent.

It was quite a party. Fortunately I have a strong and capacious stomach and have learned to accept gracefully, without the aid of alcohol, the compliment of the more unmentionable parts of a roast sheep. We swopped life stories at great length—mine being edited, of course, for comprehensibility rather than modesty, which was not a requirement. Yub al-Ali was particularly anxious to hear of all the countries I had seen.

'It is good for a man to have travelled widely,' he declared. 'It adds to his wisdom and generosity of spirit. But one should never marry a *woman* who has travelled widely. She will always be saying, 'I have seen this man. I have seen that man.'

I saved that one up for Bess.

There wasn't much of the night left when Yub al-Ali did me the honour of himself escorting me to my tent. It was empty, but the moment al-Ali left me, Black Bundle appeared and handed over Bess, doubtless feeling that it would be impolite to keep me waiting.

Bess was giggling euphorically. I suppose she'd caught that from her hostesses. Language had not been an insurmountable barrier, it seemed. Though how they'd managed to communicate some of the things she was giggling about defeated me. She tried to explain, but we lost the thread.

A sleeping bag isn't all that narrow, after all, given determination and a sense of humour.

Next morning, short night or not, we were cheerfully up with the sun. Our hosts, with typical Bedouin unpredictability, seemed to have decided to stay put for a while, and that suited us fine because we had a job to do. We struck camp and parked the Land Rover in a convenient gulley where it wouldn't' spoil the picture.

There was a hundred foot bluff overlooking the camp from the east, which gave Bess just the flat lighting her colour shots demanded. So we climbed it together, I carrying most of her gear as usual, and set up her tripod. She clicked away happily for twenty minutes, first with the standard lens, then with the Long Tom. To my professional awareness that the camp was a gold mine for her was added, this morning, a heightened personal tenderness towards her delight, I tried to keep this in reasonably manly check, but I had my work cut out.

She caught me watching her once, and teased, 'You're a sentimental old sausage, Dugald. You talk like a cynical, high-turnover philanderer, but you'd never bring yourself to do it.'

'Much too moral.'

'Much too soft-hearted. Just as well I go home next month.' I must have looked downcast, because she added, 'My own's not hard enough for both of us. Glad it's not *this* month, though.'

I put an arm round her.

'Don't forget the sparrowhawks,' she warned me.

'Talking of which, I hope we haven't offended them, sniping at them like this.'

'I don't think they've noticed. I haven't seen anyone looking this way, through old Long Tom here.'

'I wouldn't bet on it. Got all you want?'

She nodded and I collapsed the tripod for her. We clambered down the bluff together.

On the way to our Land Rover, we met Yub al-Ali, and I exchanged greetings with him. He looked at me keenly from the patriarchal drapes of his keffiyeh. 'Your woman makes pictures?' he asked.

So much for Bess' complacence. 'She does, *ya sheikh*. We work for a *jurnala* which wishes to show the beauty of your land to those who have not the good fortune to visit it.'

He considered the matter and finally said, 'This much is good.' The approval, while polite, was clearly qualified. 'I knew what your woman was doing, because I have seen the three-legged boxes with which men made pictures of the story of el-Orens.'

So that was it. You couldn't go far in Jordan in those days without hitting the backwash of *Lawrence of Arabia* (as, in

Israel, that of *Exodus*.) 'Did you know el-Orens?' I asked him.

He laughed, and launched into a bloodthirsty reminiscence of his small share, as a boy of thirteen, in one of the livelier operations of the Wrecker of Trains. He had just reached the point in his story where his father had tanned his hide for sneaking out of camp to join the ambush, but had allowed him to keep the Turkish rifle he had murderously acquired. Then he fell silent.

The sudden tension was palpable. I turned to look where he was looking.

Bess had her nose buried in the viewfinder of the Rollei with the Long Tom. The black snout of the lens was pointed unmistakably at one of the Bedouin girls—the only one I had see unveiled in this camp. She stood, momentarily unaware, and as noble as Ruth, in the mouth of one of the tents twenty feet away.

I snapped. 'Bess!' a fraction of a second too late to stop her releasing the shutter.

The Bedouin girl woke from her daydreaming at the sound of my voice and vanished into the tent. Bess lowered her lens, shamefaced. 'I couldn't resist her, Dugald.'

'Now you've torn it,' I told her, and to Yub al-Ali I said hurriedly, 'I take refuge with the Lord of the Dawn.'

It was the best I could do. The traditional exorcism of the evil eye after one has invited it by imprudently admiring something, or someone belonging to one's host. I hoped it conveyed, first, that Bess had acted out of spontaneous admiration, and second, that I deplored her breach of manners.

Yub al-Ali, impassive, said, 'That is the woman of my grandson.'

'It is as Allah pleases' – permissible admiration.

'Your woman made a picture of her naked face.'

'My woman, *ya sheikh*, meant no harm. She has not been honoured, as I have, by the opportunity to accustom herself to the ways of the bedu.'

Yub al-Ali studied me for a moment, and then said with a firm gentleness that made me feel three years old, 'I am sure that she meant no harm, my son. But you will explain to her why she must give this picture back to me.'

'I will do so, *ya sheikh*,' I agreed unhappily, 'but there are difficulties.'

'Of what kind?'

'The picture is on a roll within the box, it is true. But it cannot be seen until the roll has been taken into a room of the blackest darkness and passed through certain liquids which revealed it to the eyes.'

Yub al-Ali frowned.

'What's he saying?' Bess asked, humbly and a little frightened.

'Look,' I told her, 'he knows you have a picture of his grandson's wife in that camera. Unveiled, too. That means you have power over her.'

'Who, *me*?'

'Not only you. She'd be exposed to the evil eye and to every man you showed it to. All our readers, in fact. He knows what a newspaper is, for God's sake. He wants you to give the picture back to him. Now.'

'But Dugald, how can I? There isn't a darkroom nearer than Amman! And it's the last on the roll. The other eleven are *irreplaceable*. The best I got up there.'

Yub al-Ali was watching me. I had no doubt what he thought of women who argued, and of men who let them.

'What do we do?' Bess asked helplessly.

I told her, and she nearly wept. But she had to. She wound on the film to the end, took the roll out of the camera, sealed it, put it in its little yellow box, and handed it to me.

'In this yellow box, *ya sheikh*,' I explained, 'is the picture of the woman of your grandson. I cannot show it to your eyes, for the reasons which I have told you. But as I hope for the merciful judgement of Allah, the picture is there.'

He took the box. 'I know that you speak the truth, but why does your woman show sorrow?' he asked kindly.

'She sorrows because there are also on that roll many other pictures, which she has travelled many miles to make.'

'Let her keep them, then, and give me only that of the woman of my grandson.'

'May the angel of Allah record your compassion to my woman, *ya sheikh*, but the pictures cannot be separated from one another except in the room of darkness. But rather than offend you, she must give you them all.'

I could see he was genuinely upset, and for a moment he seemed to waver. But he said at last, 'It grieves me that I must do this. But I am the father of my people.'

'In which Allah has greatly blessed them,' I told him.

Ten minutes later we were on our way. Bess, poor girl, was wretched, and she made me feel worse by refusing to let me share the blame. 'You warned me, Dugald. I was a dam' fool, and it's cost me eleven glorious pictures that I'll never get again—never. Oh, *blast!*'

'Maybe we'll see another caravan.'

'You're very sweet, but who are you kidding?'

We drove for a mile or two in silence, with me flogging my mind trying to think of some way of cheering her up. And then, miraculously (or maybe Allah took pity on us), the answer came.

A second caravan, about the same size of Yub al-Ali's, appeared on the western horizon. It was converging on our own track.

Bess was a new woman. 'We can keep ahead of them all day,' she bubbled, 'and with any luck there'll be high ground close to where they camp. All right, Dugald?'

I was so relieved to see her smiling again. I was ready to agree to anything. But we hadn't gone another mile when a galloping horseman overtook us. It was Yub al-Ali's eldest. 'My father begs forgiveness that he delays you,' he said when I'd stopped, 'but he has a favour to ask.'

I turned the Land Rover and drove back, wondering. Yub al-Ali was waiting on the edge of the black tents. We exchanged the complicated courtesies that the occasion demanded, and then he explained.

'The men you see to the west have not always been friends

of my people. They pretend to be at peace with us now, but they are men of no trust. They may at any time again be our enemies, without cause and without warning.'

'Your enemies are my own worst enemies, *ya sheikh*,' I assured him. 'Is there a way in which I may help you?' I asked, without a thought for the neutrality which is prudent for journalists, especially in the Middle East. Perhaps Bess was right about me being a romantic.

I have not often seen a Bedouin sheikh embarrassed, but there was no mistaking Yub al-Ali's diffidence. And when he put his request, it was so out of the ordinary by his standards that I understood. 'You can indeed help us, my son, by permitting your woman to help us.'

'My woman is your servant, *ya sheikh*,' I stammered.

Yub al-Ali told me what he wanted.

We were at the top of the bluff, farther along than last time to give us a good view of the converging track. The Rollei with the Long Tom was on its tripod. Bess was checking the smooth working of the pan-and-tilt head. Around us, shielding all but her lens from view, stood half a dozen of Yub al-Ali's young men, all smiling broadly. The first camels of the approaching caravan were almost abreast of us.

The shutter clicked.

Bess wound on, swung Long Tom a fraction, and clicked again. 'Powerful stuff,' she said.

In her twelve shots, she included every man, woman, and child in the caravan. Then we went down to the waiting patriarch, escorted by his jubilant progeny.

Bess unloaded the Rollei before his eyes, but the roll into its yellow box, an passed it to me.,

'All of them are there, *ya sheikh*,' I told him, presenting the box with a formal bow.

Yub al-Ali fingered, lovingly. I thank you, Dug am-Makensi, and your woman, for the power that you have put into my hands.'

'Would you not rather,' I suggested, 'that we took the box to Amman, to the room of darkness, and came back to you, bearing pictures that your eyes can see?'

He closed both his hands round the box. 'It is not needful, my son. The box will never be opened, but I have the pictures, whether my eyes see them or not. I have in this box a piece of the soul of each of these my enemies.'

From inside his clothing he produced the other yellow box. 'And because you are a man of honour, and have done this thing for me and my people, I return to you the pictures of the woman of my grandson you will not give to your *jurnala*, but will keep safely, for your own eyes alone and those of your woman.'

'You have my word,' I told him.

As we drove away for the second time, I asked Bess (and I was only half joking), 'Doesn't the responsibility frighten you?'

'Not a bit. As I'm quite sure you told the old boy, anyone he hates, we hate too. Funny, though. It's the only time I've ever taken a whole roll of the best pictures I could—and they *were*, Dugald—knowing they'd never be processed.'

'How's that for professional pride?' I teased her.

But she was serious. 'No, it's not that.' She hesitated, and said (a little perfunctorily, I thought), 'I just wanted him to have first-rate material to work on.'

By unspoken agreement, we took a different route from the second caravan.

VIII

THE CHANLO-HERD

I am old now, Sati, and anyone who has celebrated his thousandth moon-cycle has earned the right not to be pestered with questions. At least, not with the same questions over and over again.

Tell you the truth, son of the son of my daughter, I've forgotten just how long ago I passed the thousandth. I could work it out, I suppose, but it's enough for me that the sun is still warm on my grey fur, that the lobes of my eye can still pick out the domes of the Golden City across the terraced Khrovan hills, and that my feelers can still grip the hul-leaf pipe—even though the hul they cure today hasn't the flavour I remember when I was your age. Yes, I'm still as strong as some in their nine-hundreds.

He nicknamed me Rocky, you know, because of my strength. Physical rather than moral, I'm afraid. Though he used to say I under-estimated myself. I remember the day he gave me the name. I was sticking to some point in an argument with the Brothers, and I'll admit I was beginning to wonder if I wasn't just being stubborn. But Mesaki, who was listening, suddenly smiled and said, 'What an old rock you are, Nehuri. I think I shall call you Rocky. We're going to need that strength of yours.'

He had a smile I can't forget, even now. His eye was huge and clear, and the lobes were almost luminous. He could make you smile with him, or want to shrivel into a corner from the shame. He could quell a rage that had reached murder-point, or lighten the blankness of the insane, just with a look.

Ai, ai. Shred me some more hul, lad.

When did I first meet Mesaki? That I'll never forget, either, Sati (yes, the one you were named after). Sati and I had been trapping tonraler, which were in season but not very plentiful that moon-cycle. We were trudging up the path from the river, pretty well worn out, with our catch slung from a pole between us. You know the path. It crosses the chanlo-track by Iaaha's Well. When we reached the Well, we had to halt, because there was a flock of the silly things blundering along the rack, eighty or a hundred of them mewing to each other in that pathetic way they have, and clicking their scales in panic at the slightest thing. Old Futi, the chanlo-herd, was shooing them from behind, and I remember thinking, *He'll have to be pensioned off, he's really past it.* He was bent almost double, and his feelers trembled on his stick, quite apart from the fact that he was blind in one lobe. But the chanlos loved him, and trusted him where they'd shy away from the younger villagers, so the village let him keep at it.

It was then that I saw *him.*

He was standing on the far side of the track, watching old Futi labouring in the rear of the flock. I suppose Mesaki was nothing special to look at, by ordinary standards—too loose knit and thin, and his fur was short and reddish. But even before he turned that great eye on you, you felt the gentleness and authority of him. And believe me, Sati, gentleness and authority were a flat contradiction in terms of Khrova in those days. Not much better now, you may think. And yet the Brothers have been able to achieve something. Me? Oh yes, I've been their leader since Mesake was taken from us, but it's only because I remember his words and stick to them like the stubborn old tonraler-trapper that I am. Perhaps he was wiser than I knew, when he nicknamed me Rocky.

Anyway, there he stood by the chanlo-track, waiting for old Futi to reach him. And when he was a feeler-span away, Mesaki said, 'Look at me, Futi.'

Old Futi stopped in surprise, because it wasn't a voice he knew. He strained his lobes trying to see who the stranger was, but he can't have made out more than Mesaki's foot-fur because of his bent old spine.

'Good evening, friend,' he croaked amiably. I never heard Futi snarl at anyone, before or since.

'Good evening, Futi. Look at me.'

Futi leaned on his stick and said, 'You must forgive me, but I'd have to squat down to do that.'

'Futi.'

'What, then?'

'Stand up straight.'

I remember thinking the stranger must be mad, and it was on the tip of my sucker to call out to him not to tease the old one. But something stopped me. A kind of awe, I think. And while I stared at them, old Futi began to straighten. I couldn't believe my lobes, but he did. Slowly, but with growing confidence.

'Throw away your stick.'

And Futi did that, too. At last he was standing his full height, as I'd remembered him when I was a whelp—calm and upright, looking the stranger eye to eye.

Even the chanlos had stopped their mewing an clicking.

Mesaki and Futi said nothing to each other for a while, and then Mesaki smiled. 'On your way, Futi,' he said. 'And no more hating, my friend.'

To this day I've never really understood what Mesaki meant by that. Futi had never *said* he hated anyone. But he dipped his lobes like a spear-player acknowledging a touch, returned the stranger's smile, and loped away up the track, singing to the chanlos as they tumbled around him. Mesaki looked after him till he disappeared round a rock, and then turned to us.

'Come,' he said.

And of course, we did. We took him to my father's house—

yes, Sati, this one—and cooked the tonraler for supper, while we listened to him. In the morning we left together, travelling light, and in the next thirty moon-cycles I don't there was a village in Khrova we didn't visit. We gathered more Brothers as we went along, and all of us were with him till...well, till almost the end.

I've been asleep? Nonsense. Just thinking. What if my lobes *were* sheathed, you cheeky whelp? They're old and need resting now and then.

The Golden City? No, it hasn't changed much. I don't think it ever will, not really. The rest of the Globe may change around it, but the Golden City's like a person. You know what I mean? As you grow up, Sati, you'll be wicked and conquer your wickedness. You'll triumph and the victories will fade. You'll love and forget your lovers. But you'll always be Sati. I'm an old fool and I moralise too much, perhaps, but you'll allow me to hope that by the time you're my age, you'll be wiser and better for what you've been through. The wickedness and the victories and the lost loves will have ripened you, but the whelp will still be there under the grey fur. And more than any other city, the Golden City keeps everything of itself. I don't know why, no.

But I don't mean nothing ever happens there. *Everything* happens there. That last moon-cycle, when *he* taught about the Holy Ring, it was like a blare of trumpets. The citizens were shouting for him wherever he went, and the Council were scared stiff. Absolutely terrified.

Why? Brekkek's thunder, I've told you a hundred times, lad. Oh, all right. Because of what he and the Brothers had been doing to Khrova. Sati, can you remember when this village had a wall? No, of course you can't. But every village in the khrovan hills, and down on the plain too, had a wall in those days. A high plaster wall with living griza-bushes along its top to tear the fur and poison the flesh. And from nightfall to dawn there were guards outside, to kill first and ask questions afterwards. You took a chance visiting a strange village even in the daylight, but at night it was suicide.

And you know what happened in the trail of Mesaki's progress? Apart from the straightened backs and the cleared lobes and the restored fur? The walls began to come down. I don't mean everyone stopped being suspicious altogether. There were still guards at night, but as long as you carried a light you could walk up to them, identify yourself, and be welcomed as a traveller.

Do you see why the Council were scared? No, I suppose you wouldn't. But believe me, once the rumours started reaching the Golden City, more and more every moon-cycle, they sat up and took notice. They sent a Royal squadron round to one or two of the heretic villages and made an example of them. Executed a few Elders, and stood over the villagers with naked spears while they rebuilt the walls.

Then they rode away, and most of the walls came down again. Not all, but most.

The Council had an excuse, of course. They said that without village walls, Khrova would be defenceless if the Green-furs attacked. Even though the Green-furs were more afraid of us than we were of them, and it was three thousand moon-cycles since they'd attacked anyone except the odd traveller who'd lost his way. No, the Council's real fear was if the villagers stopped hating each other, how could the Council dominate them? You see?

So more Elders were executed. Yes, that's why your mother keeps fresh jeena-flowers on your great-great-grandfather's grave, out there where the wall used to be.

Dreaming? Well, perhaps I was. It comes back to me oftener than anything else, that last night in the Golden City, when he talked to us in Aldi's little house by the chanlo-market. The Royal Guards were looking for him already, and we all knew it. I was pleading with him. All the Brothers felt the same, but I was always the most hot-headed and ready to argue, so I spoke for them all.

'Mesaki *aranu*, we can get you out of the City.'

'No, Rocky.'

'But there's so much to do! We could go to the Green-furs…' It still sounded strange, even to me. His teaching that the Green-furs were human like ourselves had been the last outrage to the ancient beliefs, bringing down the wrath of the Council on us, and it wasn't too easy even for some of the Brothers to swallow at first. 'We could go to the Green-furs and carry the word to them—to the whole Globe, where the Council can't reach you.'

'No, Rocky, that will be your task. Yours and the Brothers.'

'But it won't be the same, *aranu*. Your own task isn't finished.'

He turned his unforgettable eye on me, and once again the lobes seemed to glow with a fire of their own. 'Rocky Nehuri, what do you know of my task? That which must happen here tomorrow, must happen, and one day you will know why. But my task?'

He paused, touched my feelers with his, and then walked to the window to look out over the moonlit tiles of the Golden City. The chanlos were mewing in the market-pens, and the watch could be heard crying the hour. Mesaki listened in silence for a while.

'Rocky Nehuri,' he said at last, 'other chanlos I have, which are not of this fold. I must gather them too, and they shall hear my voice, and there shall be one fold, and one chanlo-herd.'

No Sait, I don't know what he meant. I didn't then, and I still don't today. Though I still wonder. And I never had a chance to ask him, because next morning they took him outside the wall of the Golden City and spiked him to the Wheel, to die in the sun.

But I can't bear to talk of that tonight. Leave me alone to sleep. You are young and I am very old.

CHAPTER IX

THE WITCH'S BOTTLE

Steve didn't know whether to be offended or relieved when the taxi driver waved away his money with a smile and said, 'Your uncle fixed to settle next time he sees me.' Offended in case it was implied that, at fifteen, he was too young to pay for his own taxies, or relieved in the country where the taxi driver (who was also, his conversation on the way from Colchester station had made clear, a poultry farmer, thatcher, and shopkeeper) was a neighbour of Uncle Garry's.

The many-gifted neighbour waved and drove off. Steve picked up the cases and followed Jill, who had opened the gate and was halfway up the path.

'Looks lovely!' she called back to him.

She was right. The thatched, half-timbered cottage looked surprisingly large, but was obviously the real thing, East Anglian Tudor, even if the casement windows were not discreetly metal-framed. The one-acre garden seemed huge to Steve's London eyes; a long lawn in front, vegetables to one side, and trees at the back taller than the two-story house.

They knocked on the oak front door, and nobody answered.

After a while they tried the door and found it unlocked. It

opened straight into a big lounge which must have been made out of at least two smaller rooms, because two upright beams still supported a big one in the middle of the ceiling, like black tree trunks growing out of the floor. Charred logs glowed in an open hearth. The fire didn't look as if it had been made up for an hour or two.

'Uncle Garry?' they called, several times, but obviously there was no one in.

'He *was* expecting us tonight, wasn't he?' Jill asked, frowning.

'Of course he was. I was there when Mother phoned him. And she asked him to send a taxi—which he did, didn't he?'

'Maybe he's in the garden.'

They left their cases in the lounge and went out through a glass door at the back of the room.

'Look! A pond!'

'Wonder if it's got any fish?'

It was quite a big pond, fifteen feet long at least and nearly as wide. It has been recently edged with stone, a fountain nozzle protruded from its centre, and goldfish slid about under water-lily leaves.

'I'm not surprised you want to be a psychiatrist like Uncle Garry,' Jill said, 'if this is what it gets you.'

'He's lucky,' Steve told her. 'Consultant in a Colchester hospital, so he can commute in twenty minutes. And three successful textbooks to his name. He's a big shot, Jill. I'll probably end up in Balham, analysing bed-wetters.'

'Quite a young big shot. He's thirty-six. Daddy told me.'

'Oh, well. Maybe I'll be lucky like him.'

'Bed-wetters are people, too.'

'There you go again. Always jumping two sentences back. Why can't you carry on a conversation in a logical order?'

'Because I'm practicing to be your first patient.'

He feinted a swipe at her and she pretended to cringe. It was quite fun, having a sister only a year younger than yourself, Steve thought, *you could pull each other's legs and both enjoy it.* Whereas if either of them teased nine-year-old Audrey, the other sibling (useful word he'd learned from Uncle Gerry), it usually ended in tears. A good kid, Jill, even if she did think sideways. (He was too earnest about his intended profession to say 'think like a girl', even to himself.)

They strolled round the pond, watching the goldfish.

'Steve—that tree!'

He looked up, puzzled by the sudden tension in her voice, and found she was no longer looking at the goldfish but was staring at a tall, leafless oak tree a few yards along the garden.

'It's an oak,' he said. 'Looks dead to me.'

'I don't like it.'

'What d'you mean, "don't like it"?'

'I...don't know. It gives me...an awful feeling.'

He straightened up and walked towards it. 'Oh, for heaven's sake, Jill. It's only a *tree*,' he told her, reaching out a hand towards the bark.

'Steve, don't touch it!' she cried, urgently.

Steve came back to her, concerned. 'Why ever not?' He stood facing her, obscuring her view of the tree, but she moved sideways so that she could go on looking at it. She seemed repelled but fascinated. I'm going to have to do something about this, he thought. He put an arm round her shoulder and tried to lead her gently towards the oak. 'It's only a tree. It can't hurt you. Come and see.'

'*No!*' Without warning, she became a wild thing, turning on Steve and fighting like mad, clawing at his face. It was so completely out of character that he threw up his hands to protect his eyes, stumbling backwards, not knowing what to do. She still came after him, and he tripped and fell. Jill fell beside him, and just as suddenly the fighting stopped.

She seemed herself again, but breathing heavily, looking as bewildered as he felt.

'What on earth was all *that* about?' he gasped.

'I don't know. The flames...'

'Flames? What flames?'

'There were...' She broke off, frowning.

He waited for her to go on, and when she didn't, he said,

'You haven't gone for me like that since we were kids. It wasn't *you*.'

'I know it wasn't me, but it *was*. Stevie, I'm sorry. Did I hurt you?'

Steve got up, brushing himself down and laughing a little shakily. 'I'll live.' He gave her a hand up. 'Come on. We'd better go inside.'

In the big lounge, he took of the anorak he was still wearing, helped Jill solicitously out of hers—something about her making him feel very much the older brother—and then put more logs on the fire and got it blazing. It was only just April and the evenings were still cool, and instinct told him she ought to be kept warm.

She knelt on the hearthrug beside him, gazing into the fire, and asked at last, 'Steve, what *happened?*'

'*You* tell *me*.' He tried to sound matter-of-fact but not bored, though in fact he felt neither. 'What was all that about flames?'

Jill hesitated. 'I thought the tree was on fire and that you were pushing me into it, but it wasn't me and you weren't you.'

'Sort of daytime nightmare?' he asked, carefully keeping the same tone of voice.

'Yes, only worse. Steve, I'm scared.'

'You've been watching too much telly. I wonder where Uncle Garry's got to?'

Jill looked towards him, and then past him, with a sudden little yep of surprise. He spun round, still crouching.

A strange woman was standing in the glass door from the garden, which she must have opened silently. She could have been anything from forty to sixty. A tall, trim figure in a timeless dress, close fitting to wrists and hips with a straight skirt that fell in heavy folds to her ankles. Her large dark eyes gave nothing away, except a hint of secret amusement.

'Good evening,' she said, and then walked calmly to the fire and stood towering over them, warming her hands at it. 'The night has turned quite chilly.'

'On—er, yes.' Steve remembered himself and jumped to

his feet, but Jill stayed where she was, staring up at the woman.

'I am Catherin Woodleigh. I just came in to tell you that your uncle was called away for the evening. I live next door.'

'Oh. Well, ere, thank you. We wondered where he was. I'm Steve Lancaster, and this is my sister, Jill.'

The woman nodded gravely to Steven and then gazed down at Jill. 'Hello, Jill.'

'Hello.' Jill looked confused and scrambled up. 'Sorry.'

'Sorry for what? Show me your hands, child.'

Jill hesitated a moment, then held out her hands. The woman took them in her own and studied them, first the back, then the palms. Then she looked into Jill's eyes for a few seconds.

'Yes,' she said.

'Yes, what?' Steve asked.

'Just yes.' The woman let go of Jill's hands, and suddenly became friendly and unmysterious. 'Your uncle asked me to keep an eye open for you. He had to see someone in Ipswich—his new book, you know.'

'On schizophrenia, isn't it?'

'I believe so. You want to be a psychiatrist too, don't you?'

Steve nodded. 'Yes. Did Uncle Garry tell you?'

'No.' She smiled but whether to herself or him he wasn't sure. 'Anyway, he said he'd be back before midnight, and you were to make yourselves at him. There's plenty of food in the fridge. And if you don't feel like waiting up, your bedrooms are the two at that end.' Pointing through the chimney breast, 'Jill's is the one at the back.'

'It was nice of you to come and tell us,' Steve said politely.

'Not at all. Sleep well.' And then she went through the glass door again, shutting it behind her and smiling at them briefly through it before she disappeared.

'Odd character,' Steve said.

Jill said nothing, but went on looking at the empty door.

'Come on,' Steve told her. 'Let's find that food.'

*　　　*　　　*

It was half past three in the morning when Jill's scream woke Steve up. He thought he had dreamed it—they had had a purely greedy second supper with Uncle Garry when he came home, and his stomach was uncomfortable—but as soon as he was fully awake, she screamed again. More of a squeal, really, as though she was too frightened not to scream at all, but didn't want anyone to hear it.

He jumped out of bed, threw on his dressing gown and crossing the little landing, tapped on Jill's door, then pushed it open. 'You all right? Thought I heard you yell.'

Her bed was in the corner by the window and he was sitting up, her back pressed into the angle of the wall, staring across the room at the blank white wall beside the door. A low bright moon lit the room, and she was clearly visible. She shook her head as though to clear it and looked embarrassed but glad to see him.

'Nightmare, I guess,' she told him, hugging her own shoulders to keep warm.

Steve crossed the room and made her get back under the covers, which he tucked round her. 'You don't have nightmares sitting up.'

She looked sheepish but said nothing. He sat down on the edge of the bed. 'Come on, Jill. Something in this room frightened you. What was it?'

'I saw the flames again,' she admitted.

'What? In *here*?'

'Not *in* here. Reflected on that wall, from the back garden.'

He studied the wall with its oblong patch of moonlight. Then he got up and moved the curtains back and forth so that the shape of the oblong changed. 'That's what you saw. The curtains moving in the wind. You were half awake and your imagination supplied the rest.'

'But it was red!'

'You see things in all sorts of queer colours when you've only just opened your eyes.'

'Anyway, there isn't any wind.'

'There isn't *now*, but there must have been *then*. Get a hold of yourself, Jill. It was a dream. You've got that oak tree business on your mind.' He grinned at her deliberately. 'Feeling guilty about beating me up and punishing yourself with nightmares.'

She smiled back uncertainly. 'Maybe you're right. Sorry I woke you up.'

'That's okay. Reckon you can sleep now?'

'Yes, sure. Thanks, Steve.'

'She must have got up pretty early,' Uncle Garry said through a mouthful of toast. 'She was washing up her own breakfast when I came down. Made a few social noises and then disappeared into the garden.'

'I hope she's not still brooding over that oak tree,' Steve worried.

'Odd thing, that.'

'Why, Uncle Garry?'

'You came across some weird things in our business, Steve, but I'm *still* amazed at the ticks the human mind can play. The fact is that oak tree has a history.'

'Oh?'

'Three hundred years ago—three hundred and thirty-two, to be exact—in the days of the great witch persecution, some unfortunate girl was burned alive under that tree.'

Steve stared at his uncle. 'How ghastly!'

'Yes. Local legend has it that it has never grown any leaves since it happened, but that it won't rot away.'

'I wonder if Jill read about it somewhere?'

'Could be. The case *is* mentioned in a biography of Matthew Hopkins, the notorious Witchfinder General. It went into paperback, so it's possible Jill read it and forgot it, and then some clue triggered it off. She has a vivid imagination.'

'You can say that again.'

'And there's a coincidence too, to make it stick in her mind. The girl's name—the one who was burned—just happens to have been Jill. Jill Bewlay.' He poured himself another coffee. 'I wonder where our Jill *has* got to?'

Jill was in fact next door in Catherine Woodleigh's kitchen, being told the same story, while Catherine ground herbs with a pestle and mortar.

It was a fascinating kitchen, a strange hotchpotch of antique and modern. There was an old fashioned black kitchen range, but also a modern electric cooker; an old glazed earthenware sink with a small wooden table beside it, but also a tall white refrigerator. Catherine was working at a big table of plain scrubbed wood in the middle of the room. Dozens of bottles and jars stood on homemade shelves. Their labels were neatly handwritten. Bunches of dried herbs seemed to hang everywhere. A fine pair of mounted ram's horns hug above the range. There was even a black cat warming itself by the glow of the range grate. Jill had joked, 'No, that's *too* much' when she had seen it, and Catherine had laughed with her.

But she was serious now as she told Jill the story of Oak tree Cottage. 'Old Agnes Bewlay lived there with her daughter Jill in the sixteen-forties. Jill would have been about your age, within a year or two. And when the Witchfinder General came to the village—his name is still remembered in this part of the country, you know. When he came here looking for witches, a farmer accused old Agnes of blighting his crops.'

'And had she?'

'In those days, Jill, it hardly mattered whether she had or not. For Matthew Hopkins it was enough that she had been accused. He put her to the torture. She was very stubborn, so it went on for many hours. She was almost out of her mind before she mumbled words he ordered her to say. As soon as the torture stopped, she recanted, so he condemned her to the Ordeal by Water.'

'The one they called "swimming a witch"?'

'That's right. It was supposed to be a foolproof way of testing a suspected witch. You tied her right thumb to her left big toe and threw her into deep water. You did it three times to make sure. If she floated, she was guilty. If she sank, she was innocent.'

'Head you win, tails I lose,' Jill said. 'Sick, wasn't it.'

'Very. Agnes Bewlay drowned. And what was almost as sick was this. For the good of her soul, Matthew Hopkins made Agnes' daughter watch both the torture and the swimming. They say she never spoke nor moved till her mother was finally dead. And then she cursed the village and every man, woman and child in it.'

'You can't really blame her, can you?'

'The villagers did. They were going to drown her in that pond in the garden. Hopkins had already hurried on to the next village, so they weren't going to bother with even his sort of trial. She ran into the cottage and locked herself in, but they broke the door down. Then they dragged her into the garden, tired her to the oak tree, and burned her alive.'

'Oh...*no!*'

'They still call it Jill Bewlay's Tree.'

There was silence in the kitchen except for the rhythmic grinding of the pestle and mortar. Then there was a tap at the back door, and Catherine went to answer it.

Steve was standing outside. 'I'm sorry to bother you, but have you seen my sister?'

'Come in, Steve. She's here.'

Steve came in, said, 'We wondered where you'd got to,' to Jill, and looked around curiously. 'Are you a herbalist, Mrs. Woodleigh?'

'The whole village calls me Catherine, so you might as well, too. Yes, I'm a herbalist. Don't you approve?'

'I don't know much about it, really.' He thought for a moment. 'I suppose I approve of whatever works.'

'Very sensible of you.'

Steve peered at some of the handwritten labels. 'What are they all for? Cooking or medicine?'

'Both,' Catherine told him. 'And other things as well.'

'Where did you learn about herb medicine, Mrs.—er—

Catherine?'

'From my mother, who learned it from *her* mother, and so on, back to the Garden of Eden.'

'Metaphorically speaking, I suppose,' Steve said, a little too seriously.

'Catherine smiled. 'If you wish.'

Jill asked, 'Have *you* any children?'

'No, Jill.'

'Then who will *you* teach it all to?'

Steve's back was turned as he went on reading labels. Catherine looked Jill straight in the eyes and said, 'A good question.' They went on looking at each other till Steve turned round, then Catherine went back to her grinding and Jill bent down and stroked the cat.'

'Steve,' Jill said. 'Catherine was telling me all about the oak tree. Something did happen there, during the witch persecution.'

'I know. Uncle Garry told *me*. Gruesome, wasn't it?'

'At least it wasn't my imagination.'

'Oh, come off it, Jill. Uncle says the story's mentioned in some paperback or other. You must have read it.'

'I didn't.'

'You read masses of that kind of book.'

'I didn't read this one. I knew nothing about it till we looked at that tree.'

'But Jill...'

'Your sister saw what she saw,' Catherine interrupted calmly. 'She was in tune with the other Jill. They have... a certain amount in common.'

Steve said, 'H'mm,' and turned back to reading labels.

'What should I do about it?' Jill asked Catherine.

'Do?'

'I mean, can we exorcise her, or something? So the garden's free of her?'

'Perhaps she wants to be free of the garden,' Catherine said. 'Have you thought of that?'

'Oh, look here, Jill...' Steve muttered awkwardly, but no

one listened to him.

'No, I hadn't,' Jill said. 'Perhaps she does.'

'Why don't you ask her?' Catherine suggested.

'Ask her? How?'

'You will think of a way. And you, Steve, you still think it's all coincidence and superstition, don't you?'

'Well...'

'Nevertheless, you should help your sister in whatever she decides to do. Remember what you said? "Whatever works"?'

Steve hesitated, wondering what Uncle Garry would do in the circumstances. 'All right,' he said at last.

'Good.' Catherine went to a shelf and took down a bottle of tea coloured liquid. Then she pulled a tissue from a box on the table and signalled to Jill to stand up. 'And close your eyes for a moment.' Steve moved nervously towards them as Catherine began to dab Jill's eyelids with the tissue moistened with the bottle, but Catherine said, 'Don't worry, it won't harm her. Just a herbal infusion. Look, she showed the label to Steve.

'Eyebright and camomile,' he read. 'What's it for?'

Catherine pushed back Jill's hair and dabbed her ears. 'It will help her to see and hear better.'

'But she's got sixty-sixty vision and can hear up to twenty-two kilohertz!'

Catherine laughed. 'Listen to the scientist! I'm sure you're absolutely right, Steve, but that was not what I meant. And now, off you go. The pair of you. I've work to do.'

Steve led the way out, with a polite but slightly wary good-bye, and when he had gone ahead, Jill paused in the doorway and turned. 'Please, may I come back again?'

Catherine said, 'Jill Lancaster, you may come here any time you wish.'

Uncle Garry bustled about the lounge, stuffing papers and tape cassettes into his briefcase. 'Sorry about this, chaps, I really am. I'm a lousy host.'

'Don't be silly, Uncle,' Jill told him from the armchair where she was curled up like a cat. 'We'll be all right. Won't we, Steve?'

Steve was on his knees, hunting through his uncle's L.Ps. 'Sure, we will.'

'It's just that this chap's in Colchester for three days, and he's only free in the evenings, and he's got some really splendid material for me.'

Jill smiled. 'Off you go and pick his brains, then.'

'Unkindly put, but true. Where's that dam' mike?'

'You left it on the window sill,' Steve said without turning round. 'The one on the end.'

'Oh, so I did. Well, see you about midnight, if you're still up. Don't wreck the hi-fi or burn the frying pan. Bye,' and he was out of the door almost before they could answer him.

'I like that man,' Jill said. 'He's a bit like you in twenty years' time.'

'Thanks for the compliment. So maybe I do get a lily pond after all.'

'Maybe you do.' She waited till the sound of Uncle Garry's car had faded down the lane, and then said, 'I'm glad he went out, though.'

'Oh? Why?' Steve didn't look up from his L.P. sleeves.

'Because I want to do something about that other Jill.'

Now Steven did look up. 'Oh, for goodness sake! You're not taking it seriously, are you?'

'I'd like to *try*, Steve.'

'But try what?'

'To talk to her.'

'And just how do you propose to do *that*?'

'Don't be sarcastic about it, Steve. Please.'

He asked again, more gently, 'How are you going to talk to her?'

'I don't know.'

'Vicious circle, isn't it?'

Jill bit her thumb, frowning to herself, then brightened. 'A circle! Of course!'

'Eh?'

'She was a witch, wasn't she? That other Jill?'

'I very much doubt it,' Steve said, on surer ground now. 'I doubt if one in a hundred of Hopkins' victims were. He worked his racket on mass hysteria. Somebody had it in for Agnes Bewlay, so he accused her to Hopkins. Hopkins tortures her and drowns her, and collects his fee for having "discovered" her. Typical, and then young Jill cusses the neighbours, and I don't blame her. But it doesn't make her a witch.'

'Well, *I* think she was.'

Steve sighed. 'All right, say she was. Then what?'

'Then if I cast a magic circle, she might come to it. Because I think she's still here, and wants to be free.'

'Magic circle? You don't know how, and neither do I.'

'If you *will* one, it'll work. I'm sure it'll work.'

'Don't you need lots of bits and pieces, though? Pentacles and candles and incense and things?'

Jill jumped up from her armchair. 'We've got the candles, and your pen-knife's got a black handle. We can do without the rest, I think.'

Steve watched, wondering, while she collected four candles in assorted holders, set them in the corners of the room, and lit them. He tried to make up his mind what attitude he ought to be taking, and remembered Uncle Garry talking, 'You don't lecture the patient or slap down his fantasies, because the fantasies are relevant, from the treatment point of view, they're facts. You ride along with them and bat no eyelids. Ask questions, by all means, but let it all emerge without your trying to distort it. That way you're helping the patient to analyze himself, which is what it's all about. Your guidance is very gentle, and most of it comes later.' *Okay then, maybe Jill isn't exactly a patient, but she's gone a bit odd over this thing, and somehow I've got to help her. So maybe I'd better play along for a bit.*

He closed the curtains and turned out the lights when she said so, and meekly surrendered his pen-knife, opening the blade for her first. When she asked him to choose some music, he said, 'How about the Ritual Fire Dance? It's here somewhere.'

'That'll be fine.'

So he found it and put it on the turntable.

When everything was ready, Jill stood in the middle of the room with the pen-knife in her hand, and said, 'Steve, I'm scared.'

What now, Uncle Garry? 'Call it off, then,' he told her evenly.

'No! I'd be even more scared if I *didn't* do it. I've got to. Start the music.'

He did as she said, keeping the volume down. Jill, trembling a little, moved towards one of the candles, pointing the knife in front of her. Then she began to walk clockwise round the room, the knife still pointed outwards. When she started speaking, it came out strongly and clearly, with a note of her own surprise at the sound of it.

'I conjure thee, O Circle of Power, that thou beest a boundary between the world of men and the realms of the Mighty Ones; a shield against all wickedness and evil; a rampart and protection that shall preserve and contain the power that I shall raise within thee. In the names of Herne and Diana!'

She had come back to the first candle and laid the knife in front of it.

'Where on earth did you learn that?' Steve asked.

'I... I don't know. It just sort of came. Let's sit down. You face me.' She sat cross-legged in the middle of the room, and Steve sat in front of her. Jill breathed in and out slowly a few times, apparently to calm herself. That seemed a good idea anyway, so Steve did it too.

Jill started asking very quietly, 'Jill Bewlay, are you here? Jill Bewlay, are you here?'

Steve began to worry again. It wasn't going to work, of course, so how did one *play along* then? She'd be upset. How to hand her? Then he caught his breath and frowned, watching

Jill's face. It has changed to a strange, bright-eyed intensity. Her lips were drawn back, half-baring her teeth.

'Jill? Are you all right?'

'*Why are yew caalin' me?*'

The voice just wasn't hers. Not even hers trying to imitate a village girl's accent. For a moment Steve almost panicked, almost reached out to shake her back to normality, but he knew, somehow, that he mustn't.

'Are you Jill Bewlay?' he asked carefully.

'*Yew caal me by name.*'

He was committed to playing it this way now, right or wrong. 'We want to help you.'

'*Aren't no one helps me. They drowned me marm, an' they burned me under our owd oak tree. Let 'em rot in 'ell. I told 'em!*'

'Good for you. But we weren't there. We want to help you.'

'*No one can't help me. They locked me in.*'

'I thought you locked them out, and they broke the door down.'

'*They smashed the door, an' they fetched me out an' tied me to the owd tree. Then they got out all our winter kindlin', an' they burned me dead. Then when I were dead, they locked me in.*'

'Locked you in? But how?'

'*Wi' the bottle, o' course*'—scornfully—'*How else?*'

'With a bottle? I don't understand.'

The girl lunged forwar, grabbing his shoulders, her eyes wildly pleading. '*Yew can unlock me! You ain't one o' them—yew ain't. Help me! Help me!*'

She clung to him, sobbing, while he tried to comfort her, stroking her head and murmuring, 'It's all right, take it easy. We'll help. It's all right. Please don't cry,' until at last the sobs were no longer alien, but his sister's, and growing quieter.

She straightened, still breathing quickly, and brushing her hair back with her fingers. 'I'm all right now, Steve. She's gone.'

'You had me *scared!*' he gasped. 'It was weird. Are you sure you're okay? Do you remember anything of what happened?'

'Yes. All of it. Like I was shut up inside myself and couldn't do anything while she took over, and I just listened.'

'What did all that mean, about locking her in with a bottle?'

'Didn't they make witches' bottles, with all sorts of nasty things in them? As a protection against witches, I mean?'

'Come to think of it, I do remember something.'

'That's right!' Jill said eagerly. 'You buried them under your doorstep, to keep witches out!'

'Or under a witch's doorstep, to keep her in?'

'Well, that'd make sense, wouldn't it?'

'If any of it makes sense,' he sighed. 'Hang about, though. This other Jill, she seems to be in the garden, too, doesn't she? Not just in the house.'

Jill was on her feet and making for the front door. 'Yes! Front gate, then!'

'Hey—hold on!'

'Find a flashlight and a spade!' she called back to him.

By the time he had found both and joined her at the front gate, she was hopping about impatiently. 'There's a stone step. Can you get it up, do you think?'

Steve inspected it. 'Well, i certainly looks as though it's been there three centuries. Okay, let's have a bash.' He started loosening the earth around the edges of the slab while Jill held the flashlight for him. After a while he said, 'Look, love, don't be too disappointed if there's nothing underneath. I mean, all that in there, it was pretty impressive, but...'

'But you think it was all my imagination.'

'Not deliberately, no, of course not.'

'So?'

'Just don't be too disappointed, that's all.'

She laughed, and Steven didn't know quite what to make of the laugh. 'I promise.'

At last he was able to get the spade under the slab, with its back against a biggish stone to give him some leverage. Je put all his weight on the handle and the slab came up with a jerk. Together, they tilted it upright against the gatepost.

'Steve! *Look!*' She was so excited that the flash-beam waved about, so Steve took it from her hand held it steady. There was no mistaking it. An antique green bottle, squat and uneven, obviously hand-blown, too dirty to see what was inside it, but the stopper was bound and sealed with what looked like wax.

'Imagination, Steve?'

'It's very odd, I must say.'

Catherine's voice came from behind them, startling them both. 'You want to set her free?'

They jumped up and faced her, wondering how long she had stood there. 'Yes, we do,' Jill said.

'Then smash it.'

Steve looked down again at the bottle. 'Well, that makes some kind of sense, I suppose. Right.'

He freed the bottle from the packed soil and carried it to the ditch which ran along the other side of the lane. There he found a patch of had stony bed to lay it on, and swung the spade at it till it shattered.

Jill cried out, a kind of delighted wail. 'Aaah! Steve, it's all right, she's gone! She's free! I can feel it!'

'Yes, she's gone,' Catherine said. In the darkness they could hear, rather than see, her smile. 'You have set her free. But Jill, she's left you a gift, you'll find.' She turned and walked away from them towards her own house, calling a cheerful 'Good night!' as she went.

'What did she mean, left me a gift?' Jill wondered.

Steve swung the spade on to his shoulder. 'How should I know? All I do know is I'm bloody hungry.'

He was feeling rather pleased with himself by the time they washed up after their supper. Jill was almost her normal self again. Uncle Garry was right. Riding along with the fantasy had paid off, and by God, he'd been right about the tricks the human mind could play. But weird as it had been, when Steve thought it over calmly, there could be explanations for all of it. Jill must have read that paperback and forgotten it except in her subconscious. He was sure she wasn't consciously lying. And then her imagination (with Catherine to feed it) had dramatized it, acted it out, 'trance' and all, again not consciously or deliberately. The climax of finding the bottle had been a bit of a shock to him, but by then his own imagination had been stimulated, too. And when he came to think of it sensibly, it was very probable that Jill Bewlay's superstitious neighbours would have taken steps to bind her spirit after they'd killed her. In fact, in the climate of the time, it would have been more surprising if they hadn't.

All perfectly logical, and by playing along, he'd helped Jill to work it out of her system instead of bottling it up. Full marks, Uncle Garry.

Well, almost out of her system. There was one loose end left, thanks to that wretched Catherine woman. The 'gift' the freed Jill Bewlay was supposed to have left Jill Lancaster. It was still nagging at his sister's mind, and he knew it. Damn, Catherine!

Oh, well, jolly her along and maybe she'd forget it. She was in a good mood anyway.

Uncle Garry's L.P.s were mostly classical. No pop later than Bill Haley and a couple of early Beatles. Good enough. Jill liked rock and she liked dancing, so he put on the Haley and soon had her out on the middle of the lounge floor, mimicking the jibing they'd only seen on old films, and doing it bloody well too. He had a job keeping up with her. When the record ended, he collapsed in an armchair, laughing, but Jill stayed on her feet, swaying and clicking her fingers to a private rhythm, with a mischievous smile on her face.

'What did she mean about a "gift", Steve?' she asked, still swaying and clicking and smiling.

Oh, hell. He'd hoped she'd forgotten it. Play along, then. Joke about it. 'I don't know. Her powers as a witch, maybe?'

Jill shrugged and pirouetted gracefully. Steve got out of his chair and paced dramatically round her, declaiming like a ham Shakespearian actor. 'I, Jill Bewlay, being of sound mind and three hundred years dead, do bequeath to you, Jill Lancaster, all of my supernatural powers—subject of course to estate duty and to the just debts and expenses of digging up the front garden—'

'Only a *bit* of the front garden,' Jill giggled.

'—with the solemn injunction that she use the said powers to the best advantage, which shall be deemed to include the advantage of her brother, Steven Lancaster.'

'Steve, you're an idiot.'

She was still swaying and clicking, and Steve turned his pacing into a solo ring dance around her, in time to her rhythm. 'My sister's a witch. My sister's a witch. My sister's a witch. What shall she do? What shall she do? What shall she do?'

'What do you want me to do?'

'Oh, I don't know. Whistle up a thunderstorm.'

'On a night light this? It couldn't be less thundery.'

'Call yourself a witch? You're not trying.'

They were both getting slightly hilarious, but so what, good therapy for her. Steve improved his ring dance into a kind of exaggerated minuet, and Jill raised her arms above her head, undulating like a cobra, and starting to whistle—an eerie and piercing sound like a snake-charmer's flute.

The first rumble halted them, and they stared at each other incredulously. Then they rushed to the garden door, whipping the curtains aside and stumbling out into the garden. Clouds from nowhere were obliterating the stars, and as they watched, great flashes ripped the sky, and the downpour began.

They stood gazing upwards, bewildered, while the thunder crashed and echoed and the rain drenched them.

X

LA BELLE DAME
SANS MERCI

She had me fooled right from the start, with her wide-eyed pretence of ignorance. That is to say, of ignorance of my particular subject. Even I, with my incurable tendency to accept people to their own valuation, would hardly have been taken in by a librarian who pretended to be ignorant in general.

I'd had dealings with Fay Paterson across the counter of the Borough Library for months before I even knew her name. She knew mine, of course, from my library card. She had what I always regarded as a rather charming habit of saying, 'Thank you, Mr. Smith', or Mrs. Jones, or Miss Brown, or in my case, Mr. Bellamy, when she'd date-stamped your books and handed them over, thus making the whole transaction seem more personal. In fact, I'd always found her not only pleasant, but also physically attractive, though I hadn't tried to do anything about it, because at that time I still believed that Jacqueline Newcombe and I were soul mates, and who was I to doubt it? Until Jacqueline realised that Harvey Clarke was even soul-matier and had a private income to boot, so I found myself redundant.

Anyhow, to get back to Fay. She was tallish, shapely, and incredibly fluid in her movements. She had a spine like a snake's head, and even her date-stamping was something to watch. Her eyes were a strange pearly grey, but non-communicative—receivers, not transmitters. A rosebud mouth oddly at variance with those great eyes. Her hair was black, thick, and strong, the only undisciplined thing about her, but even that had a certain wild grace, like an aristocratic Bacchante's. The total effect of these disparate elements made for what the T.V. critics call compulsive viewing.

Age, thirty-one last October the twenty-ninth. The first decan of Scorpio. I should have been warned.

That's what first took our relationship beyond the date-stamping, 'Mr. Bellamy' stage. I should explain that I am, or was, a middle-ranged employee of the Inspector of Taxes, thirty-eight years old and a bachelor. I was in the best of health, but it had been pointed out to me that I had not yet taken my annual allocation of sick leave, which omission might be regarded as unfriendly to my colleagues if not rectified before the leave-reckoning year was up. So here I was on a quiet Tuesday after-noon, the only customer in the library, except for a couple of pensioners and the resident layabout in Reference, checking out Gleadow's *The Origin of the Zodiac*, Crow's *The Arcana of Symbolism*, and Pepper and Wilcock's *Magical and Mystical Sites*, and enjoying Fay Paterson's undivided attention.

'You take out a lot of these, don't you, Mr. Bellamy?'

'Occultism, you mean? Well, yes, I do, and I've got hundreds of my own, at home.'

She smiled. 'I always feel guilty when I pass the occult section, or sections, rather, because they're scattered around, as you know.'

'Guilty? Why?'

'Oh, you know how it is. In our job, we like to have at least a superficial knowledge of most subjects, at least enough to help people find what they want. But with *that*,' waving a hand at my books, 'I'm completely at a loss.'

'You can always ring me at the Tax Inspector's office,' I told her, not entirely altruistically—Jacqueline had sacked me as a soul mate a couple of weeks earlier. 'It's 7852, extension 32.

When you're desperate for information, I can probably help.'

'I might just do that, Mr. Bellamy.' Not only being polite, because she actually got out a notebook and wrote the number down. 'Have you got a home number, too? We get queries on the evening shift as well, remember.'

'Of course, 4064. I'm in most evenings.' Then, of course, I could decently ask her name, so that I'd know who was calling, and from that we got on to birth signs (I'm Cancer, the born con-man's sucker) and astrology in general, and I blinded her with science and she asked me just the right questions to flatter my knowledgeability.

I won't bore you with the details of the spider-and-fly process of the next few weeks, because apart from the fact that my 'etchings' happened to be my knowledge of occultism (which really was quite extensive), that process was the classic one, as repeated *ad nauseam* throughout history. The mistake I made was to believe that *I* was the spider, but that mistake is classic too.

It took us a week to reach the drink-after-work stage, another week to reach the Indian-restaurant-dinner stage, and two weeks more to get her up to my flat. I'd hoped it would be hers, because mine is shared with a journalist of irregular hours and no warning of approach, but since my excuse was that she simply must see my collection of occult books, which she seemed keen to do, I resigned myself to it as a step in the right direction.

Her hobby, she gave me to understand, was antique dolls, but she was apparently in no hurry to show me *her* collection. Still, I am a very patient man, and so far was unquestionably so good. I had every intention of becoming her lover (her snake-like body, and the little intimacies she did allow, rather in the manner of a latently incestuous sister, put a definite strain on my patience) but meanwhile I was thoroughly enjoying being her guru.

For she had, eagerly and from the start, insisted on being my student. I took her through basic astrology, the elements of the Cabala, and the Theory of Levels. I introduced her (yes, actually believed I was introducing her, God help me!) to the Tarot, the I Ching, and the various methods of Scrying. I gave her, as presents, King and Skinner's *Techniques of High Magic* and Crowley's *777*, and when she had studied them we tried some simple ritual magic together.

It was then, if ever, that I should have become suspicious, because she took to it like a duck to water. She was very good at it indeed. I don't mean she produced materialisations or anything like that, but even I (psychically insensitive as I regrettably am, in spite of my knowledge) couldn't deny that she not only achieved genuine changes of consciousness, but to a certain extent took me with her. This wasn't just my imagination, either, because in these states she showed divinatory powers which I could, and did, later check against facts.

'You're marvellous, Fay,' I told her enthusiastically when we were relaxing after a particularly successful air-element ritual. 'I may have the academic knowledge, but I haven't a quarter of your natural gifts.'

The huge eyes looked remorsefully at me. 'Oh, Walter! You make me feel mean.'

'Nonsense, love. What does the man say? "He who does not surpass his teach, fails his teacher." And you're not failing *me*.'

She put a hand on my knee, and my leg tingled. 'There's one thing I'll *never* surpass you on. Psychometry. You say you're not a sensitive, but all the same you're a terrific psychometrist. You know you are—don't you?'

I had to admit that I wasn't at all bad.

It was she who had helped me discover it, and it had taken me by surprise. I'd long resigned myself to being, psychically and magically speaking, knowledgeable but devoid of powers. And then one evening, while I was lecturing her on the principles of psychometry, she had slipped a ring off her finger, held it out to me, and said, 'Show me.'

'Well, I can try,' I'd told her, 'but I probably won't get any-thing. I can tell you how one sets about it, though. Some people just hold the object in one hand. Other's hold it against the Third Eye, in the centre of the forehead, like this. But what matters it to empty your mind, to open it wide and become completely receptive. Then, whatever comes into it, you speak, without censoring it or judging it.' And to show her what I meant, I'd said whatever came into *my* head while I held her ring, assuming that it'd be complete nonsense. I'd waffled on about the ring having belonged to the younger of two sisters, with details about their love-hate relationship, and how the younger had promised it to Fay's mother when she died, and the elder sister had tried to hide it but Fay's mother had got it all the same, and so on and so on. Free association stuff, I thought. But Fay's big eyes had grown even wider, and she'd finally burst out, 'But Walter, you're spot on! Every single word of it! They were my great-aunts.' And so on and so on, point by point.

Nobody could have been more astonished than I was. But she'd refused to let me doubt myself, or believe it was coincidence. From then on, she'd brought me other things to psycho-metrise, and kept swearing that everything I read from them was accurate. Or rather, everything *she* knew the answer to, which was eighty percent of it. Cleverly, she left me with the feeling that I must be picking up facts that even she didn't know. She'd built up my confidence to the point where I'd accepted that I really was a good psychometrist. How she persuaded me to keep it a secret between ourselves, I can't quite remember, but she must have done, because I'd never tried it on anyone else. If I had, it might have removed my blinkers, and that, I realised when *everything* was too late, would not have suited her purpose.

It was after a fire-elemental ritual, which she'd elaborated with a solo dance—and what that snake-spine could do in a fire-dance was nobody's business—that my flesh and blood could stand no more and I made a serious pass at her. She'd let me get into a promising grapple, with beautiful little moans of encouragement on her part, when she suddenly broke free, claiming she could hear my flat-mate's key in the door. He wasn't there, of course, but the moment was irretrievable.

Fay was very sweet about it. 'This place of yours is impossible, darling'—her first use of the word—'Look, it's time you saw my doll collection, anyway. How about *my* place tomorrow night?'

Well, what would *you* have answered?

It was a fine collection, I had to admit. Not extensive. About a dozen of the dolls were what I would call doll-sized, a foot or more high, and she had twenty or thirty miniature ones, the smallest being only an inch or two long. But each item was a gem. The oldest was sixteenth century Dutch, and not one of them was more recent than 1850, the limit she had set herself. I do know a little about antiques, and about the methods of craftsmanship of various periods if not about dolls as such, and I'm satisfied that on this subject at least she wasn't lying.

Like all serious small-scale collectors, Fey had specialised. She might have confined herself to a given period, or to a particular country, but instead she had chosen a rather novel speciality.

Every single one of her dolls was male.

She took me along the display shelves she'd built across the whole end wall of her roomy bed-sitter, and introduced me to them one by my. 'It's been much more of an achievement this way,' she explained. 'The vast majority of dolls are female, of course—pretty dresses and curly hair and all that. But there's always been the odd gentleman in double and hose, or Restoration lace and wig—or a soldier like this Roundhead here. I don't allow model soldiers as such, only dressed dolls, and if the dress happens to be a uniform, okay. Oddly enough, the tiny ones are more common, probably because every dollhouse had to have its Papa as well as Mama.'

She made it all interesting, certainly. Yet there was something about the ranks of gentlemen dolls that made me uneasy. I hid the feeling and made suitably admiring comments, telling myself I must unconsciously have absorbed the prejudice that a doll ought to be pretty. These fellows were handsome enough, but... Somehow, they were *sad*.

'Want to see my latest?' she asked. 'I only picked him up last week, in a sale at an old house. I haven't put him on display yet.'

She took a long object wrapped in tissue paper out of a cardboard box and carefully removed the tissue. Now he *was* a handsome chap. A Regency buck about fifteen inches high, in creamy breeches and shiny boots and a finely made little tail coat. His face was of carved wood, skilfully stained with colour, except for the eyes which were enamelled, giving him a lifelike and haughty stare.

'He's splendid,' I said and meant it. 'I wonder what his history is?'

She smiled at me, enigmatically. 'Funny you should wonder that, because *I* was going to ask *you*.'

'Eh?'

'Sit down, Walter darling.' She pushed me in the direction of an armchair, and I obediently sat. 'You're the psychometrist. All right, psychometrise.'

Usually I accepted her challenge at once, and I could hardly refuse now, but for some reason I took the doll into my hands with great reluctance. He was too big to hold against my forehead, so I simply held him on my lap in my two clenched palms.

'Look at me,' Fay said, kneeling close so that her face was level with mine. Again, I obeyed. The great eyes seemed huger than ever. 'Now remember what you told me,' she went on. 'Empty your mind. Take all the shields away from it, till it is wide open—utterly receptive.'

When I regained consciousness, I seemed to be standing by the fireplace. My first thought was, *My God, astral projection! A genuine out-of-the-body experience, happening to* me! After years of fruitless trying, I've done it spontaneously!

For there was no mistaking it. My physical body was in the

armchair, apparently asleep. Fay, with her back to the fireplace, was looking down at it. And the 'silver cord', the etheric life-line between physical and astral bodies which everyone had told me you could see when you astrally projected, was unmistakably there, weaving like the stem of some water-plant between the form in the armchair and a point just below my line of vision.

I thought, *I wonder if Fay realises what I've done?*

Then Fay started to move. Purposefully, smiling to herself, she paced around the room, ignoring my unconscious body in the chair. She produced objects from drawers and cupboards. Bowls of copper and brass, salt, black and white-handled knives, wand, scourge, pentacle, candlesticks...

I watched with increasing astonishment. Fay was doing things which I had never taught her, and doing them with the smooth certainty of an adept. Setting up psychic locks and defences of a complexity even I did not understand.

And then I realised at last. Her knowledge was far beyond mine. *It had always been far beyond mine.*

But what? Why had she pretended? And what was she up to now?

I realised another thing. The Regency doll was no longer in my physical body's lap.

I could not move my astral body. She must have put some invisible lock on it, but I could move my vision around the room, as though I were swivelling my eyes without moving my head. I found the Regency doll at last, or at least its reflection, in a bit dressing mirror on the opposite wall.

The doll stood on the mantelpiece above the fireplace, and the reflection of the silver cord was clearly visible, floating up to it and vanishing into it.

I was the Regency doll. Fay had stood it on the mantelpiece and trapped my astral consciousness in it.

For an instant I panicked, and I saw the silver cord shudder. Then I pulled myself together, remembering: no shocks or the return may be unpleasant.

I tried to remember everything I had learned. I tried to will my consciousness back into my physical body. I tried to shut my eyes and envisage myself back, but I had no eyes to shut, and my vision refused to darken. I tried everything, and nothing worked.

Fay still did not look towards the mantelpiece, but now she seemed to have finished her ritual, and she went and stood again facing the armchair. She made a few passes I could not see from behind her, and then said softly, 'Walter.'

I felt a surge of hope. She's calling me back into my body. With a mighty effort of will, i tried to cooperate with what I thought she was doing.

I was wrong.

Appalled, I watched while my physical body opened its eyes and looked up at her. In a zombie-like voice, it answered, 'Yes?'

'It's time for you to go home, Walter.'

'Yes.'

'You're too weak to walk. I'll drive you there.'

'Yes.'

My body rose slowly to its feet, Fay helping it. She put on the raincoat it had come in, gently easing its arms into the sleeves. Then she left it standing for a moment while she fetched the car keys from her handbag on the table.

She opened the door, put an arm round my robot-like body and let it out, closing the door behind them. The silver cord, stretching out from my doll-prison, melted into the wall but must have continued beyond it, because bound through my consciousness was, I could still faintly feel the pulse of life that throbbed along it.

I heard the car drive away, and still the silver cord weaved and pulsed.

There was a clock on the mantel piece beside me, so by looking in the mirror I knew how long I waited before Fay came back. Forty-seven minutes, with nothing to do but think and wonder and alternate between fevered hope and dull despair.

She came back at last, humming to herself as she let herself in and closed the door. Then, for the first time, she came to the fireplace and looked me—the Regency doll which held my consciousness—straight in the eye.

She smiled the most sweetly evil smile I had ever seen. 'You're still alive, little man. Here and there.'

And while my mind screamed silently for help, for mercy, she reached out and played with the silver cord. I mean played. If ever I'd doubted that she was an adept, a black adept of the highest calibre, I knew then. Astral and physical vision and action, fingers to toy with it, pretend she would snap it. *If that cord breaks, I'm dead*, my mind screamed. *I'll never get back.*

Maybe she could hear me in her own mind, maybe not. It hardly mattered because she would know exactly what I feared, but she hadn't finished with me yet.

'You wanted me, didn't you, silly little man? Wanted me, you puny dabbler? All right, while you still have a body...'

And then, slowly and sensuously, she began to undress. At first I only felt a blind fury at her, almost enjoyable in its own intensity. But the, to my horror, I realised how complete her power over me was. I began to desire her. With each of her movements, with each almost ceremonial revelation of more of her body, my desire grew, till its intensity far outstripped that of the fury I had felt. Trapped without flesh inside a wooden doll, I desired that she-devil till I thought my mind would give way. But my mind was indestructible.

She dripped the last of her garments and stood before me, swaying a little and laughing. 'Too bad your body's a mile away, isn't it, little man? I don't think you need it anymore.'

As gracefully as a ballerina, she grasped the silver cord, my tenuous etheric lifeline, in her two hands and stretched it between them. Then she opened her rosebud mouth and bit the cord in two. The severed ends vanished.

I felt cut-off like an electric shock. A mile away, I knew beyond a shadow of a doubt, my physical body lay suddenly dead. But now, damn her, all my vitality, all my human essence, was flung back into my one remaining point of existence—fifteen inches of wooden doll on a bed-sitting-room mantelpiece. I felt twice alive, twice as aware, and twice imprisoned.

Contemptuously, Fay walked away and went behind the shower curtain in the corner. I heard the hiss of spray.

Utterly defeated, I let my gaze wander round the room. I looked towards the display shelves, and suddenly knew why I had found Fay's collection of dolls so sad. Every one of them, from the tall Dutch burgher to the smallest dollhouse Papa, was looking towards me. Their painted, enamelled, glass or porcelain eyes radiated pity and a deep fellow-feeling.

I had not been the first.

WITH MY CROSSBOW

less me, Father, for I have sinned.'

On his side of the confessional grille, Huge Drake stifled a yawn and immediately rebuked himself for he was a conscientious priest. But it had to be admitted that Angela Sutcliffe's sins, in the two and a half years during which Father Drake had been listening to them, had consistently failed to be interesting, either dramatically or theologically. At best, and Father Drake honestly tried to see the best in people, they offered a very occasional moment of unconscious humour. As for example, when Angela, having won second prize in the church fete flower-arrangement competition, had confessed simultaneously to the sin of pride at that achievement and the sin of envy for the first prizewinner, but such relief was rare. Week after week, in a cozy monotone, she unburdened herself of a featureless list of cozy little sins and was cosily grateful for cozy little penances.

Hugh had told himself, early in their acquaintance, that Angela Sutcliffe was surely too colourless for either Heaven or Hell, and that in all fairness there should be a cozy little Purgatory awaiting her, with window boxes. He did not rebuke himself for the thought because he knew that, for him at any rate, a sense of humour, even if usually private, was essential to survival in his vocation.

He was all the more startled, therefore, when it dawned on him that today was different.

Angel began predictably enough. The sin was meanness, because she'd only given a doorstep RSPCA collector 50p, when she could really have afforded a pound. The sin of uncharitability, because she had given way to the thought that the Hargreaves were pushing their young Maisie into becoming a nun, not because she was really *called*, but through family pride. And so they are, Hugh would have liked to tell her. The sin of sloth, because she'd switched off the alarm clock *twice* this week and allowed herself an extra half hour. The sin of *greed*, because...

Hugh had a good ear and a sensitive mind. The first clue that set the warning lights flashing in his subliminal awareness was the fact that emphasised words, and unexplained hesitations, were creeping into Angela's habitual smooth monotone. The tiny sins remained typically Angela's, but the delivery was less and less like her, with every passing sentence.

The conviction grew in him that she was fighting off a mounting distress. That she was stalling for time, thinking up ever tinier faults to put off the moment when she must confess to something genuinely dreadful. Father Drake, who was compassionate as well as sensitive, began to be alarmed.

At last she dried up, but the tension in her silence was painful. 'Have you anything else to tell me?' he asked as gently as he could. He had to ask her twice.

She took a deep breath and with a trembling voice, 'Father, I have broken the commandment "Thou shalt not kill".'

Canon Bellamy pushed away his empty plate and eyed his young curate thoughtfully. 'You're usually good company at dinner, Hugh, but you've hardly said a word since you came in. Is something bothering you?'

Hugh hesitated, and then said, 'Yes, there is, Father, but it involves a confession I heard this afternoon.'

'Ah... Is there something we can discuss, without your

betraying the privacy of the confessional?'

'What would you say, Father, to a penitent who confessed, with an obviously profound belief in her own guilt, to a sin that wasn't a sin at all? To something that any sensible person would laugh at?'

'Absolve her,' the Canon said promptly, 'but *without* laughing, and with a penance commensurate with *her* evaluation of the sin.'

'That's what I did,' Hugh said. 'I just wonder if I really helped her.'

'Well, using your own judgement, of course, you could try diplomatically to make her understand how and where she's got things out of proportion.'

'I tried that, too. I think she wanted to be convinced, but couldn't be.'

'Then I think you should pray for her, and unless the problem arises again, accept that you have done all you can. If her sense of guilt has been relieved by confession and absolution, then surely you have—you still look doubtful.'

'I think she needs psychiatric treatment,' Hugh said.

The Canon sighed. 'Oh, you youngster with your Freud and Jung.'

'With all respect, Father, what would *you* conclude about an otherwise apparently sensible woman—I haven't told you her name, so I'm not breaking the confessional—who is sincerely and with great distress, convinced that she has broken the Sixth Commandment by *swatting a moth?*'

'Good Lord!' the Canon said. His facial muscles twitched suspiciously for a moment, and then he added with suitable gravity, 'Perhaps we should *both* pray for her. In my case, of course, anonymously.'

Father Drake did pray for Angela Sutcliffe, and very much doubted whether the Canon did the same, even anonymously, for his superior had clearly been pulling his leg. He was a kindly old boy, and Hugh (whose first appointment after ordination this was) had learned a great deal from him about the mundane practicalities of running a parish. But his psychological attitudes were those of an age that had faded before Hugh, or even Freud, was born.

Hugh could not dismiss the problem of Angela as lightly as the Canon had. Nor did he feel justified in passing the buck entirely to God. That, by Hugh's standards, meant reducing priesthood to the level of a spiritual sub-post office.

Something was wrong with Angela, and Hugh intended to find out what it was.

He knew he must approach it carefully, so he waited a couple of days till the harvest festival arrangements gave him an excuse to call on her.

The Sutcliffe house was a pleasant double-fronted one at the more fashionable end of the Esplanade, with a fine view of the English Channel. Too big for Angela really, but she had grown up in it and was the only survivor of the family. Her father had left it to her with a comfortable income, so she had nothing to do but look after it and dabble in good works, and being healthy, middle-aged, and genteelly but impractically educated, that life suited her admirably. The only independent action she had ever taken was to become a Catholic after her father's death, naively revealing to the Vicar, and thus to the Canon who shared his taste in amontillado, that this was because the Anglican Church was father away and draftier.

Hugh's absolution must have satisfied her because it was a cheerful and smiling Angela who opened the door to him. 'Good morning, Father. Do come in. About the Brazilian Mission, is it?'

'Not this time, Miss Sutcliffe. The harvest festival.'

'Oh, of course. Nearly round again, isn't it? Doesn't time fly? I was just making a cup of tea. Do you mind the kitchen? The sitting-room's in a state. It's my day for hovering under the carpet.'

'The kitchen will be fine. Sorry to drop in on you without warning.'

'Don't give it a thought. Always welcome. There, sit down

at the table while I clear it. India or China?'

Hugh, unused these days to old-fashioned offer of a choice of teas, thought for a moment that she was on about Missions again, but he realised in time. 'Whatever you're making.'

'No, please do say.'

So he opted for China, and she made it, waffling on happily. They managed to get the harvest festival dealt with by the second cup, and Hugh was wondering how to get around to the subject which was on his mind, wondering even if Angela's light-hearted mood would make it difficult to broach at all. Perhaps he had better come back another day, and hope to catch her in a more suitable frame of mind.

The matter was decided for him by a loud *clack* from inside one of the kitchen cupboards.

Angela cried, 'Ah! Got the little brute!' and went to open the cupboard. She fell to her knees and put one hand along the floor inside, then stood up and turned to face him, proudly displaying a sprung mousetrap from which dangled a newly-dead mouse, its teeth embedded pathetically in the Judas cheese. 'Been after him for days,' Angel smiled. 'Excuse me while I put him in the dustbin.' She disappeared through the back door for a moment and then came back with the empty trap, which she proceeded to re-set at the kitchen table. 'He might have a mate, you see,' she explained.

Hugh saw his chance. 'You puzzle me a little, Miss Sutcliffe.'

'Oh? Why? Not all women are scared of mice, you know.'

'I don't mean that. But, if you'll forgive me for bringing it up again, only two days ago you came to confession terribly upset because you'd killed a moth. You seemed to regard that as murder. And yet today...'

'Oh, but that's *different!*' The light-heartedness had vanished abruptly, and her words came tumbling out in the same torrent of distress he had heard in the confessional box. 'A mouse—that's vermin. But *flying* things—God's fee creatures—it was doing no harm. It was beautiful and *free*, and I killed it, God forgive me.'

'God has forgiven you, Miss Sutcliffe. Remember?'

'I know, Father, and I'm grateful. I did my penance twice over, just to make sure, but suppose it happens again? Suppose, without thinking, or even by accident, suppose I murder one of God's flying things *again*?'

'Now Miss Sutcliffe! Try to take it easy. Calm down and we'll talk about it. Please?'

She nodded dumbly, still breathing fast, but trying to control it.

Hugh poured her another cup of tea.

'That's better. I'm sure God appreciates your care for His creatures, but if you'll forgive me for saying so, I think there's something deeper behind it. Something buried in your subconscious mind because you're not being quite logical about it, are you? Some people might say a mouse, which is a mammal like us, is a much higher form of life, or God's creation, than a moth. Yet you'll deliberately set out to kill a mouse—and believe me, no one's criticising you for that—but you feel like a murderer when you *thoughtlessly* kill a moth. It doesn't really make sense, does it?'

'But, Father—a *flying* creature...'

'What's so special about flying? God gives different gifts to different creatures. We can't fly, yet according to the Bible, God has given us dominion over—'

'I know, I *know*. I can't explain it, Father. I wish I could. I just feel in my *heart* that it's a terrible sin to kill anything that flies free. And that if I do, I'll be punished for it.'

Her distress was mounting again, and she was obviously sincere. Hugh gave up trying to convince her and concentrated on calming her and assuring her that it shouldn't be difficult to avoid killing any flying creatures, even by accident. He postponed, for the time being, any idea of attempting amateur, or suggesting professional, psychiatry to uncover the root of her obsession.

The problem of Angela Sutcliffe, he realised, was going to demand a lot more careful thought.

When she seemed almost herself again, he made his way to

the front door with her trotting behind him. Halfway down the hall, he halted suddenly. 'Miss Sutcliffe, where did you get that?' He pointed at a large glass case standing on a wall table.

'The big stuffed seagull thing?'

'It isn't a seagull—even a big one. That, Miss Sutcliffe, is an albatross. How long have you had it?'

'Oh, a couple of weeks. I love going to sales, and they had one at a house by the harbour. An old sea captain had died, and his nephew was auctioning off most of the contents. I bought that—poor thing, it looked sort of lonely—and a couple of Victorian seascapes, rather nice ones.'

A light was beginning to dawn in Father Drake's mind. A hesitant, scarcely credible thought, and yet it made sense. Father Drake was a more widely-read young man than even the Canon teased him about. He had not merely studied Freud, Jung, Adler, and many of their followers. He was also familiar with Dion Fortune, Lyall Watson, Madame Blavatsky, Israel Regardie, Christopher Neil-Smith, and many other names the Canon would not have heard of, for the Canon did not know enough about psychic research and occultism even to mock at it, and regarded exorcism as a matter for rather odd specialists authorised by the Bishop.

'Miss Sutcliffe,' Hugh asked, 'have you ever read *The Rime of the Ancient Mariner*?'

It took him twenty minutes, and two more cups of tea, to explain, but Angela finally got the message. 'You mean I'm *haunted* b this old sea captain, Father?'

'In a sense, yes, I think you may be. Or if not exactly by him, then by a strong sense of guilt which he left behind him, and which has attached itself to that bird in your hall, which was the cause of it. That's only a theory, of course. I'll have to go and see the nephew, find out more about the old captain, but it does seem to fit, you know. Sailors have a deep-rooted superstition that it's wrong to kill an albatross; that you'll bring bad luck on yourself *and* your shipmates if you do. Now that albatross was almost certainly killed deliberately, because it looks in perfect condition to me, and you don't pick up perfect corpses of sea-birds that easily. Remember how the Ancient mariner had to hang the dead albatross round his neck as a token of his guilt? Suppose our captain did the same thing; kept his albatross always near him, in a glass case, to remind him of *his* guilt? Kept it there until he died, perhaps for many years? Now psychic forces, especially when they're changed with strong emotion, can attach themselves to physical things, and to places, and to people. Otherwise the Church wouldn't have a rite of exorcism. It isn't used often, in these sceptical days, but it still exists. Miss Sutcliffe, imagine the charge of guilt and remorse that could have attached itself to that albatross over the years, if my theory is right. And when the captain died, with his sense of guilt undischarged, and you bought the bird and brought it to your house—suppose that charge transferred itself into you? Filling you with an irrational horror of the very idea of killing anything which was "flying free", as you put it?'

Angela shuddered. 'Do you think it's possible?'

'Well, tell me this. Had you a horror of killing flying things *before* you brought that albatross here?'

She frowned, thinking. 'N-no. No, Father, you're *right!* Of course I didn't. Oh, my God. Get that thing out of here. Please.'

'Now don't let's jump to conclusions, Miss Sutcliffe. I could be quite wrong. Let me go and talk to the captain's nephew and see what I can find out. Then we'll decide what to do, all right?'

But Angela would have none of it. Hugh's theory had obviously convinced her, once she understood it, and she insisted that she was frightened to have the captain's albatross in the house even for another hour. Father Drake could do what he liked with it—burn it, exorcise it, throw it in the sea—but would he *please* take it away for her? She was afraid even to touch it.

So to pacify her, Hugh carried the glass case out and put it on the back seat of his car. As soon as it was through the front gate, Angela was her old self again, as though Hugh had waved a magic wand. She beamed at him like a maiden aunt at her favourite nephew as he drove away.

He had a strong feeling that the problem of Angela Sutcliffe's obsession had been solved, though whether by non-ritual exorcism or by straight psychology, he still wasn't certain.

The Canon was out when he got back to the presbytery, and Hugh wondered what he ought to do with the albatross. If he was going to burn or bury it, now was the time. Or *should* it be exorcised, in the circumstances? Hugh sighed. That would mean one of two things. Either he must tell the Canon the whole story or perform the exorcism himself and say nothing about it. Telling the Canon would involve either getting himself laughed at—which would embarrass Hugh—or obliging the Canon to take the matter to the Bishop and ask for the official help of one of the 'odd specialists', which would embarrass the Canon. Performing the exorcism secretly himself would be a flagrant breach of the rules, and Hugh had to admit, in view of some recent much-publicised disasters arising from well-meant but inexpert exorcism attempts, that the rules made sense.

So Hugh sighed again, took the stuffed albatross out of its case, carried it to the bottom of the presbytery garden and burned it in the garden incinerator. Then he came back to the house and cleared the glass case of its papier-mâché rocks and fading grass. It would be just the job for displaying the Youth Club's team trophies.

He knew that he had done his duty. Some might say, more than his duty, as best he could, and that the sensible course now was to dismiss the whole affair from his mind.

But for good or ill, Hugh was endowed not merely with a sense of duty, but also with intellectual curiosity. And over the next few days, it nagged at him. Eventually it won.

The late captain's house was one of a row overlooking the harbour, and it looked like a retired sailor's house; cleanly whitewashed, shipshape and with a geometrical little front garden. Although terraced, it was larger than Hugh had realised from a distance, and the upper storey was set back a few feet to provide a solid walled balcony. A bushy haired young man with a Zapata moustache hailed Hugh from the balcony as he walked up the front path.

'Hang on, I'll come down.' Seconds later he opened the front door. 'Hullo. Come on in. You're Catholic, aren't you? I always get muddled over the collars.'

Non-Catholic but non-hostile, Hugh registered automatically. 'That's right, but I'm not here on business.' He smiled and explained, 'I usually change clothes when I've a whole day off, but this is only an afternoon. So forgive the uniform.'

'Forgiven. My name's Bob Cameron,' he said over his shoulder as he led the way upstairs. 'An afternoon off calls for a beer. Okay?'

'O-*kay*. Min'es Hugh Drake.'

The balcony held two chairs and a table with a typewriter on it. Cameron gestured him to one of the chairs and handed him a can of beer. 'I suppose I call you "Father", then?'

'I'd much rather you called me "Hugh". You're not a Catholic or you'd have known the collar, and we're about the same age. Cheers!'

'Okay, Hugh. Cheers. If it's not business, what's your problem?'

'You might call it nosiness, though I have a reason. I wanted to ask about your uncle, if you *are* the captain's nephew, that is? Tell me to mind my own business, if you like.'

Cameron laughed. 'No, that's all right. You've got me curious, now. Yes, Captain Alec Cameron was my uncle, God bless him. He died at a hoary old age three months ago and left me this place because he had no kids himself and he knew I'd love it.' He waved a hand at the typewriter. 'There's an old joke about house agents advertising broken-down old shacks as "suit author", but by God they'd be right about this place.' He raised his beer can. "Here's to Uncle Alec.'

Hugh did the same. 'Uncle Alec.'

'He was a marvellous old boy,' Cameron said, leaning back in his chair. 'Been retired since I was about five, and my sister and I used to come and stay with him down here for school vacations. We used to kick up the hell of a fuss if our parents wanted to take us anywhere else. It was a kids' dream, you can imagine. The sea, and the harbour, and Uncle knowing all the fishermen. We used to go out with 'em sometimes, in fair weather, and in not so fair, when we got a bit older, but it was Uncle himself, with all his marvellous yarns—and this house, with all the strange things he's collected from all over the world. I've kept most of them, of course. Just auctioned off the furniture because I've got a lot of my parents' and they're dead, and my sister's married and got plenty of her own. But I tell you, this house is a ruddy museum. Those things I *wouldn't* part with. And I know the story of every single one of them, by heart, since I was so high. I'll take you round later, if it won't bore you.'

'Bore me? I'd love it, if I'm not holding up your work.'

'Authors love being interrupted. At least, this one does, when he's been typing like the clappers all morning.'

Hugh sipped his beer for a moment and then said, 'There's one—er—museum piece you did auction off.'

'I've a feeling,' Cameron said, 'that we now come to what you're here about.'

'Afraid so, and do tell me to mind my own business if...'

'Don't be so apologetic. Which museum piece?'

'A stuffed albatross.'

Cameron looked at him with sudden interest. 'That's right. Apart from a few bad water-colour and a sextant, the old boy had two of for some reason, it was the only thing I sold except the furniture. Some old dear bought it with a couple of the pictures. I remember.'

'Yes. One of my parishioners.'

'What has she done with it? Presented it to the church hall?'

'No. She kept it for a couple of weeks, in her own house, and then begged me to get rid of it for her. Either to destroy it or to exorcise it.'

'So you...'

'Burned it. I'm not licensed to do exorcisms.'

'Interesting. Hadn't you better tell me the whole story?'

'I'm afraid I can't. At least, not all of it, because what should be the most interesting bit comes under the seal of the confessional, but I can say that I believe that albatross had a very disturbing effect on her. And that's why I came to you, hoping to find out more about it. I could be wrong, but I have a strong feeling that that bird was...' He hesitated.

'Charged?' Cameron suggested.

'The very word I used to her.'

'H'mm, and now that she's rid of it, is she all right?'

'Well, it's early days, but I've seen her a couple of times since, and I'd say she's entirely back to normal.'

'I'm glad to hear it. All right, Hugh, now I'll tell you my side. It isn't much, but I think it bears out what you say. I got rid of that bird because it gave me the willies. It was the only thing in Uncle Alec's collection that I didn't like, and that's probably because I'd always sensed, even as a kid, that it was the only thing he didn't like. He never told us any stories about it, and the couple of times we did ask him, he said, "Oh, it's just an old albatross" or something like that, and changed the subject. Kids aren't stupid, you know, not with people they love, so Molly and I left it alone. We knew it bugged him somehow, and of course we wondered why he didn't get rid of it, but we had more sense than to ask. Then of course when we got a bit older, and read the *Ancient Mariner*, I put two and two together, and whether I got the right four I still don't know. Uncle Alec only had one disaster at sea in his whole career as master—collision in fog. His ship went down with the loss of about half her company. It was the other ship's fault entirely. In fact, the official inquiry commended Uncle Alec for his seamanship, and said that but for him the losses would have been much higher. But it still seemed to haunt him. He didn't talk about it much, but when he did, it was always as though he should have been able to prevent it somehow. Right down to the end of his life, and I found out, almost by accident from something my father said, that he'd had the albatross at home from a voyage or two *before* the collision one. Oh, well, I do guessed I knew why he'd kept it, then. Not exactly round his neck, but...'

'Yes.'

'Poor old Uncle. I'm glad you burned it,'

'So am I.'

Cameron fetched two more cans of beer and said in a deliberately lighter voice, 'I'm sorry your dear had trouble. Perhaps I should have burned it myself, or even kept it. It wouldn't have done me any harm.'

'Are you sure?'

'Oh yes. I don't think anything to do with Uncle Alec could harm me. Not even his sense of guilt, which did affect your friend, if you're right about it and my guess is you are. I think he and I loved each other too much for him to harm me, even involuntarily, and alive or dead. That love is an armour.' He looked suddenly rather young and embarrassed. 'I hope that doesn't sound too naive to you, as a priest.'

'Not at all, Bob. I think it's probably the literal truth.'

'Good. Now how about that guided tour?'

Getting to know Bob Cameron brought a welcome new dimension into Hugh Drake's life. Since he became the Canon's curate, he had been starved of natural friendships of his own age. His priesthood put an inevitable gulf between him and even the most relaxed of the younger Catholics, and non-Catholics treated him with the usual varying degrees of caution. The nearest young priest, who might have been expected to talk his language, was fifteen miles away, and in any case Hugh found him unimaginative and not a little bigoted.

But at the house by the harbour, Hugh could relax, and did. He and Bob had taken to each other at once. Bob was a pagan, not by default or rebellion, but as a positive attitude to cosmic awareness, and in some strange way his philosophy was the other face of Hugh's own coin. In his company, Hugh felt he almost could—

Have sight of Proteus rising from the sea,

Or hear old triton blow his wreathed horn
—without compromising his own beliefs, at which Bob never mocked. 'Why would I?' Bob asked, when Hugh remarked on his tolerance. 'You and I, we're just on different telephone lines to the same exchange.'

'I doubt if the Canon would agree with you.'

'Never mind the Canon. This is you and me talking.'

An yet when Hugh took him up to the presbytery for dinner, Bob and the Canon got along like a house on fire. Bob treated the old priest with just the right mixture of respect and openness, and cottoned on quickly to his Victorian sense of humour, to which he replied in kind. Hugh could tell that the Canon was enjoying himself by the liberality with which he poured the whiskey. The Canon's appreciation of a guest could usually be measured in fluid ounces, and Hugh's morning hangover reassured him that Bob had rated high.

'Thanks for being so good with my P.P.,' he told Bob next time they had their feet up on the balcony wall. 'I think he was getting a little worried about me spending most of my days off in heathen company. Now he's decided you're okay.'

'Hell-bound but harmless?'

'Something like that. I've an idea he believes round-the-clock sanctity is unhealthy. You are now my approved safety valve.'

'And you said he wasn't a psychologist. Tell me, do you think I'm going to Hell?'

'No. Hell is a state of being separated from God, which I don't think you are.'

'Even though I subdivide Him?'

'Only into His aspects as you see them.'

'And Hers, remember.' And so they were at it again till the sun went down, different enough to stimulate each other, and too alike for alienation. The debate was shelved on the arrival of Heather. Bob's girlfriend and frequent bedmate. Then the atmosphere changed gear, but remained relaxed, for after an initial wariness, Heather, too, had accepted him as a friend. She as a warm unphilosophical extravert, and soon made it clear that she regarded their relationships with Bob as complementing each other, not competing. Hugh, for his part, did not feel called upon to pass judgement on Bob and Heather's sexual liaison. They were not Catholics and had not subscribed to his own set of rules, but they lived up to their own, of mutual affection and respect, and as their friend and not their priest, Hugh was quite happy about them.

Indeed, as the weeks passed, Hugh realised that he had not been so happy since he was a child. The presbytery was materially comfortable, and Canon Bellamy was benevolent, but he had never been able to think of it as home. Home had been a rambling house in faraway Wensleydale, where indeed he was still always welcome, but his brother and two sisters were married and gone from it. His mother was eight years dead, his stepmother was a well-meaning stranger, and his father, to whom he had never been close, seemed more remote than ever as the stranger's husband.

Absorbed in his work, Hugh had resigned himself to having no home. Now, unasked, the house by the harbour was beginning to fill the almost forgotten vacuum. Although he only visited it once or twice a week, here was what he had missed; a haven of human relationships, undemanding but rewarding where he could keep all his values intact but was unisolated by his status. Realising it, he at first drew away a little, aware of the danger of becoming a burden, but Bob and Heather seemed to sense this and went out of their way to draw him back in. So in the end, Hugh forgot his qualms, and the house by the harbour became accepted as his off-duty home.

Canon Bellamy, who took a very pragmatic view of trees and fruits, was more than content with the situation. Young Father Drake had always been conscientious and hard-working, but he now seemed to be tackling his pastoral duties with just that extra energy and good humour. If his off-duty friendships were fulfilling not only as a safety-valve function, but also a revitalising one, that was all right by the Canon. A cheerful and energetic curate was a great blessing to an ageing priest, and Aloysius Bellamy had always been one to count his blessings.

The weeks passed into months, and the 'family' became an established phenomenon. Hugh had his own key, and a small bedroom where he slept at least once a week, with an alarm clock to get him up for early Mass. His birthday came, and Bob and Heather threw a surprise party for him. Bob landed a six part television series, and Hugh conspired with Heather to arrange a surprise celebration for him. With the advance for the series, Bob bought an old tub of a cabin cruiser, and the three of them worked together making her seaworthy. Two or three of Hugh's younger parishioners had a great time helping with that, which he found subtly improved his standing with the Youth Club. Bob volunteered to rewrite the church's historical booklet, which was dull and out of date. He amplified it with some able research of his own, and the result got the nearest to a rave review the Diocesan Journal had ever printed. After that, Bob, heathen or not, was *persona maxima grata* with the Canon.

And when spring came, Bob and Heather asked Hugh to be best man at their wedding.

'You're going to get *married?*' Hugh said stupidly.

Bob grinned. 'Will that be letting you down by spoiling our heathen image? Pagans do marry, you know.'

Hugh smiled back, recovering himself. 'I'm sorry. I suppose I'd just got used to the way things are.' He glanced at Heather. 'Er... are you...'

'No, I'm not,' Heather told him. 'We just want to, that's all. Good enough reason?'

'The best! Oh, God, that's marvellous. I'm very happy for you both. Sorry if that sounds conventional, but I really am.'

'And you'll be our best man?'

Hugh hesitated. 'Well, I'd love to, but it does raise problems. It won't be a Catholic wedding, and...'

'It won't be a *church* wedding,' Bob corrected him. 'Surely there's nothing in your book that forbids you to happen to be in a register office at the same time as a friend happens to be getting married? Or to happen to have the ring in your pocket because he happened to leave it at home? Or to sign as witness because you happen to be around? Or to come to the party afterwards and happen to make a few witty remarks with a glass in your hand? And if the happy couple happen to think of one of their witnesses as being their best man, that's not your fault, is it?'

'You'd make a good Jesuit,' Hugh said admiringly. 'All right. You win. Let it all happen.'

So it did happen, even the Canon came to their party, bearing half a dozen Waterford sherry glasses as a present, and didn't bat an eyelid when his curate was openly referred to as the best man.

Before they drove away for their honeymoon, Bob said, 'Keep an eye on the house, Hugh, as much as you can, will you? Some of the strippers from London are right yobbos. They can sniff out empty places like bloodhounds.'

'Leave it to me,' Hugh promised. 'Enjoy yourselves.'

It was a strange feeling, moving around the house on his own night after night. In the event the Canon had worried quite independently about it being left empty, and had taken on extra duties himself for the duration of the honeymoon to free Hugh as nightly caretaker.

Strange, but peaceful. Hugh knew the house and its contents inside out by now, and with the brightness of Bob and Heather's presence removed, it was as though the house's own more subtle personality could exert its influence, like a candle after sunset. Though he missed his friends, he surrendered himself to the influence and savoured it. He watered from room to room, fingering the old sea captain's treasures, remembering the stories which Bob had passed on to him. Vivid stories for Bob, the adoring nephew and budding word-monger in his own right, had clearly captured not only the facts, but the very quality of the old sailor's telling of them.

Sometimes, even though the memory was at second hand, it seemed to Hugh almost as though the captain himself stood at his elbow. 'This now, lad. Know what it is? Right. It's a boomerang. But I know more than that. I know the old native who made it. Least, I did. He'll be dead by now, like as not. Made it for *me*, on account of a favour I once did him, and he taught me to throw it too.

'These, now. They're real castanets, none of your tourist stuff. Belonged to a gypsy flamenco dancer I was friend with in Malaga. So friendly that she gave 'em to me as hush-money, you might say, when she decided to get married.' The echo of a chuckle. 'Tell you about that when you're old enough, lad. Anyway, she could make those things *talk*, she could.

'That's a real Benin head. You won't see a finer in the British Museum. Don't you try to lift it. It'll be too heavy for you for a few years yet. Naked savages, landlubbers who put their threepenny bits in the missionary box used to call 'em. Let that be a lesson to you, boy. You ever hear people who've never left home talk like that, about other folk they've never seen. You remember the feel an' the workmanship of the bronze under your fingers, and ask yourself who's the savage.

'They say this old telescope once belonged to Captain Cook himself, and maybe that's only a sailor's yarn. I can't tell you how I laid my hands on it, 'cos that's be giving a shipmate away. Still an' all, take a look at the maker's engraving on the brass. "Juno Mablethorpe, Whitby 1762." Now bear in mind Whitby was Cook's home port, an' he was commissioned lieutenant in 1768. So if you like to believe it, who's to say you're wrong?

'Look at this now. A Jap petty officer's cap, from a submarine. Got that when I was R.N.R., Number One on a destroyer. We crept up on the sub by moonlight, west of the Nicobar Islands, while she was charging batteries. She spotted us just in time to save her skin by crash-diving, without waiting for half a dozen boor sods who were on deck at the time. She got away from us, but on the way back we picked up the three who hadn't drowned. How this feller had kept his cap on I'll never know, but he went to prison camp without it.

'Know how sailors make ships in bottles, lad? That's right.

Lay the masts and rigging flat, with a dab of wet glue at the foot of each mast. Slip her into the bottle and make her fast. Then pull the masts upright by way of a thread running to the bowsprit, an' wait for the glue to set. Not easy, you'll say, but not too hard either. Now look at this four-master, and tell me how *she* was put there. However you figure it out, she's a picture. They say the man who made her took three years to do it, an' then went mad an' never made another.'

So it went on, night after night. Hugh, increasingly fascinated, found himself marvelling at how detailed his own memory was. It was hard to believe he had absorbed, with total recall, all that Bob had told him. But after about a week, he ceased to worry. It was enough to travel the globe in the company of al old sea-dog, through a lifetime of adventure. Why question it?

One the eighth night—or was it the ninth? He was losing count—Hugh Drake lay on his bed in the harbour house, staring at the ceiling. The moon was full, and he imagined he could see not only its direct light, but even, if he looked carefully, its reflection from the barely moving waters of the harbour outside his window. In how many strange places had Captain Alec Cameron looked upon the moon, and in how many postures—her crescent frostily erect over Arctic waters, languorously supine in the tropics? What multiplicity of manifested creation had he seen? What lands, what peoples, what terror and what delight? The captain's house was full of treasures, but what treasures had died with him?

Oh, Captain, I wish I had known you face to face, not just through another's telling, however faithful. I wish I could share your joys and help you with the burden of your sorrows. Uncle Alec, i wish you were here with me, now!

Canon Bellamy was beginning to look forward a little anxiously to Bob and Heather's return. Not just because he liked them, and not because he begrudged the extra duties he had taken on so that young Hugh could look after their house at night. No, it was because he was coming to believe that their presence was necessary to his curate's peace of mind. In theory, he knew, he should find that conclusion worrying. No priest should be dependent for peace of mind on particular human beings. But the Canon was not unduly perturbed by that in itself. Huh Drake was young and maturing better than most, and the Canon had a parish to run. So please God, let the days pass quickly till the Camerons came home and his curate could be himself again.

That he had not been himself in the last day or two was undeniable. The Canon had not seen him so withdrawn, so tense, since—when was it? Oh yes, that ridiculous business over the moth-swatter. And with any luck, it would pass as quickly and completely as that seemed to have done.

'Bless me, father, for I have sinned.'

Hugh Drake's voice, coming from the penitent's side of the grille, sounded strained and harsh. And after the opening request, it paused.

'Go on, my son.'

'Father, I...' Hugh seemed to be summoning up his courage. 'Father, I have broken the commandment "Thou shalt not kill". I have wantonly and needlessly destroyed one of God's free flying-flying creatures. It was a honey bee, flying abroad on its God-given mission, harming no one. It settled on my hand, and I was unworthily afraid that it might sting me. So I brushed it off, too carelessly, and crushed it to death. One of God's creatures, flying free.

'*Mea culpa, mea culpa, mea maxima culpa.*'

And with that, Father Hugh Drake broke down and wept.

Chapter XII

THE CONFINEMENT

arak and Sleen were experienced Earth observers, with a genuine sympathy for their subject. 'Karak and Sleen' are the best I can do to represent their names as words, for Titanians communicate telepathically and have no spoken or written language as we know it. They do keep permanent records, but as thought-forms trapped in liquid crystal. So their names are mental call-signs, usually, like some Earth-names, suggesting qualities which their parents hope they will develop. Karak's mental call-sign meant roughly 'He-who-looks-both-ways-and-has-a kindly-heart', and the sharp-ended palindrome 'Karak', with its liquid centre, seems to me to match this concept. And his wife's meant 'She-who-smooths-conflicts-and-is-pleasing-to-contemplate', of if you prefer it, 'Pretty-peacemaker', so I have called her 'Sleen' because that is what it sounds like to me.

Most Titanians marry for life, which averages about seven of our centuries, not through moral compulsion, but because fully telepathic marriages develop few misunderstandings, and are difficult and painful to dismantle. Karak and Sleen had been married for fifty-three of their hundred or so years—in our terms—and had been on Earth assignment since 1947, with normal home leave.

The inhabitants of Saturn's largest moon have been keeping a whole-time eye on Earth since late Palaeolithic times out of academic interest, since Hiroshima with neighbourly concern, and since Sputnik and Apollo with growing alarm. The Earth-Observer Corps, once a mere handful, now numbers several thousand. Karak and Sleen's recruitment had been part of the major post-war expansion.

Earth creatures have always fascinated Titanians because of their permanent physical bodies. Titanians, like Earth-humans, possess the normal complement of spiritual, mental, and astral bodies, plus etheric bodies which are activated when required. But they manifest as physical bodies in three circumstances only: during recharging (an occasional day or so spent in motionless contact with the soil, be it Titan or Earth), during childbirth (an amoeba-like budding process), and during orgasm. Outside these, deliberate manifestation is possible, but very tiring. The Titanian constitution, of course, makes space travel simple. One projects the spiritual, mental and astral bodies as an integral unit to the desired destination, and if the etheric or material body is then required, either or both will naturally manifest at a new location.

The physical Titanian body, when manifested, varies from a four foot diameter sphere to about twelve feet long when extended, plus pseudopodia as needed. Its appearance is translucent silvery-white, quite attractive when you are used to it, but a little eerie to Terran eyes which are not. Titanian Earth-Observers are trained to remain undetected, but since the Corps favours married couple teams for stability, and Titanians are naturally affectionate, it must be admitted that many ghostly sightings which have scared Earth people have in fact been Titanians carried away by marital passion at an inappropriate time or place—a breach of security frowned on by the Corps directors, but apparently incurable. Karak and Sleen had themselves frightened the living daylight out of a Yorkshire farmer that way, in 1961, though their remorse was eased by the fact that it abruptly cured him of chronic alcoholism.

To Tianians, their own constitution seems normal and natural and the Earth-human state of permanent physical manifestation bizarre and exotic, exciting occasional envy.

Titanians are devoted ballet fans and would love to ski, but permanent pity. A further complication is that between incarnations, Earth-humans shed the physical body, while Titanians do the opposite, congealing into white blobs of quartz-like rock until they are ready to re-dematerialise into a new incarnation—or 'excarnation', which is closer to their concept. For this reason they try to avoid dying on Earth, since to confuse geologists would be a breach of the on-interference rule.

Karak and Sleen loved Earth and its people, and in particular the British Isles which were their allotted area. Areas are assigned in general according to language, because of Earth-humans' notorious habit of saying one thing, consciously thinking another, and subconsciously thinking yet a third. Even multi-level telepathy, of which Titanians are quite capable, is not enough in reading these contradictory creatures. One really has to understand the spoken language as well, and the fewer one has to learn the better. Karak and Sleen's grasp of English was by now comprehensive, and they had a working knowledge of Welsh and the two Gaelics—useful to Sleen especially, because she was the sociologist of the pair, while Karak was the scientist. His responsibility was monitoring the progress of astronomical research.

On autumn evening they were walking away from Jodrell Bank Radio-Astronomy Observatory, exchanging thoughts on the day's work. It was their pleasant affection to use the concepts 'walk', 'run', 'fly' for their own movements on Earth, which were in fact a kind of glide. It had been an absorbing day, though for Karak a little frustrating. He had watched two astronomers wrestling for hours with an apparent anomaly in a mass of quasar data of which he happened to know the explanation. Finally, in sympathy and exasperation, he had delicately nudged one of the two minds in the right direction. These was flagrantly against the Corps rule 'Receive only, never transmit'. They were *observers*. If concealed intervention ever became necessary, as it had, for example, during the Cuban missile crisis, that was by decision of the Titanian High

Council. It was virtually confined to preventing Earth from blowing itself up. Pretty interference was taboo, but it happened, on the quiet. Titanians are, after all, only human.

Sleen, pursuing one of her pet studies, had been watching a lesbian mathematician's fruitless wooing of a typist. Homosexuality was an unknown among Titanians. *After all, darling,* she had once joked to Karak, *imagine putting on astral body in drag,* and Sleen was preparing a lecture on the subject to deliver to the Terranology Faculty on their next home leave.

Where do you feel like resting? Karak thought to his wife. *The Pennines again?*

Okay, Sleen responded.

How about the wood near Askrigg? Nobody ever goes there after dark.

Oh, sir, what are you suggesting? (Telepathic teasing has a piquancy difficult to represent in words.)

I'm suggesting a therapeutic concentration on normality, after your day's preoccupation with... (mental caricature of an Earth-woman wearing a false moustache).

Unkind, Sleen retorted. *I sensed a congenital hormonal imbalance. If you had glands to malfunction, maybe you'd be a poof yourself.*

(Mental picture of Titanian Sky Goddess) *forbid.*

You'd never make a sociologist, with your prejudices. She extruded an affectionate astral pseudopod and entwined it with one of his. *I like your therapeutic ideas, though.*

Thus linked, they slid rapidly away from the coast and up to the western slope of the Pennines. Sleen started mentally humming a Hebridean love song—Gaelic songs mentalised particularly well, they had found—and Karak made it into a duet with his lower-frequency male harmonics.

Suddenly, in the middle of the third chorus, she broke off. Karak did too, and they halted in mid-flight.

????? he asked.

Wait.

Curiously, he began to scan with her, but she signalled *My field* and he suspended his probing at once. If whatever she was picking up was something to which she was likely to be more sensitive than he, she was like an Earth-human fly-fisher, best left to cast unaided.

There's a witch at work, she told him at last.

!!!!! he flashed, delighted for her. The British witchcraft revival movement was Sleen's speciality. Her thesis on Gardnerian witchcraft had earned her a Ph.D. in Terranology, and she was currently expanding it at the request of one of the leading liquid-crystal publishers. So every witch or coven she could observe in action was useful material. Titanians, of course, are particularly well equipped for such studies. Being continuously conscious on the astral plane, they can observe with a precision that would make any Earth-human psychical researcher green with envy.

Over here, Sleen indicated. *The big old manor house beside the river.*

'Do you think you'll be able to do anything about it?' old Mrs. Fraser asked.

'We'll see,' Carol Marsh replied cautiously. Her private view ws that the Manor was not haunted by anything more than the occasional rat, but the squire's widow was a nice old dear, and one didn't like to disappoint her. Carol could at least go through the motions to keep her happy. She started unpacking her Craft tools from the case she had brought: pentacle, athame, wand, scourge, coloured cords, white-handled knife, the private-recipe incense she used for exorcisms, the sistrum she used instead of a bell, candles, and the sword which had to be wrapped separately because it was too long for the case.

'No special robes?' Mrs. Fraser asked, watching the unpacking with interest.

'Yes. My skin. I always work skyclad, if you don't mind.'

'What a pretty word, "skyclad". I don't mind in the least, as long as you don't want me to do the same. I catch cold too easily.'

'No, of course not. Just make yourself comfortable and watch.' Carol unfolded a plum coloured velvet cloth with a pentagram embroidered on it. 'This is the altar. I lay it on the floor, at the north of the Circle.'

'How big is the Circle?'

In a serious operation, Carol would have found too many questions distracting. But since the complete absence of 'vibes' had convinced her that this was a placebo performance for Mrs. Fraser's benefit, tonight she didn't mind.

'Nine feet in diameter's traditional. But since this is the room you feel is haunted, I'll make it bigger, to include the whole room.' She fished in the case again and brought out a pocket compass. 'Ah, nice. The room runs due north and south. So we can put the altar clothe *there*, and a candle in the middle of each wall.'

She started placing the candles, and it was just at this moment that Karak and Sleen slid in through the western wall and halted, watching.

Carol paused, looking slightly puzzled.

Careful, Sleen warned. *This one is very sensitive.*

They stilled their thoughts. Carol shrugged and lit the candles. Then she began arranging her tools on the altar cloth, explaining them to Mrs. Fraser as she did so.

Gardnerian or Alexandrian, Sleen whispered mentally. *You can tell from the athame hilt markings, and the pentacle. Typical.*

Why not look into her mind and find out?

I don't want to if I can help it. I think she might feel me.

When Carol had everything arranged to her satisfaction, she started to take off her clothes and lay them neatly on an armchair.

Definitely Gardnerian or Alexandrian. Very few Traditionalists work skyclad.

Not a bad figure!

You're a dirty old man. Miscegenation, yet!

Nothing like that at all. Just that I've looked into many Earth-minds not to know what's attractive.

Sleen projected a chuckle. *Don't get any incubus ambitions, that's all.*

Goddess forbid!

Carol, still in her panties and tights, snatched up her athame. She stood in the middle of the room, and seemed to be listening.

'So you can feel the ghost, too?' Mrs. Fraser asked, her face lighting up.

'There's something here, definitely.'

Do be careful, Karak. I told you, this one's good.

What did I do?

Invoked an alien deity, stupid. One strange to her, anyway. Of course she reacted. Quiet, now.

After a moment, Carol relaxed, laid down her athame, and finished undressing.

Not bad at all.

I said, quiet!

Carol picked up the sword and began walking slowly, deosil, round the room. 'O though Circle, be though a meeting place of love, and joy, and truth; a boundary between the world of men and the realms of the Mighty Ones...'

Sleen had difficulty keeping her excitement down to a mental whisper. *Darling, I told you she was good! Just look at that Circle! Nothing, but nothing, could get through that!*

Not even us, Karak pointed out nervously. *We're stuck here till she banishes it, is my guess.*

So what? We're happy watching from the inside.

The Circle was certainly an adept's job. To the astral vision, it was a shimmering electric blue sphere, completely enclosing the room. Karak had a moment of claustrophobia. It was the first time they had been unable to go wherever they wanted, since they came to Earth, but he calmed it, realising that this was a golden opportunity for Sleen's research.

I'm a bit sorry for her, Karak signalled as Carol made the Invoking Pentagrams to the cardinal points. *I'm damned sure there's no ghost here.*

Nary a one, Sleen agreed.

But she can pick us up, and she doesn't know what we are. So she'll try to exorcise a non-existent ghost.

So what, again? We'll go away, and she'll think she's done it. Everyone will be happy, including Granny in the corner.

I suppose so. Seems like cheating, somehow.

Sleen pulsed a smile at him, and they turned their attention back to the ritual. Carol was both knowledgeable and confident, and if there had been a ghost she would certainly have got it well under control. Unfortunately she was also sensitive enough, they could tell, to know that she was not succeeding, that the unseen presence, whatever it was, was still there, and not responding to treatment. Karak worried, sensing a stalemate ahead. Carol would not banish the Circle till she felt the Presence had dispersed, which was fair enough, because a mere astral shell (which is what the average ghost would be) could have been disintegrated and neutralised within the Circle. But Sleen and Karak, two healthy living beings with astral, mental, and spiritual bodies, could not escape from it. Karak even experimented, moving towards the electric blue barrier and trying to penetrate it by sheer willpower. But it was too well set up, too strong for him altogether. Until Carol, who had cast it, chose to banish it, he and Sleen were prisoners within it.

He realised, after worrying over the problem for some time, that Sleen had fallen mentally silent. He scanned her, suddenly anxious. *Are you all right, darling?*

Karak, she replied in a small and frightened tone of thought, *I think the baby's coming.*

Karak didn't even notice that his wave of alarm rocked Carol back on her heels, gasping. *But it can't be! Not for three or four weeks yet, when we'll be home on leave.*

That's what I thought, but... Darling, what'll we do? I can't materialise here!

The surge of psychic effort from Carol, responding to their joint panic, got through to them, forcing them to steady themselves.

Not take it easy, love, Karak tried to soothe her. *If you're right, how long have we?*

She was doing her best to be calm. *If it is coming, I should start to be visible in about five minutes. Another five and I'll be fully materialised, and budding.*

Right, then. We've got to get out of here. Too late for half-measures. Tell you what, I'll get into this Carol's mind and plant the idea that to get rid of the ghost, she's got to banish the Circle.

Yes, perhaps you'd better. Remember, I won't be able to help. Once it really starts, I'll switch to automatic. I'll be a sort of vegetable till it's actually budded off.

I know, he replied shakily. *Here we go, then.*

He got into Carol's mind easily enough, but then his trouble started. He would never have believed how tough she was, or how well trained. He put his suggestion, and knew she understood it, and immediately she interpreted it as a trap. Just the kind of trap a threatened entity would set. Karak felt her mind harden and hang on to the single thought like a bulldog: *I must not banish the Circle. I must not banish the Circle.*

He increased the mental pressure, felt her waver, then felt her rally. He did not know how long they stayed locked in struggle till a cry from Mrs. Fraser startled them both.

'Carol! Look!'

In their own different manners, Carol and Karak both whipped round and looked where the old lady was pointing. And Karak knew that he was too late.

Before the West candle, Sleen was rapidly materialising into the characteristic shape of a Titanian female approaching childbirth. An upright ovoid, about six feet tall and two and a half wide, her normal translucence shot through with flickers of colour like a turning opal, through which the candle flame could be plainly seen. Karak flung her a determined burst of reassurance, but got back no more than a loving whimper of thought in return. Inexorably Nature had but her beyond his reach, or anyone's until the child was born.

It was all up to him now.

He jumped back into Carol's mind, ready to fight, ruth-lessly if need be, to defend Sleen and the child. But Carol seemed paralysed at last. For all her experience and genuine power, she had never seen a visual manifestation in the Circle before. He could feel her wondering whether to pick up the sword and challenge the phenomenon, demand its obedience. He was able to quash that for the time being—the sword was too psychically changed and might damage Sleen's aura—but wondered how long he could hold Carol once she had pulled herself together.

Then he had an idea, and turned to Mrs. Fraser, who had half-risen in her chair and was staring at Sleen, wide-eyed. She could be his way in into her mind. *It is beautiful and it is friendly.*

'It's lovely, Carol,' the old lady breathed at last. 'Absolutely lovely. Look at those colours!'

'But Mrs. Fraser, we have to be careful.'

'Oh, I'm sure it wouldn't harm us. Not something as beautiful as that can stay. Please, Carol, don't even think of exorcising it!'

Gaining confidence, Karak flicked into Carol's mind. *Well, it's your house.* And withdrew quickly.

'Well, it's your house, Mrs. Fraser,' Carol said. 'and maybe you're right. It certainly doesn't look maleficent. I'll be honest with you. I've never seen anything like it.'

So far, so good. But Karak knew there were at least twenty minutes to go before budding was over, and a few minutes more after that before Sleen and her newborn child would cease to be visible to the women. How to keep things steady meanwhile?

Then Mrs. Fraser left her chair and tiptoed over to sit on the floor beside Carol, and suddenly he knew he had nothing to worry about. Unreachable or not, Sleen would do it all for him, because she had the women spellbound.

Even to Earth-human eyes—and there is no other recorded case of them having watched it—Titanian parturition is a beautiful sight. The opal tints in Sleen's symmetrical ovoid body became, minute by minute, more intense, while always remaining translucent. The candle flame never ceased to shine through them. Then gentle waves began to run up her surface, the colours pulsing in harmony with their movement, and soon afterwards, the symmetry of the ovoid began to change, one side swelling outwards and the other straightening, till she stood poised like a shining bow. At first the curve of the bow was a smooth arc, then it began to swell downwards into the shape of one side of a pear.

It was Mrs. Fraser, mother of five and grandmother of three, who understood first. 'Carol, look! I do believe the darling's having a baby!'

And, of course, have a baby the darling did. The swelling turned into a bud, the bud into a two-foot high miniature Sleen attached to its mother by a dwindling isthmus, and at last, with a final brilliant flare of the opal colours, into an independent being, wobbling a little uncertainly where it stood.

Sleen was herself again at once, swaying back into her ovoid shape and putting a protective and supporting pseudopod round the child. The gesture would have been un-mistakeable to any species on any planet, and Mrs. Fraser gave a crow of delight.

Karak, my love, we have a daughter, Sleen pulsed triumphantly.

I know, Sleen. Goddess bless you.

Then she became aware of the two women, sitting wide-eyed in the middle of the Circle, and Karak felt her sudden quiver of tension. *It's all right, darling,* he signalled hurriedly. *It's all right. Bring her forward and show them.*

Reassured, Sleen moved forward in front of Mrs. Fraser and Carol, with the child held to her side. Then, with a smooth pseudopodic gesture, she held the baby cradled a couple of feet from their eyes.

All Mrs. Fraser could say was, 'Oh. Oh. Oh!'

Almost fearfully, Carol reached out her right hand and traced a figure in the air over the child.

What's that? Karak wanted to know.

It's the ankh, the Egyptian symbol of life. She means it as a blessing.

Thank her, then. You're beginning to fade from them.

Sleen bade another unmistakable gesture, she bowed. Then, as she and the child began to fade from the women's sight, she projected as clearly as she could into Carol's mind. *Thank you. And thank you for looking after us. Please banish the Circle now, so that we may go home.*

By the time Carol, with a suspicion of moisture about her eyes, had made the four Banishing Pentagrams, Sleen and her daughter were invisible.

When the Titanian family had found a secluded spot in the woods near Askrigg, and settled for the night, Sleen asked happily, *How many rules have we broken today?*

Goddess knows, and I don't care. I'm on top of both worlds.

Me too. Isn't she adorable?

Adorable. The image of her mother.

They shared a contented silence for a while, then Sleen suddenly came up with, *Oh* (four letter thought), *I meant to ask Carol if she was Gardnerian or Alexandrian.*

Drop in on her next Circle, then. Hey, darling, do you realise we haven't given our daughter a name yet?

Sleen thought a smile. *I think we'll call her "Born-in-a-meeting-place-of-love-and-joy-and-truth".'*

Yes, why not? I'll bet she's the first Titanian child with an Earth-human goddessmother, and a witch at that.

She ought to have an English name as well, then. You choose.

"Carol", obviously, Karak decided.

Yes. Yes, I like it. You know what, darling? It sounds rather like the feel of your name, Sleen told him.

XIII

BRIGID

She put the mug of coffee where Frank could reach it, passing behind him on her way to the terrace, without touching him because he was working. He thanked her in Irish, and since his back was to her she could allow herself an affectionate smile. After twelve years of perseverance his accent was still unmistakably Home Counties. Fluency and idiom he had achieved, but not the native timbre. His sensuous awareness was all in his eyes and his hands, not in his ears. In shaping wood, stone, or clay, or in loving herself, his sensitivity was a constant source of wonder to her, whether his mood was bold, delicate, or light-hearted. But he was touchily resigned to his own tone deafness, and she was careful not to pull his leg about it.

She also allowed herself a quick glance at the oak panel he was carving, without pausing in her steps. Twelve years of marriage to Frank had made her a skilled navigator of his creative process. First the seedling stage, the slight frown of germination which must be ignored and enveloped in normality. Then the growth of an idea, which he needed her to react to it, to contribute her own perception, to argue even, till the idea was consolidated. Then, as this morning, the blocking-out stage, the first cuts between the pencil lines, the first hand-fuls of clay slapped on to the armature. Now he must be left to himself. He needed her presence, but her eyes must not be

181

seen to watch. After a while—a day, a week—would come the looked for moment when he stood back from the growing shape with a sidelong expectancy, and she would come and stand behind him, her arms round his waist, gazing at it with him, and say what she thought—honestly, for she had very early been gratified to learn that false praise made him stiffen and withdraw mentally. After that he would attack his material with a new vigour, thrusting ahead to the day when he would fetch her by the hand to stand with him and contemplate their 'child'. For theirs was, and they both knew it.

But right now there was their living child to think of.

Brigid walked out of the studio on to the terrace, to sit on the low stone wall and look along the boreen that hugged the shore, inland towards the quay and the little town. A minute later Nuala appeared round the bend from the back of the house, swinging her shopping bag of schoolbooks—she would not use a satchel—all ten-year-old legginess but somehow graceful with it, her dark hair long in the morning breeze, looking back to see that Brigid was there to be waved to.

'Frank!' Brigid called.

She heard him put down his chisel. This interruption was permitted, indeed obligatory. He was beside her before Nuala reached the corner, and they waved together.

'I must draw her like that,' Frank said. He had said it many times, and one of these days he would do it, without warning. Brigid knew better than to hurry him.

They stood together looking at the morning, after their daughter had gone. Half a mile away, the little quay was busy with fishing boats preparing to catch the tide. Beyond it, the river glistened its way towards them among the houses of Bunross. The little town was well named. *Bun an Rosa*, the Base of the Promontory. It nestled close to the northern face of Binn Bhrid, whose headland hooked inwards and sheltered it from the southwesterly gales. Frank and Brigid's house was the last on the inside of the hook, at the very end of the boreen, facing east across the bay. They had bought it for a song soon after their marriage, for such houses were no longer deemed convenient by fishermen and farmers and their wives, when compared with the neat cement block bungalows of Bunross' inland outskirts. But London-born Frank and Dublin-born Brigid had loved it on sight when they had come searching the West for a settled home.

'It's hot already,' Frank said. 'Are you going to sunbathe?'

'I've got laundry to do.'

'Let it wait,' he coaxed, and she smiled, knowing what he wanted. Herself near him, stretched on the terrace, her sunlit flesh visible from his studio as he worked. 'I have a visual need for your loveliness,' he had told her once in a rare mood of poetry, for words were not his primary means of expressing his devotion. She could feel that need of his, and it warned her to fulfill it. Besides, it was true. The laundry could wait. They had enough clean things to wear, this weather.

'It's very near the tide, though,' she pointed out. 'Should I really bless the boats in a bikini? I could wait till they've gone.'

'Why? A *maighdean mhara* should really be naked.'

'Mermaids have fish-tails Anyhow, mermaids don't bless ships. They lure them, surely.'

He said 'Sea Goddess, then', with such serious thoughtfulness that she could not answer with a joke. She went indoors and changed into a bikini.

Twenty minutes later she was aroused from her sun-drunkeness by the far thump, thump of the diesels starting. She sat up, blinking until she could see again, and then rose and looked in through the studio door, meaning to find a hairbrush. Bug Frank forestalled her as he so often did. The brush already in his hand, he pushed her gently back into the sunlight and then stood behind her, working on her hair which was even longer and darker than Nuala's, till it lay shining almost the length of her bare spine. When it was ready, they could see over the rim of the wall that the line of boats was almost level with the house.

Brigid knew an unexpected moment of stage-fright. That boat blessing had grown had grown imperceptibly over the years, without comment on either side, from a casual greeting to an essential function. Once, three summers ago, she had been compelled to miss it because she had been in bed with a flu. She had been disturbed to learn that the boats, seeing her terrace empty, had turned back, though the sea smiled and the mackerel were riffling the surface in the thousands. For next morning's tide, she had begged and pleaded to be allowed to wrap up and go out. But Frank had been adamant, and on an intuitive impulse she had sent Nuala out instead. Frank reported that the leading boat had slowed its engine for a moment, as though hesitating at this new development, but the girl had raised her hand in solemn imitation of her mother's salute, and the boats had forged ahead to bring in a good catch. 'Obviously a matrilineal function,' Frank had smiled. From then on, Brigid knew she had an acceptable deputy. Maybe Frank was right.

Only once had the role really frightened her, and that had been the turning point between friendly custom and serious responsibility. It had been two years ago. Brigid had stood as usual on the terrace watching the boats, waiting for them to draw abreast of her before she gave her ritual salute. The sky had been cloudless and the wind a mere whisper, and the forecast had been unalarming, but suddenly she had known the boats must not go out. She had been paralyzed for a moment, then she had urgently waved them back, keeping up the imperious gesture till the last of them had gone about. The doubts, the fear that she had made a fool of herself, had come flooding over her as the line headed for the quay. Two hours later the freak storm had struck, lashing Binn Bhrid from the northwest and stripping tiles off roofs in the town. One of the boats had even been damaged at her moorings.

Frank had said nothing. But from that day, neither of them had let anything stand in the way of blessing the boats. Only in darkness did the small fleet venture out with Brigid's salute. As long as she could be seen, even under a clear full moon, Brigid was there.

Never, though had she done it like this, and for a moment she quailed. Should she go in for a housecoat? Then she shrugged and said, 'Stand by her, Frank.'

Frank nodded and walked ahead of her to the wall. She straightened her shoulders and came forward, and he gave her his hand to step above him on the top of the stones.

She could be Queen Medb herself, in her near-naked splendour, Frank thought as she looked up at her with the awe that often tinged his love. At thirty-two, her body, though it was of a kind that would never degenerate even in old age, must be near the peak of its perfection. Slim, yet roundly   modelled, strong yet utterly female, she had never ceased to delight him as both husband and sculptor. But he had never before seen her thus performing a ritual act, and the pagan rightness of it, and of her, took his breath away. She raised her right arm in salute across the water, and his eye was held by the way the movement sculpted her deep armpit and altered the cascade of her breeze-stirred hair.

Tearing his gaze away, he looked down on the boats. He knew every one of the upturned faces; the MacGowan brothers, Paddy Walsh, Tommy Kirwan... hard workers and hard drinkers, generous-hearted but crudely direct in their masculinity. Yet here and now their eyes reflected his own awe. The eyes not of lechers, but of worshippers vouchsafed an unlooked for vision, almost terrible in its wonder.

Gradually the boats drew away, only the helmsmen looking ahead, till the faces were mere white dots. Then Brigid turned and jumped down, and although strangely quiet, was his own human wife again.

Father Nolan was always disturbed by Brigid Thomas, and angry with himself over the disturbance. She was not one of his flock, not even a lapsed Catholic, for her Dublin parents had never had her baptised. Nor was she a Protestant, and anyone who fell into neither category was unpigeonholed, disturbing enough in this predictable community. But he knew this was not the source of his unease. Bunross had had lone wolves before, men and women who acknowledged neither discipline, but they were always rebels, negative reflections on the very thing they rejected. Brigid rebelled against nothing. She carried no chip on her shoulder. She simply went her own way, with a warmth that included everybody.

So did Frank, but him father Nolan—always a welcome visitor in the Thomas household—could accept and understand. Frank had his own pigeonhole. English immigrant in love with his adopted country. The West scattered with them. The Thomases' friends and neighbours John and Sylvia Garrett, for instance. Again, Frank was an artist, and therefore odd man out by definition. Brigid had no such escape clause, being simply housewife and mother, if 'simply' was the word for one whose husband and daughter were so obviously contented with her.

The parish priest was intelligently self-analytical, so he had asked himself sometimes if it was Brigid's shining tough unprovocative sexuality that disturbed him as a man. But in all honesty he felt he could dismiss that explanation. Now nearing retirement, he had come to terms with celibacy as a young priest and believed he could say the sublimation process was long ago satisfactorily completed. He could appraise, even appreciate, without envy.

No, there was more to it than that, and as he watched Brigid coming towards him up the aisle of his church, he wondered yet again what it was.

She had come, he had no doubt, to commune with the Blessed Virgin Mary, or as she always called her, the Madonna. Unless she was looking for Father Nolan himself, she never entered the church for any other purpose.

Again, disturbing, though in this case understandable. For the undeniably beautiful statue of the Virgin had been carved in oak by Frank, on Father Nolan's own commission, and the model for it had naturally been Brigid herself.

They exchanged greetings, and he stood beside her for a moment as she gazed inscrutably up at her own image.

'If you were a Catholic, Brigid,' he said on impulse, without sternness, 'I might have to lecture you a little.'

'On what, Father?'

'Oh pride, perhaps.' He felt unjustified even as he said it, and went on quickly, 'And on the true nature of Our Lady.'

Brigid smiled. 'The pride's all for Frank.'

'I know. I'm sorry. I shouldn't have said that. I know you too well to believe it.'

'Don't be too forgiving,' she teased him. 'I might be just a little pleased that I contributed something. And the other?'

'The true nature of Our Lady?'

'Yes. Do *you* understand it, Father?'

He hesitated, a little taken aback. 'I could give you the stock answers, and they would all be truth, but I doubt if they would satisfy you.'

'Because I'm not a Christian?'

'Well, outside of the Christian context, she would be nothing. Or in this case, just a beautiful stature.'

'Oh, *no*, Father. She's universal.'

The priest sighed. 'The Goddess heresy.'

Brigid considered, her head on one side. 'You might say that, I suppose. And yet she *is* human, isn't she?'

'To me, certainly. The immaculate chosen human vessel, but that is rather different from the pagan macrocosmic-microcosmic approach.'

'Now you've lost me, I'm afraid,' she smiled. 'Yes, I suppose I *am* a pagan. As a positive thing, I mean, not just by default. I'm sorry if I contaminate your lovely church.'

'You do *not*, because you are so transparently good.' He surprised himself with his own spontaneous vehemence.

'Now Father!' Her mockery was very gentle. 'I'm sure that's a heretical statement, as well as being a shocking exaggeration.' She turned her attention back to the oaken figure. 'I wonder why she almost obsesses me? I have to keep visiting her, trying to find out what it is she has to tell me, and I still don't know.'

'Are you sure you're not just trying to understand yourself? After all, that statue is an image of yourself, seen and interpreted by the very gifted husband who loves you, and whom you love. Isn't it *that* you try to communicate with and not Our Lady at all?'

Brigid shook her head. 'I've thought of that, of course, but you know what, Father? Sometimes I don't visit this one. I go to the wayside Madonna on the bog road, and she's a pretty plump blond little thing, not like me at all. More like Kathy Bready in the post office. And yet she... she asks me the same riddles. There or here, I'm talking to the same person.'

She obviously meant it, and the priest was nonplussed. After a pause, he asked, 'Why do you always call her the Madonna? It's not a name that's used much in these parts.'

'I know. I suppose "Our Lady" muddles her up too much with other people's ideas about her. The official ideas, if you like, and "Virgin"...' She glanced at him apologetically, reluctant to shock him. 'No, Father, I can't call her that. I see her as *whole*. What you call immaculate, I would call dried-up. You know what? Whenever I hear the... the official story, I think "Poor Joseph" and I know it can't really have *been* like that. A universal embodiment of love who doesn't give and receive, with all herself? No, Father. I'm sorry. Not "Virgin".' She looked at him sadly. 'Now I've shocked you, and I *am* sorry. I didn't want to do that.'

He shook his head dumbly, unconvincingly.

'I saw you cross yourself,' she pointed out.

'Involuntary, I'm afraid. I shouldn't be shocked, really. Because when it comes down to it, I don't think we're talking about the same Lady.'

'Aren't we?' She laid a hand briefly on his arm, smiled at him, and walked away down the aisle into the sunshine. Father Nolan watched her go and knew that he was more disturbed than ever.

'What puzzles me about this girl,' John said over the leisurely remains of dinner, 'is what the hell she's got left in the way of karma to work out.'

'She can cook, too,' Sylvia mused.

'No, seriously, love, I mean it. All these incarnations you've been pumping out of her.'

'*Pumping?* Jesus, i just switch on the tape and get out from under. Brigid's the most prolific subject I've ever worked with. Since the first couple of times, I don't even have to hypnotise her. I make sure she's comfortable and draw the curtains. Instant regression, practically.'

'Sorry I'm such a freak,' Brigid said.

'God send me more freaks like you. Though John'd be so busy writing it all up, he'd have no time for his television plays. And they're what pays the mortgage.'

'It's not just the writing,' her husband pointed out. 'It's the research. Look at that Etruscan one you coughed up a few months ago. I had to go all the way to Dublin to check on the facts in the R.D.S. library. You'd got 'em all right, as usually— things you couldn't possibly have known. Almost boring.'

'I'm sorry,' Brigid said again. 'I'm only trying to help Sylvia with her thesis.'

'Don't you dare apologise,' Sylvia told her. 'And John doesn't mean it either. You're a gold mine, darling. And it's got a lot bigger than my ruddy Ph.D., or *he* wouldn't be working on it too. I only hope it doesn't bore *you*.'

Brigid seemed to ponder for a moment. 'No, it doesn't bore me at all. Puzzles me, a little.'

'Why puzzles? You accept reincarnation. You couldn't help it, the way John's checking-up keeps proving you right.'

'Oh, yes, I accept it. I think I always have. And not just because of John's proofs. These lives you take me back to...'

'No, Brigid. *You* take *me* back to them. I'm just an observer.'

'All right, these lives, anyway. Five now, or is it six? Well, five and a half, because that Celtic one was a bit vague. Funny, that, being a Celt myself, now...'

'Harder to stand back fro, perhaps. Overlaid by today's images.'

'Could be. What I'm trying to say is, I *know* they're all me. I can feel it at the time, even though it's kind of misty when I come back to ordinary consciousness, and when we play the tapes back, it's all clear and vivid as though it were last week.'

'What puzzles you, then?'

'That it's sort of *irrelevant*. Interesting, yes, like a history lesson, but as far as the "me" bit is concerned, it's over and done with. Finished. No loose ends.'

'That,' John said, serious now, 'is what I mean about karma.'

Frank, who had been listening without speaking since the subject came up, asked, 'Explain?'

'You know the theory of reincarnation,' John told him. 'that our karma's a sort of spiritual bank balance we carry from life to life till it's all evened up. Reincarnation is a whole web of loose ends. In a way, that's what it's all about. Yet Brigid isn't aware of any.'

Brigid frowned. 'Perhaps I'm unconsciously repressing them because i don't want to face them.'

'I doubt it,' Sylvia said. 'Incarnation recall doesn't work like that, in my experience. Almost always, a recalled life explains things in *this* life. Apparently undeserved suffering, for instance, or advantages we don't feel we've earned, feelings of déjà-vu, maybe some relationship that should be casual, on the face of it, but is charged with emotion that seems out of proportion. And I know what John means. We haven't come across anything like that with Brigid. Like she says, her past lives seem interesting but personally irrelevant. It hadn't dawned on me before, and I should have done. I guess I was too enthralled to notice.'

'Don't get me wrong,' Brigid told her. 'Irrelevant in a sense, but I'm not *indifferent* to them. That sixteenth century one in Segovia, for instance. Once I'd recalled them, Ramon and Isabella and Miguel, it was like yesterday. I could recapture the love, even the quality and texture of the love, and feel marvellous about it, but still know it was *then*. They're somewhere else now, loving someone else, just as I'm loving Frank and Nuala *now*. And now is what's relevant, isn't it?'

'No loose ends?

Brigid shook her head. 'None at all.'

'What goes on?' Sylvia asked John.

'A sort of unconscious recurrent bodhisattva? Knowing Brigid, it would almost make sense.'

'Don't blind us with science,' Frank said. 'Explain that one, too.'

John was silent for a while, and then answered, 'I think I'd rather not, Frank. Like pinning a butterfly to a museum shelf, you know? Forget I said it.'

Frank too was silent, studying John's face. Whatever he read there, he did not press the point, but turned to Brigid and asked, 'This afternoon's session with Sylvia, what did you get?'

'A Victorian one, darling. It must have been almost my last. My husband was a doctor in a Somerset village. We had a huge family. Seven boys and four girls.'

In bed that night, her head on his shoulder, she asked, 'Do you mind me having these sessions with Sylvia?'

'Why should I? They're only once every six weeks or so.'

'That wasn't what I meant, darling.'

He smiled in the dark. 'You want to know if I'm jealous of these dead loves.'

'Well, are you? If you were, I'd stop, you know that.'

'With a woman like you...' He broke off, and started again. 'Put it this way. The sun shone on me today. Wouldn't it be a waste of good sunshine to be jealous of whoever it shone on yesterday?'

She rubbed her cheek against him. 'I love you, Frank. Love you. Love you. Don't ever leave me.'

'Leave you?' He buried all his fingers in her hair. 'You must be crazy.'

'Good day to you, Frank. What'll you be having?'

Frank had only just bought one, but knew it was useless to refuse Seamus MacGowan. 'Hullo, Seamus. A glass of the dark, thank you. How's the fishing?'

'Can't complain, at all. And the carving?'

'Not bad. And only myself to complain of, if it were. I can't blame the weather, like you.'

Seamus grinned. 'Hadn't thought of it that way, but isn't it the truth? I don't envy you, boyo. It's a rough old yoke, having nothing to blame but yourself when things go wrong.'

They teased each other according to habit until the drinks arrived, then to Frank's surprise Seamus led the way almost too casually to the window, which was not his usual spot. Tuffy's Bar was nearly empty, so every conversation at the bar counter was audible. He seemed to be seeking privacy.

'*Slainte, a Sheamus.* Something on your mind?'

'*Slainte mhaith.* Now why should there be? It's the fine day I want to be looking at.'

'Fine it is. Why aren't you out after the fish?'

'Diesel misbehaving, dammit. Mike's seeing to it now.'

'Oh. Bad luck.'

Seamus shrugged and went on looking out the window. After a while he said, 'It's a day like Wednesday, and a grand catch we had of it then. Grand.'

'Too bad you're stuck ashore, in that case.'

Frank had almost as good a weather eye as most fishermen, and he tried to remember what way Wednesday had been particularly like today, in a run of what seemed to him unusually settled weather. He was on the point of asking Seamus when the fisherman changed the subject abruptly. 'And how is Brigid, herself?'

'Fine, thank you. And Maire?'

Seamus nodded briefly, as though his own wife's health was irrelevant to the discussion. 'A remarkable woman, your *Bean an Ti.*'

'I think so.'

'A fine figure of a woman, too, and no disrespect at all.' He seemed both embarrassed and serious, neither of which was like him. 'No disrespect at all, Frank. If anyone laid a finger on her, or spoke a word amiss, every man in Bunross would have the guts of him. Do you understand me?'

'I understand you, Seamus.' He did not, quite, but the man obviously wanted reassurance that he was giving no offence.

'There is a power in the presence of her.' Seamus puckered his brow, still embarrassed. 'They say that in the old times, before shame laid its gray hand upon the innocence of us, the magic of a woman was a holy thing, protected by *geasa* that no man of the tribe would think of breaking.'

God, how slow I was being, Frank thought. 'And Wednesday's was a grand catch, you tell me,' he said. 'I remember which day was Wednesday, now.'

'It is a lot to ask of a husband.'

Frank smiled. 'I realised long ago that the husband of a woman like Brigid has much responsibility, as well as much happiness. Is your diesel really out of order?'

'It is not.'

'So you speak for the men.'

'I do. Are you angry with them, Frank?'

'Neither with them nor with you. I will ask her. The decision must be hers, of course.'

'Of course.'

'And I will lay a *geis* on the fishermen. A holy thing, you said, and so it is. There will be no wagging of tongues in Tuffy's bar or such places.'

'Is it savages you think we are?' Seamus asked indignantly.

Frank and Brigid talked long into the night. Not about the thing itself, so much as about the uncanny way in which they both accepted it as right, as inevitable almost. Nuala even more so. She had been resent when Frank had reported his conversation with Seamus.

'Everybody knows Mammy's magic brings in the fish. So the more of Mammy that's showing, the more fish. It's only sense,' she had told them firmly. 'Me, too, I suppose, though I might be a bit shy because I haven't got proper tits yet. Still, if mammy ever can't, I'll have to.' She had grinned. 'It'll get a bit goosepimply when the autumn comes, won't it? Dad'" have to build us a big picture window upstairs, with lights.' She had wandered away soon after that, bored with her parents' protracted analysis of the obvious.

There was a part of the terrace, round the corner of the house, which was visible from the sea but not from the town or from the hill behind the house. Next morning, Frank lugged a packing case there, turning it on end to make sure it would raise Brigid higher than the wall.

Today's ride was at high noon, and when the boats came out, Brigid, shy but proud, wearing nothing but a crown of marigolds which Nuala had woven for her before she left for school, mounted the case and saluted her fleet.

Over the next few days, frank built her a stepped plinth of cemented stones to replace the packing-case, and when that was done, he set to work on the floor-to-ceiling picture window at the seaward end of the upstairs landing. With lights. The window served also for sailings in the hours of darkness, because as soon as it was finished Brigid, unasked, extended her duties round the clock.

Now and then, out of school hours, Nuala took her mother's place on the stone plinth or in the lighted window, a maiden nymph as slender as a reed. She must have had her own kind of magic, for the gifts which appeared anonymously on their doorstep from time to time—a stone of potatoes, a sack of split logs or of turf, a bag of groceries, a bottle of poteen, a poached salmon—now often included a pop L.P., a children's book, or an 'in' tee-shirt.

Frank's *geis* was hardly needed. No jokes were made in Tuffy's Bar or on the streets of Bunross. But not even a *geis* could silence the pillow-talk of husbands and wives, or the turf-hearth murmurs, and when Brigid and Frank found themselves being treated with the kind of awed respect hitherto only accorded to Father Nolan, they realised the whole town knew.

One young man, a notorious flouter of public opinion, tried one day to flank the fishing-boats as they rode out with the tide, in his sailing dinghy and with binoculars round his neck. The flotilla turned and drove him ashore, where a silent crowd of men and women dragged his dingy up the beach and burned it in front of his eyes, flinging his binoculars into the sea. Sergeant Devlin, passing on his Honda, looked carefully the other way. No Peeping Tom tried again.

And that season the sea yielded a harvest second to none that the oldest fishermen in Bunross could remember.

'That was a strange one,' Slyvia said after they had played back the tape.

'How do you mean?' Brigid asked.

'Well, at the start you couldn't stop talking. Marvellous stuff. All that detail about the procession. Have you ever read "The Golden Ass", by the way?'

'No.'

'All the better. And the description of the temple, and what everybody was wearing and carrying, and the countryside around you. Cyprus, is my guess, but John'll do his detective work on the facts you gave. *And* well into A.D., because you mentioned a servant of the Emperor who'd come from Byzantium to pay his respects to you.'

'Not to *me*. To the Temple of Isis. It was quite an important one, I knew.'

'But you were its High Priestess. That was clear.'

'Oh, yes. It used to be called after Aphrodite, once.'

'Yes, you said that, and it was one of the things that made me think of Cyprus. And Isis had taken it over?'

Brigid sounded surprised. 'But there's only one!'

'Only one what?'

'I mean, she has lots of names. If it *was* Cyprus, it'd be natural for them to call her Aphrodite. But by my time, that place, I didn't think its name, just "our city", had become sort of cosmopolitan, so it'd be just as natural to call her Isis. What did you mean by "strange"?'

'Oh. After all that talking, you suddenly fell silent. I

thought you'd gone to sleep, so after a minute or so I switched the tape off and left you to come round in your own time. It must have been nearly an hour, because I read three whole chapters of the new Wilson, and made notes on it. Then all of a sudden you said, "We're coming into the sunshine now", clear as a bell, so I switched on again quick and you talked for another ten minutes, nineteen to the dozen. Were you asleep?'

'Of course not. Was it really one an hour of your time? It was much longer there, in the temple.'

'Was there anything happening?'

'Anything? Everything! It was an initiation.'

'Yes, so I gathered. Then why didn't you describe it?'

'But I knew you were listening!'

This time it was Sylvia's turn to sound surprised. 'But for heaven's sake...'

Brigid smiled apologetically. 'I see what you mean about "strange". But don't you understand? An Isis initiation can only be described to another initiate. And you're not. I certainly wouldn't be allowed to put it on tape.'

'Allowed by whom?' Sylvia asked, carefully.

'By myself. By my oath. By my function as a...' She trailed off.

'As a High Priestess of Isis?'

'As a High Priestess of *Her*.'

Sylvia waited, not daring to prompt. After a while Brigid smiled again. 'I don't think I know quite what I'm saying. That just came out.'

'But you still feel bound by an oath taken, say, sixteen centuries ago? That'd be the nearest thing to a karmic loose end you've given us, so far.'

'No, not a loose end,' Brigid said emphatically. 'Just something that doesn't change, ever. *I* know what happened in that temple. I'd forgotten it in my Brigid Thomas mind till today, but it was *me* knowing everything I had to do, and doing it. I learned quite a lot, remembering, and I'm glad I went back. It was wonderful. But...'

'But you can't tell it.'

'Of course not.' Then suddenly she laughed, a very Brigid Thomas laugh. 'Poor John, he'll be furious. Let's be extra nice to him, shall we?'

Father Nolan had long been in the habit of dropping in at the Thomases' for half an hour every week or ten days, purely socially. For although they were not of his faith, he seemed to enjoy their company as much as they enjoyed his. He was one of the few whom Frank allowed to watch him at his work, by which he was fascinated. He would ask technical questions, and finger finished pieces with a delight tinged with wistfulness that suggested an artist manqué. The timing of his visits used to be haphazard, and he had been quite accustomed to Brigid leaving them to wave to the boats if he happened to be there round high tide. A habit which he had smiled upon as 'very friendly.' But Frank noticed that this summer his visits no longer coincided with high tide, ever, and that if they happened to walk out on to the terrace together, the old priest's eyes avoided the stone plinth by the corner of the house. Nor did he look up at the new window, or comment on it.

Frank and Brigid were embarrassed for their old friend, sensing the unwonted constraint in his choice of subjects to talk about. Amiable theological sparring, which they had occasionally indulged in, no longer arose, and the size of the current fishing catch was never mentioned, as it would be in three out of four Bunross conversations.

This morning, a cool day in early September, Father Nolan was not merely constrained, he was patently ill at ease.

The four of them were gathered over mugs of tea and coffee in the studio. Nuala, still on vacation, was the only one who was chattering unrestrainedly, and Brigid noticed that the priest kept glancing at the girl with a hit of frustration. In itself untypical because he was very fond of her.

'You know what?' Brigid said at last. 'I feel like some of those coconut biscuit things, and we're out of them. Darling, would you run down to Carney's and get some? Take a pound from my bag.'

Nuala said, 'Sure,' and jumped to her feet. Her back to Father Nolan, she winked at her parents.

That kid doesn't miss much, Frank thought, smiling at her as she went out.

There was a brief silence after the door closed. Brigid broke it with, 'Well, Father?'

The priest smiled ruefully. 'Is it so obvious?'

'That you came here with something to say? It is, rather.'

'I wish I knew what to do about you three,' Father Nolan sighed. 'As non-Catholics, I can't command you. Nut in the circumstances, neither can I ignore you.'

'You say "three"?' Frank asked.

'Do you think I'm unaware that the people of Bunross regard Nuala as being... shall we say, of the same *nature* as her mother, albeit junior? And regard you, Frank, as being their guardian priest? That must sound strange, coming from me, but I don't know what other word to use.'

'If you can't either command us or ignore us,' Brigid said, 'you can surely talk to us. We've always been your friends.'

'Indeed you have. I love you all very dearly, which makes it harder. I suppose in the old days you would have been called witches.'

'White ones, I hope?'

'What as snow, and in a way that's the trouble. If my bishop could hear this conversation, which, God forgive me, I'm grateful he can't, he would say that the white are more dangerous than the black. At least the black are identifiable with the Enemy. But you... even if I were to preach against you, which that same bishop would doubtless tell me is my duty, what could I say to my people that would not alienate them? Since you began that unashamedly pagan ritual for the boats, their catch has increased, and you cannot expect men like the MacGowans to understand the *post ergo propter* fallacy. For them, it has happened, so you have caused it. And of course, I know it has not stopped there. *I* know which houses you have been begged to visit when someone was sick, and that almost all of those people have got better. Psychosomatic maybe, but who would believe me? *I know about the matter of Brian O'Noone's ailing barley field.*'

'Oh dear. I hoped you wouldn't hear about that. For your own peace of mind.'

'Brigid, every man and boy may have stayed honourably indoors, behind closed curtains, while the women and girls took you and Nuala out, and you walked the boundary of the field in the same condition as that in which you salute the boats. But did you really imagine it would never reach my ears? Especially when the field began to thrive from then on.'

'I suppose not.'

'My dear, in this "Land of Saints and Scholars" paganism is never far below the surface. A wise priest learns to accept it, to keep it in check at a relatively harmless level, to transform and transcend it where possible. But you... you have drawn it joyously into the open, and with a pure heart, too. And thanks to your personal power (in which I too have to believe, for all my talk of coincidence and psychosomatic phenomena) the people acknowledge you and treasure you. If i did my theoretical duty and preached against it, they would not attack me, they would simply bypass me. My relationship with them would become an empty shell, a thing of outward convention, while they turned to you for everything I was once able to give them. And that I am not prepared to risk, because I believe I am needed.'

'Of *course* you are, Father, but what can I do?'

Father Nolan sighed again. 'There have been times, this summer, when I almost begged you to leave Bunross, to move away and leave us in peace. A legend I could have coped with, more easily than a living presence.'

'I couldn't leave, Father, you know I couldn't. Whether this thing came from inside me, or was thrust upon me, or both, I couldn't abandon it.'

'I know, Brigid. That's why I said "almost". So since I admit to a certain helplessness, may I suggest a compromise?'

'With the Enemy?' Her smile softened the mockery.

'With *you*. And with Frank in particular. I want him—and I will pay for it myself—to make a new stature of Our Lady for the church, but not using you, Brigid, as a model. Sylvia, perhaps. She is a very different type, and it would be embarrassing to use a member of my congregation. That very beautiful stature of you has, I'm afraid, become the focus of my church. It is your image, and your symbolic presence, which dominate the place in the minds of my people. And that is too much to ask of me, and of my God. It must go, Brigid.'

Brigid came across and put a hand on his shoulder. 'Of course it must go. I wouldn't steal your church from you, Father. I hadn't realised... Frank?'

Frank nodded. 'I'll start on the new one tomorrow. I'm sure Sylvia will pose for it. And there'll be no charge.'

Before Father Nolan could protest, Nuala came in with the coconut biscuits. 'Hope i took long enough,' she grinned. 'Have you finished your private bit?'

Six weeks later, Father Nolan stood alone in his church looking up at his new Mary, and told himself that Frank had certainly kept to the spirit of their bargain, including the unspoken implications. Sylvia Garrett had been a model, to be sure, and an echo of her sharp birdlike appearance could still be sensed in the finished carving by anyone who knew Sylvia well. But this was not Sylvia in the oaken flesh and spirit, as the earlier one had been Brigid. Using Sylvia as a starting point, frank had deliberately departed from her personal essence to create something unique, not identifiable with any living woman. Human, yet ethereal, coolly wise.

Father Nolan thought, a little wryly, that not even Brigid would have any hesitation in calling this one Virgin. The one stood where he believed Our Lady belonged, Mediatrix between unreachable Heaven and inescapable Earth. Frank had done his work well, and Father Nolan no longer felt disturbed in his own church.

Outside of it, his unease remained, and he blamed himself

for at least one aspect of it. It had seemed natural to offer Frank the original carving back, in exchange for the new one which he had executed free. It was, after all, an uncannily faithful portrait of his own wife, as well as a work of which he had every reason to be proud. Unfortunately, the fries had not thought to ask, until after the offer had been made and accepted and the carving itself duly collected, where Frank proposed to stand it. When he did, Frank said, 'Oh, didn't they tell you? I gave it to the I.C.A. they asked if they could have it.'

Why the Bunross branch of the Irish Countrywomen's Association should want the figure, Father Nolan did not like to conjecture. Unexcitedly concerned with handicrafts, visiting lecturers, and occasional socials, the I.C.A.'s formal acknowledgement of religion seemed confined to asking Father Nolan to say grace at their teas and to judge their jam or cake-making competitions. Why should they suddenly want a life sixed figure of Our Lady? The thought nagged at him that the I.C.A. was the only representative organisation of Bunross women as a whole, but he shied away from the possible implications of that fact.

On October the thirty-first, the eve of Samhain, he found himself wishing he had faced it more squarely. Though even if he had, he did not altogether see what he could have done about it.

He had filled his pocket with nuts and stood a box of apples inside the front door, ready for the laughing Hallowe'en gangs of children who would be roaming the streets long before dark. But when night had already fallen without a single knock on the door, or even a sound of them in the street, Father Nolan began to wonder. He went to the kitchen where his housekeeper was busy ironing. 'Where are they all, Eithne? The children?'

'I wouldn't be knowing, Father.' She seemed to be avoiding his eye, Father Nolan thought, so he deliberately went on looking at her till she said uncomfortably, 'Unless they've all gone to the Square.'

He said, 'Thank you, Eithne,' and went to put on his coat and hat.

The Square was the heart of Bunross, an acre of paving dominated by the 1798 Memorial on which an idealised Erin presented a pike to an even more idealised peasant. (Someone had suggested once that Frank be commissioned to design a better one, but he had declared ambiguously that he wouldn't have the heart.) Once side of the Square was also the landward side of the quay, and the other three accommodated everything from the Garda barracks and the tiny Town Hall (for Bunross was really little more than a village) to Tuffy's Bar and the office end of the Fishery Co-op sheds. Except on market day, the Square was a cheerfully unorganised car park, innocent of painted lines of even of accepted custom; the whim of the first vehicles to arrive set the pattern for the day.

But tonight, as Father Nolan walked towards the Square though inexplicably empty streets, the first thing he came across was not people, but cars. Cars parked nose-to-tail, like Church Street during Mass, in all the approaches to the Square, silently informing him that they had been diverted from it for a reason. When he came unnoticed, because nobody was looking his way, within sight of the Square itself, the reason became clear.

Almost the entire population of Bunross—men, women, and children—were packed into the Square. They made little sound, because they were all watching the centre, waiting.

At first, Father Nolan could not see what they were waiting for. Then, in front of the Memorial, somebody began lighting torches. One by one the flaming brands were held head-high until there were a dozen of them which formed into a double line. Between the lines, something began to rise. The oaken Madonna, garlanded with late autumn flowers, secured upright on a stretcher and borne on the shoulders of six strong young fishermen.

The crowd swirled gently as the bearers and their torchlight escort began to move away from the sea towards Main Street. Over their heads the calm smiling face—Brigid in oak—towered high, swaying very little as the bearers kept careful step. Behind them, family by family, the people of Bunross formed their procession.

A religious procession, bearing a flower-garlanded Madonna to God knew where—and he, the parish priest, had been neither invited nor informed.

I have no place in this, he thought, *or if I have, I am not brave enough to take it.* He turned, still unnoticed, and went home to his supper, which Eithne served to him like a mute but concerned mother.

Halfway between the town and the promontory, above the boreen that ended at the Thomases' house, stood a little hill. It was known as *An Coilean,* the Puppy, because it nestled against the incurving bulk of *Binn Bhrid* like a suckling whelp. Fittingly enough, in the hollow where *An Coilean* adjoined its towering mother, there rose a clear spring known for untold centuries, like a thousand others in Ireland, as *Tobar Bhrid,* the Well of Brigid. The name was a great deal older than Christianity, because such wells had been sacred to Brid, Goddess of inspiration and fertility, long before that lady had merged into St. Brigid with little more change than the added title. And small knots of cloth or significant garments, tied to nearby bushes, spoke of the supplicants who still came to her Well with their private pleas.

A mediaeval wall and steps surrounded the Well, and since they had been built, nothing in the hollow had changed for six hundred years, until the past four weeks.

The mortar in the new shrine had barely had time to dry, but the volunteer builders—and everybody had wanted a hand in it—had made a pleasing job. Three-sided and roofed, lovingly assembled from *Bin Bhrid*'s native stone, it looked down on the Well like a little stage.

To this new home, in solemn torch lit procession on Samhain Eve, the people of Bunross bore their Madonna of druidic oak.

It was the twin Samhain fires, blazing on the summit of *An Coilean*, that brought Frank and Brigid from their house to see what was happening. A communal Bealtaine fire, on May Day Eve, they were used to, as they were to the Midsummer one on St. John's eve. But these were traditionally lit on another hillock, inland from the town and closer to the farmlands, because there were still a few old fashioned farmers who would drive cattle between the twin fires as they sank to patches of glowing embers in the early dawn. But the Samhain fires—Hallowe'en fires, as most people now called them—had become family ones; much like the Guy Fawkes' Night bonfires Frank had known in his London boyhood.

Tonight, though, no family bonfires dotted the landscape. Some unusual pretext must have brought everyone together on *An Coilean*.

On their way, they met Seamus MacGowan and his wife, Maire. 'We were coming up to fetch you,' Seamus explained. 'There is something you'll be wanting to see.' He would say no more until he brought them face to face with the new shrine and the familiar figure that smiled down on the Well.

Brigid halted, staring across the Well at the candlelit Madonna, and was silent for a long drawn out moment. Then she asked, 'Where's Father Nolan?'

Seamus seemed suddenly less confident. 'He's not here, Brigid. We... To tell you the truth, we didn't ask him. We thought maybe he wouldn't entirely understand it.'

'Do *you* understand it, Seamus? Maire?'

She faced them questioningly, her eyes unnaturally bright. They looked uncomfortable and nonplussed. Seamus said at last, 'Some things you just feel you have to do, without understanding them. We thought you'd be pleased. A fine thing like that, now, it shouldn't be hidden away in a dusty cupboard. And if Father Nolan didn't want it in the church, what's wrong with Tobar Bhrid and God's open air?'

Brigid sighed. 'No. I suppose it can't be hidden.'

'Will you be coming up to the fires?' Maire asked. 'Everybody is there.'

'I don't think we will, Maire, if you don't mind. I feel very tired. You go up and enjoy yourselves.'

She turned away. Frank gave Seamus and Maire what he hoped was a reassuring smile, and went with her.

'But why, Frank? Why?'

'It's like Seamus said, darling. People do what they feel, without always knowing why.'

'They're trying to make me into some kind of...' She paused, groping for the right word.

'Power source?' Frank suggested. 'You can hardly blame them. You've shown yourself to be one.'

'I'm *human*, my love. Maybe there's something inside me which can't help coming out, but I'm still a woman, not a sort of minor Goddess.'

'Don't get it out of proportion,' he tried to soothe her. 'They're fond of that carving. They always have been. And if I say it myself, it's the best thing I've ever done. So when Father Nolan banishes it, what's so surprising about them putting it somewhere else, where they can go on seeing it?'

She shook her head. 'You know it's not just that. They put it there, in the most pagan place in Bunross, for the same reason that Father Nolan banished it from the most Christian place in Bunross. Because it's *me*, their... whatever they think I am. If it had just been the carving, they'd have brought him along to install it. You know I'm right, darling. And it scares me stiff.'

Frank drew a long breath, and said, 'Yes, I know you're right, but why does it scare you, exactly?'

'Because if I *do* have gift, I want to enrich things, not tear them apart. Because I can't stop doing whatever it is I can do, and have to do, but I want to be seen as *me*, human me, not as some Being to light candles in front of.'

He went and put his arms around her. 'You're human all

right. I can vouch for that. But you are also something rather special. I can vouch for that, too.'

She clung to him. 'Oh God, darling, I'm so tired.'

'Come to bed, then. You've got a session with Sylvia in the morning, remember?'

'I know.'

'Shall I ask her to put it off?'

She hesitated, and then said, 'No, Frank. I promised. I don't like letting her down.'

In the event, Brigid was so deeply asleep when he got up next morning that he let her lie. He and Nuala had breakfast, and Nuala left for school, and still Brigid slept. It was almost unprecedented, but she looked so peaceful and breathed so evenly that he was unalarmed. He walked the hundred yards to the Garretts' house, where Sylvia said of course the session must be put off. She had plenty of other work to get on with.

Frank worked all morning, peeping into the bedroom every now and then to make sure Brigid was all right. When midday came and she was still asleep, he began to wonder if he had been right not to worry, but just as he decided he really must go and wake her and ask her if she was unwell, she walked into the studio, tumble-haired and smiling in her housecoat.

'Darling, whatever possessed me? Why didn't you get me up? It's half past twelve!'

'You must have needed it, that's why.' He kissed her. 'Want some breakfast?'

'Yes, *please*. I'm starving.'

'Good. I'll have my lunch alongside you.'

'And Sylvia! I—'

'Not to worry. I went and told her. She said it was quite okay. This evening will do instead—or if you're still tired, some other day.'

'No, I'm fine. I had a marvellous sleep. I think I dreamed, but I can't remember at thing.'

'Not still worried, after last night?'

'Oh, yes, I'm still worried. But not scared, somehow. We'll cope.'

'Those dreams must have been therapeutic,' he told her, and they went into the kitchen and shared the cooking.

Brigid went to Sylvia's after the evening meal, and Frank and Nuala played Scrabble till almost midnight. High tide was due at half past, and it was fine fishing weather, so Nuala firmly stopped the game and announced she would have to get ready to stand in the window if Mammy wasn't home in time.

But they had scarcely cleared the board when Brigid came home. She stood in the doorway with a strange expression on her face, and said, 'Hello, my darlings' with such a quiet and warm intensity that Frank's heart jumped.

'Hello, Mammy! Are you going to do the boats, or shall I?'

'No, *a thaisce*. I'll do it tonight.'

'Yes, I think you should,' Nuala told her. 'You look extra beautiful.'

'Good session?' Frank asked. For some reason, his throat felt dry.

Brigid just smiled at him, in a way that made him agree with his daughter, and said, 'Bed, Nuala. Help me, Frank?'

They went into their own bedroom after Nuala had gone, and when Brigid had undressed, Frank brushed her hair. He wanted to speak to her but was tongue-tied, not knowing why. He felt the brush tremble in his hand. Brigid caught his eye in the mirror and reached up her hand to steady his, and he found it stopped trembling at once.

'Are you sure you want to go through with it tonight?' he heard himself asking. 'I thought maybe, after yesterday, and you saying...'

She squeezed his hand which she was still holding and said, 'Yes, darling. I must.'

He finished brushing her hair, and they went and stood in the tall picture window together in the darkness, watching for the boats' lights to ride out of the little harbour. He put an arm round her warm, naked body, with an unfamiliar and unexplained diffidence, and she shifted her weight from one foot to the other to lean against him.'

'I love you, Frank.'

He tightened his arm for a second or two by way of answer, for he still could not speak.

Brigid went on, 'And don't *you* ever doubt my humanity. I couldn't bear it if you did.'

At that moment, the first of the boats appeared—white mast light, red port light—so he squeezed her again and withdrew as always to the back of the landing where the switches were, and sat on the floor where he would not be visible from outside. He could see Brigid silhouetted against the stars. Somehow she looked taller and slenderer than usual, and quite motionless. After a while, she said, as she always did, simply, 'Now.'

Frank reached up and threw the switch. She was bathed in brilliant light, a warm living statue of a woman, and Frank gasped. It was as though he had never seen her before. He did not know why or how, but every known and loved line and curve and plane seemed fractionally more beautiful. And when she raised her arm in salute, the movement was like that of a Goddess.

He caught himself up, almost in a panic, suddenly her plea, 'Don't *you* ever doubt my humanity' had a real and urgent meaning. To fail in that would be to betray her.

She lowered her hand, and Frank turned off the lights.

Blinded momentarily, he still jumped up and ran towards her, almost stumbling, but she was there reaching out for him, and he enfolded her in his arms, holding her as though he would never dare let her go.

He never knew why he asked the question, at the moment for all moments. He simply knew he had to ask it. 'Brigid, your session with Sylvia tonight, where did it take you? Where did you find yourself?'

For a time she did not answer. Yet he knew it was not hesitation, but preparation. A long moment while her closeness strengthened him and her love and gentleness flowed into every part of his being.

'In a stable in Bethlehem,' she said.

BOOKS

To see a full list of our amazing books,
please check our website:

www. darkdragonpublishing.com/books.html

All Books Available At The Following Retailers:
Amazon.ca
Amazon.com
Amazon.co.uk
Amazon.com.au
Barnes and Noble
Books A Million
Book Depository
Powell's Books
Chapters/Indigo

And other fine book retailers.

www.ingramcontent.com/pod-product-compliance
Lightning Source LLC
Chambersburg PA
CBHW060551310726
48982CB00008B/1091/J